Mohamad Ahmad was born in Syria, of Circassian descent, holds a law degree from Damascus University, worked at Prime Ministry in Syria as executive manager for twelve years, immigrated from Syria during the war, and is currently living in Britain.

This is a work of fiction. Names, characters, businesses, places, events and incidents are either the products of the author's imagination or are used in a fictitious manner. Any resemblance to actual persons, living or dead, or actual events is purely coincidental.

It Goes On

Mohamad Ahmad
Translated by Hoda Fadl

It Goes On

Vanguard Press

VANGUARD PAPERBACK

© Copyright 2023
Mohamad Ahmad

The right of Mohamad Ahmad to be identified as author of
this work has been asserted by him in accordance with the
Copyright, Designs and Patents Act 1988.

All Rights Reserved

No reproduction, copy or transmission of this publication
may be made without written permission.
No paragraph of this publication may be reproduced,
copied or transmitted save with the written permission of the publisher, or
in accordance with the provisions
of the Copyright Act 1956 (as amended).

Any person who commits any unauthorised act in relation to
this publication may be liable to criminal
prosecution and civil claims for damages.

A CIP catalogue record for this title is
available from the British Library.

ISBN 978-1-80016-633-2

*Vanguard Press is an imprint of
Pegasus Elliot Mackenzie Publishers Ltd.*
www.pegasuspublishers.com

First Published in 2023

**Vanguard Press
Sheraton House Castle Park
Cambridge England**

Printed & Bound in Great Britain

I have to say thank you
to the one who brought me back to the life I love so I wrote and
drew.

The Melia Zaedarach tree cast its shadow on the unmoving swing in the yard.

In that faraway place, she sat on the porch of her rural house in a small village at the entrance of the Nassara valley surrounded by the beauty of nature. As was the norm in that valley in Syria, Christians inhabited the village, and it was in the jurisdiction of Homs Governorate. The people of the village were farmers, but the youngest generations who had higher education found it hard to follow in the footsteps of their fathers and they had to leave the village to work as public officials or to enlist with the army.

That area had been mentioned in the wall writing of the Pharaohs as the place where a treaty between them and the Hittites had been signed after a months-long battle where no one won.

Destiny would deem it to have this village as the starting point of this novel, and perhaps the battle which would begin there would end the same way it did with the Pharaohs and the Hittites.

She sat on the swing and started to move after leaving her phone near her. She received an unexpected message; it read, "Happy birthday, you're twenty-two years old now, twenty of them are yours, and the remaining two are mine."

Yona could not believe that she would receive a message from that man. She did not understand him!

She spent two years dreaming of receiving a call from him, even if by mistake. Dreaming that he would say anything that was only meant for her; something not work-related. She often made fun of that dream and of herself.

Two days earlier, Yona had celebrated her twenty-second birthday. She was an average girl; nothing special about her, and yet nothing wrong with her. You might think she was a teenager, when, in reality, she was an ancient icon, well drawn by priests, mixed with the smell of incense and the holiness of the monastery. The glow in her eyes answered the prayers of the believers. The soul would see her before the eyes. She always knew the right thing to do. She was not envious. She was generous. She would open doors for you to choose the path you wanted her to take so that she would end up with you. Generous. Affectionate. Amicable. Never angry, and if she ever was, she would be so only for a few minutes. Understanding. Jealous. Clean. Organised. She always knew what to wear. She never cared for make-up or for showing off her charms, but eyes would follow her, nonetheless. She was not beautiful nor had a slim and elegant body, yet she was never overweight. She was a light story, like Fairouz the Lebanese singer's songs in the morning, and like children's stories at night. You could not but love her.

She looked at her phone and remembered the first time she met him. She had been drying her tears. Perhaps she wanted to seem strong and nonchalant. She never took much notice of him, when he asked her to accompany him so that he would show her the workplace where she would work in one of the administrations inside the main building of the Prime Ministry in Syria. She did not even remember whether she walked by his side, or behind him, but she clearly remembered that he had never asked for her name or for anything else. After a short tour of the place, he took her number and told her that he would contact her with a date to come after all her papers were ready.

His name was Jawad, a forty-two-year-old man with long grey hair; he inherited that premature greying from his father. He mostly wore a navy-blue suit, and had a good position in the Prime Ministry: he worked closely with the Prime Minister, who used to entrust him with secret tasks. He loved his job to the extent that sometimes he would remain there working until the sun was up. He used to work in a silence which everyone feared. He advocated his colleagues of lower status. Never knew fear and was always honest to a fault. His hobby was drawing, but he never had the time to enjoy it. Listened to people while scribbling on a paper — by the end of the meeting, he would finish a small drawing which he always threw away. A Muslim, married with three children of Circassian origin. Simple workers always made use of Ramadan to make use of his services. Despite not being a religious person, he never punished any of his subordinates during the holy month of Ramadan and tried his best to answer their requests.

Yona tried with all her strength to answer his message and to forget who he was. For two years, she kept on daydreaming about him. Her dreams would take her away, further away than she should have. Sometimes, she would punish her imagination for taking her where she sincerely wanted to be. She tried more than once to confess to herself that she loved him, but that photo of his family stood in the face of her desires.

For a moment, she contemplated not answering his message.

The swing gained more speed. Thoughts jumped around in her head. Sentences scattered around her. Even her words deserted her. She felt surrounded. Her hands shook and she asked herself whether destiny would grant her wishes.

But what did she want?

She remembered how she cried for a whole week when Jawad calmly said his goodbyes to everyone. He quit his job and she never saw him again. Everyone kept on mentioning his name. They remembered him. Why did he suddenly send her a message?

For two years, they worked closely in the halls of the Prime Ministry. Two whole years! She realised that his message mentioned "the remaining two are mine". What did he mean by that?

The conclusion she reached made her even more nervous to the extent that she could hear the beating of her heart. Did he dream of her as well? Or was it just a teenager's conclusion?

"He is a decent man and an expert in life, but does he love me?"

Yona's mind was filled with random thoughts, despite having Destiny grant her what she wanted. She composed herself a little and stopped her swing, then picked up her phone and wrote, "Thank you for your wishes, and thank you for remembering even though you are busy."

She hesitated whether to hit 'send'. She hesitated because it was thirty minutes after midnight. Why did he send his message at that time?

Night, the time to think of your loved one. She felt happy and replied with her message.

He sat down on the windowsill of his daughter's room in the hospital, looking at the cross lit blue and hanging against the window. That cross had been his main motivation to send that message.

Yona said goodbye to him before he left his job after a Cabinet reshuffle which followed the start of the crisis in Syria. Her tears and her red lips were the only image that occupied Jawad's thoughts. He was sure she would never answer him because it was late, and she might be sleeping or reading. As usual, his message was met with silence. He had always known that she never spoke much and he even tried sometimes to make her talk and get her to speak out all the sentences which would express her feelings and all that was taking place inside her head. He got her to sit around with her friends at work to talk and comment on whatever topic they discussed, so that she would get out of that sad halo surrounding her. Her answers were always short. That had got to be the reason why her reply to his message was so late.

Jawad hungrily read her words and reread them in joy and calmness. He tried to find any clue that she was not disturbed by his message. His only way out was to reply to her; nothing was keeping him busy so as not to remember her birthday.

He knew it was her birthday from one of her friends. She was not at work that day because she had to go back to her village for her aunt's wedding. An over-fifty-years-old woman who had to take care of her mother when her siblings got busy with life, the main reason for remaining unmarried till she reached that age. Her mother's name is Amal. Ten years earlier, Alzheimer's got hold of her and she forgot all; her home and her children. Heaven rewarded that aunt by sending her a groom whom she regarded as her knight in shining armour — to be honest, any man who would get her out of her misery (she never complained, though) would be her knight in shining armour. The groom was widowed, had children, some of them were married. He was a grandfather, and he was her knight!

Jawad answered her message, "You are far more precious to me than to forget you." He pressed 'send'.

For a moment he felt that his soul went out with the electric wave of the message on its way to her. He felt himself reach her phone and hear the peep of her phone receiving a new message.

Her heart skipped a beat when his second message reached her.

She replied at once, "Why are you still awake?"

He answered that he was in the hospital. It was a relief, because she could chat with him without embarrassing him in front of his wife. He had been married for more than twelve years.

After he told her of the reason he was at the hospital, they kept on exchanging text messages until dawn.

Their messages were formal and contained nothing but casual exchanges. However, each one of them struggled to reach what they wanted and to avoid any possibility of ruining the exchanged respect they had maintained between them for two years when he was still working.

The happiness Yona felt that day because of talking with him for that long was unprecedented for her.

After her father's death, and for two years, sadness had been her constant companion. Her father had been her friend, and his death horrified her because it came after the new fashion devised by some murdering cowards. A suicide bomber blew himself up on a public road near a police station. It happened that her father, her older brother, and their driver were on the way to their work and they were near the car bomb.

A car bomb from Lebanon, in 2008, the dawn of the Muslims' celebration of "Al-Qadir Night".[1]

The originally targeted police station was not harmed; instead, all the injured and the dead were civilians. It was true that her father had been a military officer, but destiny led him to that disaster, and he was not even the target.

The failed bombing operation had been planned in Lebanon by extremist Islamist losers who do not know Allah, and it is a shame to call them Muslims.

The investigations declared that the car had been rigged and the suicide bomber had been recruited in Tripoli, Lebanon. The attack had been an attempt at avenging the death of Al Hariri, the previous Prime Minister of Lebanon. His son was convinced that Syria had planned the assassination of his father. In ignorance, he avenged his father's death by killing civilians and thus emphasising the existence of stupidity and the law of fanatical and irresponsible revenge.

That day, Yona found no consolation, not even from her exploitative boyfriend, the university professor teaching French. That stupid man who

---

[1] Muslims celebrate this night mostly on the twenty-seventh day of Ramadan. It is a holy night mentioned in the Qur'an as a night which is better than thousands of months. During that night, Muslims pray to Allah and ask for His forgiveness. Many of them pray that He answers their prayers.

abandoned her after a year of courting and night phone calls, and who for no apparent reason ended up marrying another girl.

She never expressed her sadness to anyone. Never showed her wounds off. She remained silent, but allowed her eyes to scream all her oppression, with hot tears wetting her pillow for long days and nights. Sometimes, she even wondered why she shed all those tears; was it for the death of her father, or perhaps because her family is all females now, or was it because she was furious at the world and all those living in it? She cursed all the laws and political parties; she even stopped believing in all religions because they took everything she ever loved from her. She stood before the cross in the church one day and asked Jesus, "Have you ever loved someone and suffered their parting?

"Had your father and brother been murdered by an unknown man, and you did not know how to avenge them?

"Had destiny taken your little brother from you in a car accident?

"Were you alone, friendless?

"Give me redemption, Jesus, because I now feel the pain from thousands of nails in my wrist, and the thorns of the crown of thorns are digging into my head and to the end of my back.

"Why don't you redeem me from this torture?

"Why do you want me to carry all these pains?

"Islamists killed my brother and my father; should I take my revenge from all Muslims?

"Give me redemption, Jesus; rid me of this torture, or at least answer me: why me, why give me all this grief?"

Yona slept when birds were waking up and the sun was out. For the first time, she slept without crying or whining. Jawad's words were the reason. She dreamed that she had said what she wanted to say to him, and she repeatedly blamed herself because she never admitted her true feelings for him in her text messages. She felt cold, but warmth filled her heart.

She quickly fell asleep due to the little spider weaving its meticulous thread to salvage her from the torture of the dark sadness which overtook her during the past two years. The spider started weaving threads that would put a barrier between her and her fear of the unknown, which for her had turned into a game she could play with. Perhaps that unknown would be some new events which would break the routine of her sad days. However, her hero did not have a horse, no. He was a father and a husband. He was older than her, from an older generation. His armour was old, and the most hideous truth of it all was that he had a wife, and he was a Muslim; his sword was curved, not straight like the sword of the Crusaders. All that did not stop her from talking to Jawad; it would never be worse than what she was already going through.

If you have nothing to lose, do as you wish!

What would you do if you were one of those unfortunates whom life dealt them the misfortune of losing the most beloved people to their hearts?

Yona welcomed her nineteenth birthday with the death of both her father and brother. A hysterical and difficult situation, and it left her lost and unbalanced.

It is impossible to win a battle in which your enemy has allied with the unknown.

Should Jawad try to heal that massive floundering in Yona's personality? She was harbouring a secret; she and her family curse all Muslims and everything related to them, or so he believed.

Jawad, the Muslim, entered Yona's dark and horrifying tunnel. He wanted to light it up, but he did not have the fire that would help him light this darkness.

Jawad was spontaneous like grandmothers' tales; he had always done everything without planning. He never expected praise, and never cared for any criticism.

At noon, preparations for the aunt's wedding began.

Her sister went to the hairdresser. Her mother kept on calling out everyone there, and all were busy going around in the wheel of the wedding. Moving around like ants after a rainy day. Clothes were laid down on beds, the smell of perfumes everywhere, and smiles on everyone's face, their first chance of happiness after the loss that broke their hearts.

Yona never expected that day would be carrying all the noise roaming freely inside her head. She originally came back to her village carrying the heavy burden of her oppressive sadness, and not to show off her clothes or any of her femininity as all girls did. She only attended the wedding because of the duty she felt towards her family. But Destiny may have written down a new symphony that would start playing from that day on.

Today, anything can be said, and anything can be worn, because it was her fifty-year-old aunt's wedding. A bride incarnation. A bride who battled life and ended up tired. She needed to be a bride even if for only a year, just to know the feeling of sharing a bed with a man. The feeling of thinking with two minds, not just the mind of a woman, to always think of what he loved and what would make him comfortable, to take care of her home and cook for the man who would thank her because the food was delicious.

Yona chose a white dress which was neither long nor short, the same as Jawad, who was neither a friend nor anything more than that. The dress had a long slit at one of its sides to attract the eyes of any young man; so was her last messages with Jawad. When she sat, the slit showed her charms; and when he read her messages, he would be infatuated with her and would try to understand the hidden meanings of her words. Thoughts were roaming freely in her head, but those messages took control of everything and brought forward the past with all its details.

For two years he had been calling her, and she always went to him. He consulted her and she responded. Sometimes, they exchanged glances. She knew that when he asked for her, it had not been for work, but she never succeeded in finding a justification for that.

She remembered the little agate on which he engraved her name and age: twenty-one. She also remembered that he said, "Now, in the eyes of the law, you're free of any restrictions and are responsible for your actions. Now, you are an adult who can do whatever she wants; you can even get married without a legal guardian." They were law terms he learned from his studies.

She remembered when he asked her on Valentine's Day, "Has anyone got you a gift?"

She answered, "No," and he calmly put in her hand a small plastic figurine. When she pressed its feet, its eyes turned into two small red hearts. She was surprised at this gift and almost screamed in joy, but he never stayed long enough; he quickly left without saying anything.

Yona could not look him in the eyes that day. Jawad hoped she would call his name, and say something; but, as usual, she remained silent.

Yona never went to the hairdresser; no one called her to put nail polish on her nails. She did everything, even her simple make-up. She was not aware that her black shoes might not suit her white dress, and that they were of classic design, more like the shoes the Spanish Flamenco dancers wore. They were tightly bound on her feet. Perhaps her shoes never believed that she would wear them, and when she did, they clung to her feet like leeches.

All the little mistakes she made that night were because she was swimming in the words of his messages, and wondering whether he would text her again later that night.

She attended the wedding ceremony with her body, but her heart was standing at the gates of the village, waiting for a tiny single message from him that would make her heart beat again. She desperately wanted the wedding to be over and for night to come. She wanted a message that would express her thoughts and feelings. She wanted to remain wakeful until the end of her time, doing nothing but exchange words with him.

Yes, she could explain all his previous actions, now she knew their true meaning. She felt stupid for not understanding all the signals back then.

That day, she organised her thoughts, refined her sentences; they might be clearer than the ones she exchanged with him the night before. She was like all girls, practising by herself the rotten and shy pride which made lots of chances go astray. That happened because those girls never knew that there were lots of young men who had a despicable bashfulness which stopped them from saying what they felt, and so their words were lost. In the end, both young men and women are separated, burned, and the only happy one would be the regret which conquered them both. She, too, was that kind of young woman, playful and coquettish. She was of strong character, never talked much and always knew what she wanted.

Everyone danced until they could not any more, and eventually, the aunt went to her bridal nest.

The swing did not move that day, as if it shared Yona's sadness. She sat waiting for someone to sit with her. Night fell like precious black pearls with so many stars lighting it.

The night before, she told him about the moon and the sky and how it was filled with more stars here than it was in the city. Maybe the sky was happy because of his message; that was what she had told herself. She told him of the morning breeze and all the flowers opening up in her garden, and the Melia Zaedarach tree which cast its shadow upon her swing. She told him of all she was seeing, because she could not tell him of all that was in her heart. She bravely pretended that it was merely a chat between friends and nothing more.

She became aware that she denied herself all rights because she blamed her pretended willingness in handling all that had been going on in her mind; she branded herself a traitor; she betrayed herself. A greater fear than the one her aunt had overtook her. She feared losing him and remaining a lying virgin.

The fever of pain in the world; to be a virgin of love and not a virgin of body.

Jawad tried a lot to sleep during the day so that he could stay awake at night, but her words occupied his mind. He tried deciphering their meanings and secrets. He could always do that; to devise all that was hidden, and he was never wrong in doing so, except for some rare times when he could not. He felt that he was heading into a battle which might go on for a long time and in which victory might be the same as defeat. Having this little angel Yona into the laborious labours of a foolish love might make the mother's love of her baby bigger and her fear fiercer. That travail which carried the wailing of the feminine pain might shatter his heart if he ever abandoned her. However, her acceptance of his love might lead to tragedy.

He decided to stop that exchange! Logic forced him to take that step, but logic was never Jawad's companion in his life.

Specifically, at that point, memories were brought forward. They accompanied him, and he started talking to himself, remembering the way all his past love stories began, or maybe he thought they were real love. He tried recalling the details of the first time he started a new romantic relationship; his constant question had been: "Have I ever planned to have a girl fall for me?" Or ever thought of and organised his words so that he could have a girl fall for him? He reached the conclusion that he never even asked himself that question before having a relationship with a girl, whether that relationship was transient or went on for years. He was aware that he never pretended to have a quality that was not in him, and never hid anything, nor lied. He had always been accused of being overly rude. But why now, why did he stop to study all the possibilities? He had always been the leader of his battles in life. He had always been recklessly brave, and never thought of the consequences tomorrow would bring with it. He lived day by day and always searched for all that he had always lacked in others; always looking for real tenderness. A tenderness that would embrace him and give him a mother, a sister, and a lover.

He finally noticed that a certain girl had lived in his imagination since his birth. He creatively drew her, and she always sheltered him whenever he had nowhere to go. He befriended her and loved her, but he never touched her; and that girl was... Yona! Yes, she was the woman of his dreams, the friend he had always imagined. Yes, in likeness, she looked like Yona and no one else. She was drawn on the folds of his mind, talked with none but him, befriended none but him, faithful to him, the companion of his soul.

A fierce battle between letters, all wanted to be the chosen ones to form words, and words raced to form sentences.

When night fell, he returned to the hospital. He did not sleep. He joked with his daughter. She seemed better that day. The doctor told him she could get out the next day. That news made him happy and unhappy at the same time. When the clock struck twelve a.m., his daughter finally fell asleep, and he sat tired at the windowpane, playing with his phone and words inside of him still fiercely battling. For a moment, he felt that some of those words were gravely wounded and were admitted to his own hospital, into the extensive care ward. It was imperative to not let those words leave that ward; they were in danger. He smiled to himself and started his text message, "Congratulations, hope you'd get married soon as well." That had been the message he started the second day of texting with.

There, deep within the Summer breeze, she received his message. She jumped and went out to her swing, to tell it that the message she had been waiting for had finally reached her. She could not find the place where she could press to open his message. She read, hesitated, then started writing.

"I will marry after at least ten years from now."

He replied, "Even if a groom with all the needed qualities wanted your hand in marriage?"

She answered, "I do not have any requests. I only want him to be open-minded, beautiful, with lots of money, and would always love me."

"All this and you don't have any requests."

"Honestly, I only wish him to love me and that I would love him back."

"No matter his other qualities?"

"Yes."

"Even if he is a little older than you?"

"It doesn't matter."

"Even if he's not Christian?"

"I can forgive that."

"Even if he has a life-long disability?"

"No one is without fault."

"Even if he's on edge."

"I love a masculine strong man."

"So, you do not want to marry now and yet here you are in a hurry to marry unconditionally."

"As I said, I want to marry in ten years at least, but I also want to fall in love as soon as possible."

"Why haven't you fallen in love until now?"

"No one has stolen my heart yet."

"How stupid the young men of your village are; they have you and yet no one ever approached you."

"And what do you believe I have that they might want to marry me for?"

"I see in you all the dreams, all the women, and all the miracles of the world. I see in you a medicine to all the diseases. Oh, how I wish you would come now to the hospital so that all the pain may end."

She hesitated to answer, and some time went by without a reply from her. He was scared that she might not have received his message, so he sent her another one.

She replied that his message had reached her, but her mother called her to tell her that it was almost dawn, and that she had to sleep. She lied. Her mother slept three hours earlier, and only she had been awake. Even her aunt, the one who got married recently, slept as well. Only she in the whole village was awake. Yona just did not know how to answer him!

He caught her off-guard with another message, "Then answer my message."

"You're exaggerating."

"The day when you would learn your true self may come."

"And what is my true self?"

"And why are you in a hurry like all women?"

"Answer me!"

"You would answer me honestly if I asked you?"

"Yes."

He asked her, "What am I to you?"

"You are the most precious person after my family."

"What I mean is, what are your true feelings towards me?"

"Precious; and you, what are your true feelings towards me?"

He immediately answered, "I love you!"

She answered as fast as he did, "I, too, love you."

"Then, why have you lied to me before?"

"I was afraid to admit it to you."

Her phone rang and broke the absolute silence which filled the few minutes before dawn."

She hastily and nervously answered, "Yes?"

He said, "I want to hear it from you first, because I wrote it first."

"Yes, I love you, and I am not afraid any more. I love you."

"I have to shut off my phone, I do not want to hear anything else today after what I heard from you. I love you, too."

Jawad ended the call and went to the extensive care ward not knowing the reason for doing so. Perhaps he felt that his lungs were too heavy, or that his heart went still; no, it was actually dancing, or maybe he just wanted to take out all the words which were admitted into the extensive care ward, because they no longer wished to remain there.

He never imagined that he would write that word, nor that he would say it. Now, it was no longer necessary to keep it in. He said it, and she said it, and now, anything can be said, no restraints or shackles holding words down any more.

The key to an honest relationship is one phrase: I love you.

At that precise moment, the Adhan calling to the Fajr prayer started, and when he looked out the window, he saw at the end of the passageway a church and its blue crosses, and he said, "God, in the name of all those who kneel in praying to your greatness, and in the name of those who call out to your Jesus, I pray you to be our strength. Do not make me a traitor in front of myself and my family. I never planned for this to happen, but you made me admit it out loud."

He sat on the waiting chair outside in the corridor, and a few seconds later he was lost to sleep. He was so tired, and happy. All those who saw him thought that he was just another one who just fell asleep.

In his coma, he went back in time, twenty-five years ago. His memory took him back to his second year in college when he had been playing volleyball with his friends, barefooted and shirtless because it had been Summer. He had screamed his friends' names while playing and joked by calling them strange names. Suddenly, one of the girls had brought them back the ball that went flying outside the court.

For a fleeting moment, he had not seen the ball, because the blackness of her eyes, her plaited hair that went down to her waist and her softness, all that impressed his masculinity. She had been more beautiful than all the girls woven inside his imagination. He never said anything to her, but later on, he deliberately sent the ball outside the court, where she had been. His friends had noticed and scolded him. She had not cared, which made him ask her boldly to "come and play with us".

That had been all that he said, and her answer had been unexpected: "Thanks, but no! I do not like these things, and if you please, never talk to me again."

Then, she walked away. She had been deadly serious, and he never knew what he did wrong, or what it was that had annoyed her like that. Her friends noticed that he was trying to draw her attention, or that his eyes lingered on her, and so she got shy. It was true that he hadn't known what he did wrong, but that huskiness in her voice made him forget all the negativity which came out of her mouth.

On the second day, he sat down at the gates of the faculty. He was sad and wanted to make sure whether she had meant what she said the day before. He waited for her, and when she finally showed up, she went to him with her friend. He was a little nervous, but determined at the same time to stand up face to face with her and to stop any nonsense she might say. He had not slept the night before because he did not know the mistake he had committed.

She said, "Good morning." He nodded nervously, which made her hopeful.

She continued, "I want to apologise for what I said yesterday. I was cruel to you and I wasn't aware that I've hurt your feelings."

Jawad remained silent, just like the day before; then he asked her to wait a little while for him, as he ran to the restroom, washed his face and went back to her with water splashed all over his face and clothes.

She asked, "What's with you?"

He replied, "Nothing. I thought I was dreaming and wanted to make sure that it was you standing in front of me apologising."

That was how Jawad managed to be loved by anyone new; he would do something simple and yet unusual, and perhaps even somewhat stupid.

The two girls laughed for a long time, then he added, "Any time you feel upset, and wish to breathe out your anger, I will be waiting for you, and the happiest man on Earth for that matter."

She smiled again, and before she left him to go to the lecture, she told him that her name was Samar.

Jawad went to his usual place in campus and started replaying what had happened with her over and over and to compare the day before with his present day, and wonder what it was that changed. Do women think the same way men do?

He was twenty-two years old that year, in his second year at the university; it had been due to his failure in primary and high school. He had been a lazy and naughty boy. Girls had always excited him since he was little. He was ten years old when he first saw the body of a fully grown girl. He got into the bathroom with his neighbour. She was six years older than him, and she stood there naked, not shy. Water drops did not run on her body the same way they did with men; perhaps they did not like being parted away from that young teenage body, and also because the layout of her body is different from men's. For a moment he shied away from looking at her body, but he could not take his eyes off her full breasts. As for her, she pretentiously closed her eyes to allow him the chance to look his full at her body which she boasted about. She, too, enjoyed this and was practising a strange kind of sensual sex. She imagined him sleeping with her, and he, too, felt as if he had hugged her and almost did that for real. But her mother's voice forced him to get out quickly. Her breasts, however, remained in his eyes, and he went back so many times and boldly asked her one time to show him her breasts, but she did not, which forced him to suddenly pull at her yellow cotton blouse when she was not paying him attention. He saw them, and when she got nearer to him, he thought she would slap him, but instead, she kissed him and told him that he was a naughty boy, then she was gone. That was how his childhood began, and how his school years were delayed.

Since women do not have the same bodies as men, then they do not think the same way men do.

Samar quickly realised her mistake. Had she taken notice of something about him, the same way he noticed her eyes?

Did beauty mean the same to girls as it did to men?

Did girls notice things like the huskiness of the voice, the eyes, the lips, the nails, the hair?

He never found an answer to these questions, because he never knew anything about the components of women. He only had a teenager's love experiences in which lovers did not speak much, and, mostly, it was a one-sided love affair where the girl did not know anything about him and they had never even exchanged one word. Such had been his romantic relationships with Nora, Setta, Sawasan, and Hayam.

The lecture ended, and Samar left quickly. She looked for him in the place where he usually sat. A university student had a place where he would always hang out, and always protected it, just like animals did for nothing more than to have privacy.

During the lecture, both kept on exchanging looks, and she seemed to have not understood anything from the lecture. That time they were not ashamed and openly exchanged looks for a long time. He signalled for her to go to him; he decided to let her in his special zone. She did not hesitate and calmly went to him and sat down near him; no, she sat down so close to him to the extent that he felt her body's heat and could smell her perfume. Silence prevailed for a moment.

As if he was in a trance, he sat there in the waiting area in the hospital with all these thoughts going through his mind like a dream; what Yona said reminded him of what Samar also said in their first encounter, and during their second day together.

Yona directly said it and did not need an explanation, and she also emphasised the word, leaving no chance for a second thought. And Samar, she had said it after a moment's silence, "I love you!" — and when he had turned around to look at her with his surprised eyes, she continued her sentence, "I love to sit close to you, but I am scared that I might bother you."

He had replied then, "I called your name, how would I be bothered by a star that fell from the sky just to accompany me?"

He had asked her about her family. She answered him that they were two daughters, a little brother, and she was the eldest. Her father had been an employee in an airline, and she told him all there was to know since the day she was born. She also told him of how much she blamed herself for being that harsh on him the day before, then she apologised again. The whole day went on with both sitting together. That had been the first day on which Samar missed a lecture.

In the end, she told him that she felt a kind of relief towards him, and that she felt as if she was confessing to the Father in church, and also as if mercy and blessing had filled her whole. She finally asked him whether he went to the Sunday mass. Up until that moment, she never noticed that he did not tell her his name.

He answered her that he goes, but on Friday!

Her friends Faten, Kenda, and Abeer came to pick her up, because it was time to go back home. Abeer told him to accompany them. "Come with us, Jawad, we want to go home by foot. You can get us to our homes, and then go back to yours. Tomorrow is Friday and you do not wake up before it is twelve for Al Gomaa's prayer."

Samar looked back at him; at first, she thought he had been joking, but Abeer confirmed it. They all walked, the four girls and Jawad. Samar was absent-mindedly blaming herself for her wrong choice; everyone called him

Abu Nassif, and she thought he was a Christian, but no, she had been mistaken, mistaken.

Jawad woke up screaming "mistake", then he realised that he was in the hospital, and that it was morning. He asked himself whether Samar had truly mistakenly thought him a Christian; but Yona knew everything, and there had been no chance of any mistake like that.

Life is strange in what it gives; gives when we do not need its giving and takes when we strongly need it to give. It made a huge amount of prohibitions. Made religions, customs, traditions, rules. Life took it as a chance to make rules so as not to allow people to live in chaos; but at the same time, it created total chaos when it brought on us all these religions, and thousands of sectors. It should have set one religion to control and not religions, and one rule instead of so many rules. Life mixed the cards to confuse all the players in finding the right way to live their lives.

Jawad argued a lot with his professors at the faculty of law, that all laws were useless because they did nothing but produce criminals who aggravate the innocents, and never actually stopped the corrupt but made them more cautious. There was no use for laws because they were only made to classify and not to fix the society. He believed in what one of the previous prime ministers whom he worked with once told him, "The righteous individual does not even need to pray."

Yona never did any wrong, because she was one of those girls who always knew what they wanted; but perhaps, this time, she was a little hasty. She did not realise the consequences. She said the word and started her story without knowing that her story had no ending. However, the present was full of a huge number of obstacles, and her story had all the contradictions. The non-logical sat there cross-legged on the title of a love story that had seemingly started already.

Samar was the first to get to her house. She said goodbye to everyone without looking to Jawad. He wondered whether this, too, would be a sleepless night which she would spend sadly. He blamed himself for that.

He walked the rest of the girls to their houses, and Abeer had been the last one. She advised him before she went into her house, "Samar did not know that you were a Muslim because everyone called you Abu Nassif. You need to excuse her." Then she left him feeling a bit surprised because of her concern and because she knew what he was going through. It seemed that before going to the university that day, Samar had told her friends of what happened and the embarrassment between them, and they could deduce from the way she talked that she liked him, but they did not tell her that he was a Muslim.

Abeer was the cuddliest. A family of a father, a mother, three girls, and she was the youngest one. All her sisters got married except for her. She was a naughty brunette who knew everything going on. She had the pretense of being a strong woman, but like all other women, she was weak, sensitive, cried most of the time, and was lonely. Jawad once made fun of her when she got a sanitary pad out of her purse in front of the other students. The girls around her were shy and walked away, while she bravely exclaimed, "Are you satisfied now? You know now that I… Get it back to my bag, I will need it." Jawad promptly returned it because he knew what Abeer's looks and words meant.

Later on, when they were alone, he knew that she would roast him, but surprisingly, she said, "You are the only one whom I allow to do whatever he wants, because I consider you a brother. Only if you accept to be a brother to me?"

Jawad answered, "And I need a little sister to whom I can confess my secrets."

Samar never slept that night. She kept on tossing and turning in her bed, hugging her thoughts, and trying to reconsider Jawad from multiple angles. She tried to break free from all the stereotyping of the fact that he was a Muslim. Finally, she conquered her thoughts because she decided to not accept defeat in her first experience of love. She wanted to go all the way despite being young; she had been only eighteen.

With a simple manoeuvre, Samar succeeded in doing away with all the fears which took over her, and on which all children, no matter their religion, were raised on; religious doctrines were the basis of life, and anyone who would defy them would be walking down the road to hell and would infuriate God because you smiled at a Muslim, or a Christian, or talked to an atheist. Each house had these doctrines deep within their walls, festering there, blinding people from seeing humanity. Neighbours in

Damascus were either Muslims or Christians. They visited each other, showed mercy and love towards each other; but when something serious took place, like a girl would fall in love with a Muslim, his father would be mad at him, and the Christian family would leave the alley because a Muslim fox was hunting down their daughter. And the other way around: if a Muslim girl fell in love with a Christian, the fires of hell would be raised to burn her and kill her as they deem the right thing to do. As if the Christian young man was created by another God. All this went through Samar's head when she kept thinking about the validity of having Jawad as a boyfriend, and so she mixed religions together with love to come out with a solution to the fruitless discussions of the imaginary trial she had in her head. He was her first love; would religion be a hindrance? She decided to take a step back, which was a sort of cowardice. She got out of her bed, brought a paper and a pen, and decided to write her first letter.

She began…

"I had been rude to you yesterday. I did not know your name, and yet I apologised. You were the one who told me to vent all my frustrations at you. Today, I was also rude to you because I have come to know your religion, and so I left you without saying goodbye. I knowingly did that, because I knew that tomorrow you would forgive me, but before you do that, I want to confess something to you; yesterday, while sitting near you, I said that I love you, and when you followed that confession with looks which confused and scared me, I lied to you. I said that I loved sitting and talking with you. From the first sentence, I cowered. Now, I am confessing to you: I love you; I love you with my soul. I love you. Be whoever you can be, I will still love you, and you have the right to reply however you like to this."

Samar never wrote more than these lines, but they were enough for her to know that she had won over herself, and that she had been stronger than all the premonitions which took over her. She carried the letter to her bed as if carrying a sword. She put it on her cheek and prayed, "Our Father, who are in heaven…" When she finished, she felt safe. This prayer laid peace upon her soul, and turned her letter into a weapon to protect her from going back in her decision. She hastily fell asleep in a hurry to start the new day.

After he left Abeer, Jawad walked more than eight kilometers back to his home. He never stopped thinking about what had happened. Did it make any sense that she does not know who he is? Or did her friends trick her into this situation to make fun of her? But she was calm, her hair as dark as the night, her back erect like a soldier. The glint in her eyes was almost mythical. The huskiness of her voice miraculous. He was about to compare her to more than that when, suddenly, he remembered that she rejected him. He was not the kind to sail out to the sea without having a compass. He convinced himself that he did not need love this early in life.

Love is a commitment before all else, and it is also a machine which presses down the soul and takes out of it all the needed values in a love relationship.

Yona and her family prepared themselves to come back from the village after they spent the morning congratulating her aunt on her wedding. Yona never drove the car while travelling — her older sister did because she was more stable than her, or so she believed; even her mother always encouraged her sister to drive. This time she said nothing because she would be sitting alone in the back, lost in her thoughts; she was living the first day of a love story she would have never believed to be possible. Jawad, the wondrous and faultless lover. One hundred and eighty-five kilometers went by, the same scene running outside the slightly opened car window her mother opened to release her cigarette smoke. Yona tried to organise her thoughts; she was still in denial, she still had not believed that something like that happened. In the past, she wished it would. She used to talk to herself over and over, and would just fall in love with him in her dreams. She wished she would love him, and that one day, in her daydreams, she would dare to get naked and sleep on his chest; but as soon as she did, she would wake her soul up and blame it, and she made herself forget such thoughts. Then, the next morning, she would go back to her dreams; she would bring him back and make him stand in front of her and watch while she put her clothes back on. She would make him pick the clothes he would like for her, or the clothes she thought he would like. She did not even look at the mirror much before leaving the house like all other girls do; but since she met him, she started taking care of herself and she befriended her mirror. When she reached her workplace, she would not care for anything except for the moment she would meet him.

Yona remembered all the details of the past few days and she blamed herself because she could not bring herself to admit to him even once that she liked him. How could she when he never once took notice of her and when he treated everyone the same way? True, he had treated her differently, but perhaps he only did so because she had been grieving after the death of her father and brother.

When morning came, Samar woke up from a deep sleep that relieved her body of all the pains. Today, if she could not tell him all that she wanted to say and confess, she would just hand him her letter. She was prepared for all kinds of scenarios because, usually, when she was in a confrontation with someone else, she would stop talking, or she would just utter some nonsensical and incomprehensive words — same as Yona — or maybe all women had that cursed habit just to get themselves out of any situation. They would make excuses that it was not the time to talk now, or that they did not want to talk, or just leave without any excuses. Finally, their strongest weapon, they would become totally silent, to the extent that you would believe them to have turned into walls.

Women forget the beautiful things you do for them the moment you upset them, because women are like lizards: they accommodate themselves accordingly to the place they find themselves in.

Samar knew herself well, and so she readied herself, got her apple and walked down the road. He had not been waiting for her the day before at the gate of the faculty and she did not find him in his usual place, and missed her first lecture and kept on looking for him in all the corridors, and spent more than an hour waiting for him, hoping to meet him; instead, she met Soliman.

Soliman was the poorest, but the wealthiest in his sensitivity. A poet walking his first steps in life, carrying all the goodness of life within him, believing in Communism and, like all the oppressed, he wanted everyone to be a communist, but Jawad convinced him to abandon these thoughts, which were under attack back then from religions and the state. He had been Jawad's closest friend. They shared the same room in the students' dorm, even though Jawad's family lived in Damascus. They never separated, except when they reached the faculty, because each had his own friends, and when they met at night, each one would tell the other how his day went on. Usually, their talks were mostly about girls.

Samar asked him, "Where is Jawad?"

He replied that he went with her three friends to have breakfast.

She thanked him and went to where Jawad usually sat. In less than half an hour, they all returned. He looked at her sitting there, unaware that they had come back. On her part, she felt something strange piercing her body and she tried to explain it, but she had never felt this way before. It was jealousy, which started eating away at the leaves of friendship like a silkworm. Was she jealous? And so soon? They were not lovers yet. Despite all that, jealousy ignited her anger. She tried hard to control herself and to contain that strange feeling which no doubt meant that she loved him.

He did not go to her even when their eyes met.

She liked that jealousy she felt because it assured her that she was heading in the right direction. She was not delusional, she really loved him, and because she was not used to defeat, she jumped up and walked in his direction. He felt her coming towards him. She arrived, and said, "Good morning. Can I talk to you alone?" He replied that there was no need to because he hid nothing from his friends. He never had secrets.

Samar controlled her anger after this underlying insult because she intended to win. "I want to apologise again for what happened yesterday."

"If you insult me in front of everyone, then why do you want to apologise away from their eyes?" he replied without thinking.

She smiled and rearranged her cards. She almost lost her nerve, but she did not want to lose him. She had been determined to win. She carried her sword and stood facing her night with two options, and both were bitter. If she won and caught him with the net of her love, she would make him a loser in front of everyone; and if she did not throw her net, she would lose her precious hunt.

In the heart of all these silent and scary looks, Soliman stood there, joking around; but when he heard his friend's reckless and stupid reply to her, he tried to interfere, but stopped when he saw in his friend's eyes a look which threatened of a reckless storm, and so he thought the better of it and remained silent.

Samar never shied away from a challenge; she bravely chose to hit with her sword. She said, "You told me to talk to you of all the worries within me, and here I am doing just that; but what I am seeing now is you shying away from your promise, or was it the word of a boy and not a man?"

It was the bullet that hit its target, the sentences which were the heavy volley at the beginning of a historical battle to scare the enemy.

Jawad did not know how to reply to that attack; it had been him who started this battle and now he lost it in front of everyone and there was no way out of this tight situation.

Samar wanted to assert her victory, so she said, "I wish to tell you something else before everyone here."

She was to finish the battle that just started with a decisive victory, and because withdrawal is considered sometimes a tactic, he gave her a surprising reply: "I don't want to know what you want to say," and he walked away.

She followed him. "Just take this paper, and read what I wanted to tell you."

"No, I… I don't want to," and he walked away.

Samar looked around her and saw that everyone was looking at her and appreciating how she managed this war brilliantly and so bravely, because her proud enemy and his words and his constant solutions to all problems had been silenced and humiliated by her. Honestly, though, she never wished to do that, but that was the way with these kinds of battles; they manoeuvred you and not the other way around.

She went to Soliman and asked him to give the letter to Jawad. Then she said loudly so that everyone present would hear, "I wanted to tell him that I love him. You can read what's written in here in front of all those present."

Spontaneously, Soliman took the paper from her. Everyone admired her final victory; even her Christian friends reluctantly liked her frankness and strength of character, her bravery and the way she threw her sword and knocked down her knight. She could have stuck it in his heart and then cut off his neck, but she had the manners of the strong. She preferred to put all her cards face-up, because she was not fighting any enemy; she wanted to win over an angry lover from whose eyes she could tell he loved her. She wished to hug him and enter his heat. She wanted Jawad's crescent to hug her cross.

She went home early to take a break after that tiresome fight.

Yona reached her home safely without finding the answer to her question: why did he choose her? Finally, she said to herself that he did not actually choose her and not someone else, she only felt that way and nothing else. Instead of emptying her bags, she relaxed on her bed and talked to herself; she still could not believe that what took place a couple of days ago was real. A kind of confusion engulfed her.

Her mother interrupted her by asking, "What are you doing? You slept the whole way here, and your sister who drove all the way has already finished unpacking and there you are still relaxing, you lazy bone."

Yona got up, whining, "Driving is not that hard. I am tired of her boring driving."

Yona could not tell her friends about this love; she could not even utter the name of her lover, nor walk by his side in the streets of Damascus. She could not even daydream of completing her love with him. She would not even think of taking a hold of her knight because he was already tied to a wife and children; the children of the lover who carried all her wishes. He was disabled to the extent that she would never be able to walk down the aisle with him in a white dress and carrying flowers like all girls. She could never dream of a wedding because he would never be her groom. A lover outside the circle of targets, with defaults no one would accept. No one would accept the story of his love and he would turn into an outcast.

All that Yona had been going through, Samar experienced twenty years earlier.

When Samar went back home, happiness filled her, because she was in love, and because she let everyone know that she loved him, and that from then on she did not need to justify herself for standing with him. She even laid down traps and landmines around him to not let anyone near him. However, she felt a bitter taste in her mouth because she went back home without knowing his answer. She would have to wait until the end of the week.

Soliman caught up to Jawad and walked by his side without saying a word, because his friend's veins were still visible under his skin. He preferred to walk silently and kept on focusing on the road taking them back to the dorm. When they crossed the gate, Jawad said, "I do not want to go up to our room." Instead, he went to the garden and sat down on a chair, and added, "Don't blame me and don't comment on what I did, because I know I did wrong. However, I did it on purpose, for I have seen in her revolutionary attack on me a chance to throw a net. Her nets are strong to the extent that they could catch the strongest of prey, and I am a big and strong one, but I fear that she would catch me with her silken love-knitted net. I would not be able to escape unless I tear apart her love net. I would not be able to hurt her with my pride. Do you understand me? That was the reason why I drew back."

Soliman said, "I have a question before I say anything: did you not want to be the prey of her love?"

"Yes," he answered without thinking, "that is the reason for all this incomprehensive exchange which took place in front of everyone today. All this confusion is but a sign that logic was not part of today's event. My thoughts are confused, and what's oppressing me is that I have never fallen in love because I have always been afraid to fall in love, because if I did, I would remain faithful to that love and I would not back down from it even if it carried all the faults of the world. She is beautiful and I am aware that she is way better than men in everything, even in her humanity. I was the one who started all this, and up until yesterday I thought she was the girl of my dreams, the one I always dreamed of when I was a teenager. But, last night, I went back to the hut I built in the jungle of my dreams, the one where the girl of my dreams has been living for a very long time. I asked her whether her name was Samar. Do not be surprised that I know the name of the girl of my dreams. I never dared before to know her name, because I made her up and have never given her a name. When she answered me that her name was not Samar, I panicked and came back to the physical world. Poverty can live along with the girl of your dreams, but not with a real girl in the physical world, even if that poverty was mixed with love. How could I keep a relationship with Samar when her eyes are filled with love, and if I did love her, how would this end? To what end would all this lead us, my friend? Believe me, the barrier of religion has never been one for me. I did not even think of it. That is not the reason, but the main obstacle is how would I make her happy? How would I walk by her side knowing that I might not be able to provide her with something she wishes to have? How would we have a house, children, how would we make ends meet, how, and how and how?"

Tears filled his eyes, fighting to be released into a stream down his face, as if they were the tears of a sinner confessing his sin.

When he became calmer and his tears turned into drops of dew on his cheeks, he continued, "I love the girl in my dreams because she is not demanding, and she does not need the material world; she even knows everything about me, she knows that I can't bring her what she asks for, and she also knows that I would give her everything once I become a rich man. She is beautiful, but not as beautiful as Samar is, because Samar was artistically created by God. I am in love with the huskiness in her voice. I even fear looking in her eyes, where the holiness of the Creator's ingenuity lies. As for my dream girl, I am the one who created her. Her skin is white, her hair is colourless, or it has a colour that you cannot name. Her eyes are two drops of honey in a mountain of flowers. Her eyelids are velvety and made from the Damask rose. Their ends are as red as dawn, as if an explosion of red apples is about to take place. For her, I plucked an icon from the Orthodox Church and put it in the middle of her upper lip. Her body is small, but it has all the sexual appeal you think of. When I finished creating her, I feared someone would rob me of her, and so I mixed the remaining colours and threw them on her face and body to hide her magical beauty. The unexpected happened, and instead they were like freckles that made her even more beautiful. When she is longing for love, she gives you secret messages that she wants a hug, because she does not know how to utter this request. For me, she is the answer to the question of the ultimate beauty."

Soliman interrupted him, "Don't boast of falling in the sea of love without getting wet. I can see in your eyes the opposite of what you are saying. That who drinks from the cup of love even if it is just a drop, gets drunk, and you are drunk; not just that, the rain of love has drenched you. Unfortunately, you do not realise that she threw her net in front of everyone and caught you. You are the only one who still does not realise that. She caught you, you poor whale."

Soliman took out her letter and told Jawad to read it. Silence prevailed for a moment. When Jawad read it all, Soliman said, "Sir, she said that she loved you in front of everyone, and she asked me to read this in front of everyone; with that, she proved that she would not repeat the previous two days with you, because she ended everything now. Your answer is what remains now. Have you known that women are a thousand times more talkative than men and they still would not easily utter the phrase 'I love you'? Women look at how you look first, and they try to accept you, then they would imagine making love with you in all kinds of positions. When they are finally convinced of the man, they start evaluating his way of thinking, and his lifestyle, and if they are convinced, they would start loving him. Unfortunately, their female pride prevents them from saying 'I love you' even when the man passes all these tests. That is why they most likely lose the man they love, and their life becomes unstable, because women never forget the perfect love which suits their personality if they do not get it even when they meet other men, or get married and have children. This is the art all women excel at from the day they hit puberty. Today, Samar made a miracle and broke the pride code of women after she put you under test and found you to be an excellent student. After all that, she would not wait for destiny or time to make you say that you love her. She decided to make it short, even if it meant to insult her pride and admitted her love to you in front of everyone. She is a girl who is worthy of appreciation and respect. Do not let her go."

Soliman stopped for a moment, before adding, "Think, and by the time you have done so, I would be finished with preparing our lunch. Come to eat and continue our talk."

Jawad screamed at him, "Dreams are not fertilised, they would only give birth to a disfigured baby. Dreams only birth dreams."

Soliman laughed and said, "You took your decision pretty quickly. You are as I've always known you: you never fear to take difficult decisions, but why do you hesitate to think this deeply this time? Go back to your spontaneity and recklessness, they are who you are. Now, to the *Kawaag*."[2]

To which Jawad replied with, "*Kawaag* today, too, *Kawaag* every day."

Yona made herself a cup of coffee and sat in the balcony. She wanted to be alone and talk to herself to find the perfect way to reach him now that she was in Damascus and he still had not called her.

---

[2] It's a dish which consists of eggs, tomatoes, onion, salt, and pepper.

Was she able to call him?

She realised that she did not even have the ability to text him."

How would this love live in such yearning without her being able to touch, see or talk to him on the phone?

That was how she started weaving the strings of the barriers separating them, even if they seemed weak, but they hampered the logical flow which humans had been used to in love stories since the beginning of creation, but these strings might become harder.

Flowers wither with the passing of days, but thorns become harder.

She blinked for two seconds and tried to not think of this saying, because she was in a good mood. She said to herself, "Light exists even in the darkest of nights, even in the pieces of coal that shine like diamonds."

Yona listened to her heart and nothing else, and because its beats were becoming faster and louder, she allowed herself to fly with the breeze of her positive thoughts. For a moment, she felt the whole of her body quiver. It all astonished her, and she could not stop all that went through her. Suddenly, her phone vibrated, notifying her of a new message. She quickly opened it.

It read, "Look out, I am standing beneath your balcony."

When she read his message, she stood up abruptly and looked down at the street crowded with cars, people, shop banners, and thousands of intertwining chaotic electric cords that somehow looked like the human nervous system. He stood at a place she could distinguish him from despite all the chaos and the crowdedness inside that scenery.

Jawad stood at the beginning of the cemented road and right beneath her balcony. It was four thirty p.m. and the hot sun of July was still blazing.

She could not believe her eyes, and she did not make a move. Her body calmed down. She knew why her body had been restless; he came to her. She waved at him. She wished she could fly out of her balcony with an umbrella that would be in all the colours of her joy towards him. She wished to fall on the land of that lover who knew when to flare up the fire of his recklessness and his boyishness, and when to turn that fire into the candles of respect.

Foolish love is what makes you evolve and rebel against everything. Love is the master of all feelings, and there it is, eating away at Yona's little heart.

Samar had a call from her friend Abeer and she told her that she and Kenda would visit her. Kenda is a friend in their group. Afterwards, they would all go to visit Faten, who lived near Samar.

Samar hesitated because it was not usual that they would exchange visits, and because usually the reason behind their visit would be to discuss all that happened that day, and they would blame her and advise her to stay away from him because he was a Muslim.

Anyway, she agreed to their visit because she wanted to get out of the house and did not want to stay all day long alone and thinking of what had taken place, especially that her little sister never came back home early on Thursday, because after she comes from school she goes to the church, where lots of activities were held, like caring for orphans and people with special needs.

Faten waited for them at the doors of her building. She was a beautiful girl whose big, uneven white teeth distinguished her but never ruined her smile. When she laughed, she used to make that gentle voice mixed with a unique giggle, since she rarely laughed; her mood was as unstable as the month of May. When talking to her, one had to be alert because her answers were usually unexpected. She was a kind of an Aristocrat, or so she believed since she lived in the second most beautiful neighbourhood in Damascus, Al Ghassani. Every evening she would be standing on her balcony, looking at a group of teenagers who liked to show off all that was new in the markets.

Faten asked, "What is going on? What is urgent?"

Kenda answered, "You ask as if you weren't with us today and saw what Samar did!"

Samar did not comment, and silence befell them all for a moment.

Faten said, "Did you mean what you said today, or you just wanted to have fun?"

Samar answered, "Do you see me as the kind of girl who wants to play on others' feelings, or that I am a prostitute who hunts men this way? Why do you ask this strange question? Rest assured, I love him, and I love him a lot. I tried to stay away from him, but I could not, even when I found out that he was a Muslim. That fact, however, did not affect my love for him. I know that my confession to him today made me seem shameless, but I could not but admit what I felt towards him. You are now hiding so many feelings and you suppress them either because of your pride, or your religion or even your traditions. You do not want to challenge any of them, and you prefer to kill your feelings instead of recognising them. You are controlled by things you do not love, and you don't even allow your minds to discuss them or to know the reasons behind your holding on to them. You claim to be open to the world, that you're not religiously, socially or personally fanatics, but honestly, you are. An open-minded person would accept the other no matter what. When a Christian girl marries a Christian man who is twenty years older than her or who is a womaniser, you all say how beautiful that is because she is truly in love since she accepts that; but when it comes to religion, which, to be honest, we no longer belong to, but just carry it in name, then we are no longer tolerant, and no number of justifications would make us change our minds. Being religiously different is the problem and nothing else is, but let me ask you, why all this rush and having every one of you here for an urgent meeting, and who called for it? If Faten did not know why we are here, and Abeer did not care for all this before, then was it you, Kenda?"

Kenda almost said yes, but Samar did not give her a chance to do so, and continued, "If you were me and you loved a man and shared your dreams with him and you suddenly discover that he is a Muslim, would you abandon him? In all cases, your answer would not be accurate, because you would do so without being in the situation yourself. Your answer would come out of the darkness in your heart, an answer that would carry the blackness of the extremism planted in our minds since we were born in this country. Or, you will stop because your Maronite will lock all doors. But, what I am asking you is whether your heart would stop loving someone because he is a Muslim or would you marry a Maronite and imagine him to be your lover? Answer me honestly."

Kenda was two years older than the other girls. She was the youngest in her family. Her sister was five years older than her, and her brother was married and eight years older than her. One time, she tried to fall in love, but she was fooled by the man when she realised that he pretended to love her and only wanted her body. She did not possess any kind of beauty, was a little bit chubby, with sharp features and thin lips. She liked wearing loafers, even though it did not go with her height. She was also taciturn, and only God knew what was inside her. She had always tried to be the one to advise all, a fox in a sheep's skin; always discreet in planning her little conspiracies, and she did it in a way that never proved her to be the culprit.

Kenda could not answer her for a moment; then she got hold of herself after a moment of daydreaming and analysed what Samar had said.

Will love remain in the heart, or go away when we leave our lovers for whatever reason, even when we break up with no chance of getting back together?

She did not find an answer to that question.

However, she answered, "I am not telling you to stop loving, but I am saying that you should be careful of whom you fall in love with; you should not begin a love relationship which has no end. If you want to swim in this love, then do not dive in it, just walk, and be certain that you can stop it whenever you want. Do not trust men because, at this young age, they only care for having fun. We love you and you are still young and beautiful, and today we could not take it to see you say what you said in front of everybody else with such boldness. He left you and walked away, so does he really deserve your sacrifice?"

Samar interrupted her, because she could not take it any more. She said, "Yes, he deserves it. You were having breakfast with him this morning; if he was that bad, then why did you go with him? Do you think I am like you? Love and then stop loving whenever I want? Are you kidding yourself? Love is unstoppable, because originally it is not in the circle of moving forward. It creates and never dies; its carrier does, though, and we do not know what will happen after death; we might carry it with us, who knows? When I am in love, I do not realise that I am.

"Because whoever knowingly loves, does not know what real love is...

"That is why abandoning true love is not as easy as you claim it to be, because in the first place, you do not know the route love takes to enter your heart, so how would you know how to get it out?

"Love is a desired restriction, it is lovable solicitude, an endless wakefulness. It is the Djinn controlling everybody else. Strong, controlling, delicate, charming. Love is not an idea, not a principle, nor a belief, but it is an utter surrender. It is more of a secret, like death; you cannot expect it or avoid it. It is indeed an inescapable destiny."

The three girls knew that after her words, Samar had already fallen in the swamp of the crocodiles of love, and to get her out would take exceptional effort, or perhaps there was not any way to save her, because she had already fallen in love within two days, and it had already made her sick with it to the extent that she described it this way. The largest crocodile in the swamp had swallowed her.

Did Jawad really have the charms, or did it just turn into a challenge?

Yona never imagined that she would one day be in that kind of situation. She was looking at him, and he was smiling at her. The sun heating him, and the dust surrounding him. He sat down on the pavement which looked blacker than the car exhaust. When he looked at her, he signalled her to answer her phone, because he wanted to talk to her while she was there where he could see her. Initially, she did not understand what he wanted because she was still shocked. He screamed that she should answer her phone, until she finally did.

He said, "Thank God you understood that I wanted to talk to you. The whole street understood me, and you still did not notice your phone ringing."

She said, "I did not expect that." She stopped for a moment to get a hold of herself, then she said, feigning nonchalance, "What are you doing in our neighbourhood?"

He answered, "I was given the job of cleaning the streets."

She laughed because she felt that her question was extremely stupid.

Jawad added, "I love you. I just want to see you to calm down my restless soul; it had gone crazy and it almost devoured me."

Then, he cut off the call without giving her the chance to say anything and he walked away until she could not see him any more. She tried to catch him with her eyes even for a few seconds, just like the day tries to catch the setting sun, but he vanished quicker than she expected. She looked at her phone, then looked back to the street; maybe she could see him even for a moment. She thought it was all a dream. Did he really come? She checked her recent calls over and over, and each time she found his number in the callers' list. She remained this way for more than four hours, during which she kept on looking at the street, the pedestrians, and her eyes always lingered on the spot he stood at.

When it was eight thirty at night, he called again and said, "I want you to look out the balcony."

She asked, "Where are you?"

He replied, "At the same spot."

She said, "I am out, buying some stuff for the house, but I do not want to see you, nor do I want you to see me."

He asked, "Why?"

She answered, "Because I am not wearing suitable clothes, and I…"

He did not let her finish her sentence; he could feel where she was, and said, "I can see you. Can I give you something and leave as soon as I do? Won't I cause you any embarrassment?"

She did not answer him; instead, she nodded towards the place they would meet, because he could see her, but she could not see him. When they met down the street, he gave her a bag with three small paintings he had done.

She said, "We could walk down this direction a little if you want…"

There it is again, destiny had them meet in a situation so similar to Samar's.

Yona was walking by his side when he tried to avoid a passing car, and their shoulders touched. She was wearing a sleeveless shirt, so when this happened, her body shivered because of his first gentle touch. Yona considered it to be accidental and unintended, but he did it again for no reason.

He said, smiling, "Why are you trying to harass me?"

She said, "As if you're the one who is trying to…"

At that point, he was completely touching her. Stuck to her.

She continued, "And what should we call this?"

He said, "I love you."

She laughed. "Its name is 'I love you'?" Then she held tightly to his waist.

They walked for ten minutes, during which each of them watered the seeds of love that had fallen in a land full of sand, where no plant can grow. Where the air is burning with the sun of intolerance and a thousand storms that might blow and destroy this forbidden love — but love blinded them to all these dangers.

When they got to the initial meeting point where each one of them would go on his and her way, he said, "I wanted to tell you so many things, but I turned into a teenager with his first girl, and I was just content to walk near you."

He walked away for a little distance, got in his car, and drove to her. She was standing there waiting for him, because this time she would not let him out of her sight that easily. She happily watched him until he completely vanished. She went into her building and took the stairs instead of the lift, because she had been completely lost in all that had happened.

Yona loved three times…

Mohanad had been the first. She only agreed to meet him twice just to please her mother; then she ended it all with a nice text: "Please understand that I only see you as a friend." She said that she had not felt any attraction towards him; she wanted a cultured fighter who would make her listen to him from the first punch.

The second one remained for a little bit longer; she had fallen in love with her teacher at the languages institute. His name was Kamal. At first, she did not realise that she loved him, because he had been a kind of a strict Muslim; but for some reason, when he had told her stories from his daily life, and his suffering with his mother, she had felt that he wanted to keep his secrets safe with her.

If you want to own a woman, give her absolute trust, and let her take control of all the details in your life. Ask her opinion all the time, no matter the subject, then do whatever you want later. This way you will remain the sole winner of your life's battle because she will lovingly stand behind you and will think she is the one making you. There is no harm in that.

She did not remember how exactly she got out of his love, or maybe it just stopped before it even began. At that time, she had started college, and disaffection grew more and more every time they did not meet. In all ways, when he looked at her, he only saw someone who was just passing through his life, since he was from a strict Muslim family, and it was impossible for him to marry a Christian girl.

    Her third and last love had been her professor, Samer, and she loved him early on. She had loved him, and he had loved her. They tried to make it work and to have a lasting relationship that would end with marriage. He was a Christian, so there had not been any kind of obstacle; but for some reason, he left her and married another. She desperately needed him, especially as her father's horrific accident coincided with his break-up from her. She had made herself believe that she was the one who broke up with him, but she kept his pictures, and she even saved his wedding pictures from Facebook and put them in a secret folder with a password, which was the date they broke up. No doubt he was a petty professor, if what Yona had said about him was true.

Culture and education do not make you a balanced human being, because respecting love is the alphabet of life. That who does not respect his love, or the love stories of others, is outside the circle of humanity.

    Yona loved three times, but none of them touched her. That had been what she said to Jawad one day.

    She did not know the reason she loved him; it was a love full of paradoxes, but she loved him. She wondered whether she would have ever allowed the others to touch her.

    She entered the house, then her room, and sat down on the couch across her bed; then she took out the three paintings and put them in front of her.

    The first one was of a girl in a red dress. Her facial features were not clear, but she seemed as if she had been walking under the rain.

    The second one was of a sunflower. Part of it was dying and the other brimming with life as if in a painting by Van Gogh.

    The third one was of a boat sailing in a raging sea.

    She contemplated the three paintings for a long time. She wanted to understand what he wanted to say through them, but before she could, she found something else in the bag: they were stuffed toys, a laughing spider being one of them. The toys made her happy and made her forget trying to understand his messages from all this.

Jawad left his first encounter with her. Yanni's music was playing on his radio and his fingers were automatically tapping on the driving wheel. He had delivered his message with those three paintings. The girl in red who was loved by everyone, but she gave her love to one man only, and it was clear that he was that man.

The sunflower, following the sun which nothing but death would stop. Yona was his sun.

The boat sailing in a raging sea is a metaphor of all the hardships facing their days-old love story, but the boat would not stop as long as there was a sea and a captain.

The first day of the week. Everyone was nervous and everyone stood alert in the campus.

With all the calm Samar had possessed, she walked towards Jawad. He did the same with his unique way of walking. Girls exchanged looks; some accusing her of insolence, and some who thought Samar had learned her lesson and that she would end it all boldly.

A loving smile adorned Jawad's lips: it was a smile that many writers wrote about. It seemed that day as if all the drums of love were beating inside their hearts.

They stood close to each other, and Samar wanted to be the first to talk.

However, he took the initiative and asked, "Why, when, and how, from hatred to a proclaimed love? What is the reason behind all these chaotic feelings which confuse the one perceiving them?"

Samar did not answer him; instead, she walked away from campus. He walked by her side. The other girls were very incensed by her and Soliman jumped as if a goal had been scored in a football match.

Samar continued her previous talk with him about her family. She asked him to tell her about his family. He answered in quick, unclear words. She understood from them that he was the youngest in a family of five boys.

Samar's long and black braid made her look way younger that she was. Her rosy wet lips were the obsession of her male colleagues. When she talked, her words were like hymns; with her calm sentences and husky voice, she talked with an honesty that almost turned into rudeness in the ears of those hearing but not listening to her words. Some others would consider her to be immoral, but she never cared for all this; she had always been as clear as the sun in all she did.

She wanted to meet a hero who would sacrifice everything for her, because he had let himself fall in love with her. She wanted someone who did not want something material, but wanted to nurture his love from the water of looking at her, and by doing so would find his paradise and desire — her. She wanted someone who would identify her as his "lover".

What kind of creature was Samar? She was no more than a seventeen-year-old girl, and yet she had mastered the most beautiful art in the world: the art of confessing love.

They did not attend their lectures that day, and instead they spent the whole day in a phantasy of fireworks that almost exploded, announcing that there was a love growing up between two people.

He walked her to the house, and before they parted, each of them had their image engraved within their eyes, and parts of their souls within each other. After a fight that lasted less than four days, they both decided to remain in the love arena despite its danger, just for the sake of them being there together.

Jawad said to himself, "We strive to start a love story, and when it does start, we only think of the way it'll end. Thoughts and fears jump around screaming inside our heads, wondering what would happen next."

Would the future be ominous or promising? All types of thoughts rushed through his head, challenging him and his masculinity. They bound him with commitments which time had yet to come.

All of this made you remember your past, and all the fruitless experiences you had back then. You strip your past and lay all kinds of hindrances in your future so that your already broken-down car would get off the road into the rocky unpaved path of the future; the lighthouse of your love was far away, and your car could not overcome all the obstacles to reach it.

To those who want to be honest with love, they need to understand that love is a conflict between truth and mirage.

Jawad stopped at the small yard which he always passed on his way to the students' dorms. He wondered why he felt darkness surrounding him despite the love he breathed in and out. Did masculinity require us to be lovers and at the same time to take responsibility for love and its demands, or to just love, and when it was time to take these responsibilities, we just run away?

A shiver went through him because of all these questions. He was taken by surprise when he found himself in front of Soliman's door. He went in and lay down on the bed. Soliman closed the door and followed him and slept next to him. Both kept on looking at the ceiling for some time, then Soliman asked him, "Are you hungry?"

He nodded in confirmation without talking or interrupting his thoughts which were still with Samar, whose image was still in his eyes. He wanted to keep it somewhere else; he did not want her to be lost inside his chaotic body which had been filled with his contradictory ideas. At last, he imagined it there on the ceiling. Doing that, he got up to eat from his *Makdous* plate, which was overflowing with chopped tomatoes.[3] He had not asked what would they be eating just because his mind had been occupied with all those thoughts, or was it because it had been the only food available in Soliman's room? Still he loved it more than anything else.

"Did you love her more when you got closer to her?" Soliman surprised him with that question.

He replied, "I am like a bird right now, but wingless. I've lost my wings. I don't know how to walk on earth, and I am no longer able to fly. I can't control my thoughts. They've turned into marionettes which were left by their puppeteer, thrown into a faceless and soulless heap. We were created from the same dirt, the same soul was breathed into us, but religion separated us. If we were some soulless dirt, we would be like status, and only then we'd become similar. One soul had been breathed into us, and we had landed on this Earth to be humans together, but religion separated us and forced us to forget that the same creator breathed His soul into us, the One whom all religions worshipped.

"Are religions God's weapon which we should avoid, being normal human beings? Is that what we understood to be the correct thing?

"I wish we did not know how to speak or express ourselves so that the teachings of religions would not…"

---

[3] A dish of oil-cured aubergines. They are tiny, tangy eggplants stuffed with walnuts, red pepper, garlic, olive oil and salt.

Soliman interrupted him, "But, my friend, without speech, what would I do? Do I become a poet of the language of the mute?"

Jawad continued, "If you had just listened to the huskiness in her voice when she started talking her heart out to me. If only you saw her eyes and those deep-sea pearls shining a thousand colours within them. This story, my friend, carries discomfort within its folds. I am like a man lost in the desert and suddenly he came upon a well of the sweet water of love, but it's poisoned."

Soliman listened carefully to him, then he said, "It appears you're drunk with love. Your thoughts are in shambles, and you blabber on and on. Do not think of everything all at once. Days come and they bring solutions with them. I believe that it is not religion that worries you in all that. You can easily overcome it because your family is not even that strict. You only converted to Islam one hundred and fifty years ago, you Circassian. What really worries you and occupies your thoughts is kept secret within you. Anyway, don't give this more weight — even though you already did that — because that would weigh you down more."

Jawad finished his food and started washing the dishes, then he wrapped what was left of the bread, and said, "Do you believe in a love stricken with poverty?"

He did not wait for an answer and continued, "How could I, and you as well, love even when we do not have enough money to last us just one day, when we're still living off our families? Shame is suffocating us because we still take our pocket money from our families. Do you think we are real men? Don't you think that a person who loves should either be a female waiting to be requested, or a man who is able to demand and fulfil the female's demands? How could we love and involve the ones we love with people like us? You and I were created just to die or to be struck by luck and turn into real men.

"I wish we were eggs; to be eaten before we have the chance to fully grow. Then we would not be tested in life."

Soliman laughed and said, "Eggs? Nice idea. Did you know that my destiny today has somehow been tied to yours? After you went away with Samar, the girl with the blue scarf came to me and said that if I did not mind, she would like to go out with me. At first, I did not believe her and thought someone had sent her to play a prank on me."

Jawad interrupted him, "You mean that tall and beautiful white girl who came from Beirut? Her father worked there and retuned to Damascus to settle down. What's her name?"

"Laila."

"Wasn't she the girlfriend of that boy, Abo Saleh?"

"Yes, and today he saw me sitting with her and he wanted to get her away from me, saying that there was something he wanted to talk with her about, but she said no."

Jawad asked him, "Maybe they quarrelled, and she used you to make him jealous?"

"But she refused to go with him and told me that he has been stalking her, and that she wanted me to protect her from him. She wanted us to be just friends and I did not mind that. She is beautiful and her skin is so white that it is scary. Her beauty scared me, man, and I suddenly felt nervous and could not talk to her."

Jawad laughed.

Soliman continued, "It is said that whoever wants to know how far he is fallen in love, he should evaluate himself after the first date with his girl, and as much as that person stutters, he is equally in love. Today, I was the master of stuttering and idiocy."

"Do you really mean what you're saying?" Jawad asked him.

Soliman evaded his question and said, "We need eggs for dinner. Let us leave this talk at that and go out to get eggs."

There, at the place where they met the time before, Yona asked him to wait for her. She would come to him.

He was hesitant to ask her to go somewhere with him and to be alone for the first time in his car. Yona did not hesitate to agree; she, too, craved this meeting. It seemed that this relationship had been controlled by a single idea; or, to be more accurate, it had only one direction. Neither of them thought of anything and kept it secret, but they opened up to each other, just like any beginning of a love story. Spontaneity was the main feature of their love and not the usual pretence.

Women's perfumes are beautiful, they remind us that there is a female nearby.

It was her scent; he had always been familiar with it.

Calmly and assuredly, she closed the door of the car and they drove off, as if they had been dating for months. He even held her hand the moment she sat in his car. He drove to a place which only exists in their love story. She did not say anything; instead, she pressed his hand with her magical hand. She held onto him and allowed her eyes to speak for her. The silence within their depths implored him to never leave her.

He answered her the same way: that she should never think for a second that he would leave her. He finally said, "You are not scared that someone might see you?"

She answered, "No one scares me."

The coldness of shyness, of love's shock engulfed her hand. He wanted to ease her fast-beating heart. He said, "Don't fear anyone, and do whatever you can to be with me."

"Yes, anything," she confirmed.

"Anything?"

She nodded.

"Then kiss my cheek."

She never hesitated, like a lioness attacking a larger prey. She was scared but hungry and did not want to lose this time. She closed her eyes before she came closer to kiss his cheek, but he quickly turned his face and she kissed his mouth instead.

She smiled and uttered her first words, "You scoundrel!"

That day she never left his hand. He kissed her and she kissed him a thousand times over. He almost tore her upper lip, with that gentle pearl-like Cupid's bow. It had been her unique feature. The first thing his eyes fell upon when he first met her. They had not talked much, then he broke their silence and reminded her of her birthday which had been five days earlier.

He told her that he feared her. His grandmother had told him when he was a child that those born during the Winter knew the meaning of love, unlike those born during the Summer: they only knew misery.

He made up that story because his grandmother never talked about such a topic. She had never known love or passion to begin with. She had even married the brother of the man she wanted to marry, and she never knew that until her wedding day, in their bed. Despite that, she slept with him and bore children. She confessed of this later to her grandchildren when her husband and his brother had died.

Life becomes an imposition when social traditions are what lead you in life, or when you become religiously strict and thus oppress yourself into giving up life.

She said, "I respect your grandmother, but from now on, my birthday is 13th July, and not the one you're familiar with, even if it means that your grandmother's theory still applies to me. On that day, I had been born, baptised, and all the bells of the world were rung, and all of creation prayed for me, while all lanterns shone their lights on my path. The path that had been dark with a tragic sadness which engulfed all my days and my soul. If it was not for you, I would have slipped into a coma of hatred towards all the Muslims of the Earth. I love you. Today, I was born to be yours. Today, I was born to be a woman tempted by all kinds of foolishness in this universe. Today, I was born to touch your hand and kiss your mouth. Today, I felt like a woman…"

Her words surprised him. He said, "Each one of us, when he or she is born, has what we call a consort, an angel companion to one's soul. They grow and live life together. That angel sometimes disagrees with our decisions, but they do not remain in dispute for long. That angel sows the seeds of good, and when the fruits of life's ethics are ripe, he picks them. He also protects us and is always ready with his bow and arrow to attack whatever threatens us. He is constantly flying around us, and when life gets too hard, we find only him to go to. We go with our faces to the ground, but we come back with our heads held up high. Everyone looks for that creature and they seek to embody him. They search among all creatures, hoping that they might find even a small part of him to lay their heads on his shoulder peacefully, to thank God through him. People of old saw him in their statues; some said that he was the sun or the moon, others thought he was fire because they could not touch him. He is fire, but without its pains. The one who finds this angel is the luckiest on earth."

She said, "I do not understand a word of that maze of strange words you just uttered."

"I will make it easier for you. Any man who gets to know a girl and falls in love with her, waits for the perfect chance to ask for her hand. In all cases, you imagine the scene when he kneels and offers her the ring. That act of kneeling down is the beginning of metamorphosing into an angel. That's what I am trying to explain."

Yona raised her eyebrows in exclamation because of his description, and her little heart wondered of the time he would kneel to offer her the ring.

Or was it that Muslims only kneel to Allah, to God?

Their love would not include kneeling because it was against their basic Muslim teaching. Kneeling to give your lover a ring was a strange habit, foreign to their culture and religion. Marrying him was impossible, as impossible as the existence of the ghoul, the phoenix, and the good honest friend. All the prayers of believers would not absolve them of that love, and it would not be allowed into existence because it was an atheist love.

Their date ended. He drove her to the palace where he picked her up. On their way back, she relentlessly stared at him.

He said, "Today, I am one of the lucky ones."

She silently left after she snatched her hand from his as if she was taking it out of a heap of needles.

Soliman sat on a flowery ledge full of fallen leaves and warm flower buds that seemed prepared for the stormy autumn leaves which were no doubt coming.
He arrived unusually early and sat there to be able to see everyone entering the university. His heart was still in denial of what happened with him the previous day. Jawad's words had worried him; that she was using him to make whom she truly loves jealous. He still could not get rid of her image all night. She lived in his eyes and with it came all the worries of humanity.

The beautiful stones forming his crush on her fell down and caused the land of her crush on him to shake below his feet. He said to himself, "But, if it happened and she did not end up with me, it would be horrible to live alone with my love. Alone without the one I love taking me in, without touching her body which tempted me from the moment I laid eyes on her. I wish I had held her hand yesterday. I wish I had shaken her hand in farewell." Laila occupied Soliman's thoughts and turned his eyes into a radar searching for her everywhere.

Before entering the university, Jawad signalled to him with his head that she was right behind him. He stood from afar and watched them. Soliman shook her hand, and she let him do it. He was high up in the skies of his love, and God only knew what had been going on inside his head at that moment.

Samar stopped Jawad in the garden of their faculty. She had spent all night writing about everything she felt towards him. She read him her letter, and after she finished, he said to her, "I will tell you something, but you have to promise me first that you won't forget that promise; if we ever broke up, and I was the reason, then know that it would be because I could not provide you with all you need and not because I did not love you. I do not deserve you. Not because I do not love you, I don't…"

She interrupted him, "Why are you making me that promise, and have I ever asked you to provide me with anything? Why are you saying this strange thing to me? Have I upset you?"

"No, no," he said.

She continued, "And I would never upset you. I will be by your side, near you. I don't want anything from this world except for you. I love you and I have been dreaming of this day for months, dreaming of walking by your side and to talk my heart out with you. Yesterday, after we separated, I did not finish what I wanted to tell you and so I wrote it down for you in a letter, and I will write a letter to you every day." She was agitated because of that promise of his. She continued, "Don't ever think this way. I don't care for anything but being with you, however you want us to be."

Jawad thought she was getting more nervous, so he interrupted her, saying, "Your handwriting is as beautiful as you are." When he talked to her of what his friends had been saying about her beauty, she forgot the pain his promise caused her. He told her of a friend of his who said she was like a Swiss mermaid because of the beauty of her body. He made her happy, but she could not forget what he said; that promise and the timing of when he said it, all this worried her.

Laila sat by his side. The blue of her eyes reminded Soliman of the sea he left back in his coastal hometown: Jebla. The sea had always been the source of his inspiration. It had helped him take his first steps towards writing his own poetry, looking and searching in that vast blueness of sky and water for the face of his muse; the angel he had been looking for. When he used to go out daily to the sea, he would sit on the rocks facing it, listening to the sounds of the waves calling him, providing him with poetic vocabulary which was organised according to its importance in his mind until the day would come when he wrote the master poem in which words would mix and produce a musical meter that would be his first source of pride. Perhaps in those days he could not find the right moment to get out his poetry, because his muse was never satisfied with his teenage girlfriends or his childish adventures, even though he thought it silly to be able to write something that a reader would like in case he found his muse. Was it possible that destiny had easily led Laila to him so that she could be his muse?

He gave her the poem he wrote for her and which he seemed to have spent all night writing, and she asked him to recite it for her. Soliman did not mind because he added feelings to his words when reciting his poem. He mentioned her name more than once in the poem; he had made her his wave, his light and guide in everything. For a moment, he even made her responsible for having the moon so large or so little, he made her the secret behind the heat of the sun. He had her understand that he could exchange his religion with the one she believes in. With all the energy his love possessed, Soliman rushed forward without a moment's thought that he would rethink the whole matter.

Soliman was from the Alawite community, which believed that the Sunni Muslims were at fault concerning the Caliph, and they considered Ali, Prophet Muhammad's cousin, to be the rightful first Khalifa of the Muslims. They only believed in God, Allah, and few of them even considered Ali to be the god who accompanied Prophet Muhammad and taught him. Sunni Muslims considered the Alawite community to be nonbelievers.

However, all religions and doctrines were of no importance when it came to the love which young people believed in more. The students at the university were always alert to the matter of the differences of religions and sectarianism and how humans had played on their rules to get what they desired.

At the university, everyone loved everyone, but a small number of them would not continue their romantic relationship if the other party had had different religion or doctrine or ideology. Unfortunately, after graduation, few students would continue their relationships and remain civilised as they had claimed when they first got into the university and proclaimed to challenge anything that would object to their love to the girls they met. The majority, however, considered the whole thing to be entirely religious, and they would become fanatics even more than their parents, because they considered abandoning this kind of love a sacrifice in the name of religion. They would become stricter, and at the same time unable to admit that they had lost their love. In the end, they would turn into fanatic fools who would actually be proud of themselves. When the mind accepts a new idea as the norm, it is almost impossible to demand it erases it. That idea would just fall into a deep well, leaving in its wake a kind of stale water that would touch everybody, and that would never dry out; instead, day by day its rank would get stronger and future generations would carry it with them.

All religions should unite in the name of love.

Love is the master of all religions, because the Creator ordered religions into being to organise the matters of all living beings, to make them love each other; love is the master of all religions, because the Creator laid the foundations of religions to organise the world of all creation. He had made them into beings that love each other and make love in the womb of their religions and ideologies. Only if their religions were different, they would suffer a kind of sterility in their understanding that at the end they are only humans made by God. As for fanatics, they only believe in words and ignore reality and values.

Soliman dived into the depths of the sea of his love, and it had become clear to him that no matter the words rescue ships would throw to him, they would not work with him.

Yona had grown up today; she did things she had never done before. She kissed a mouth for the first time, she even rested her head on his shoulder when he clearly wanted her to do that every time he took a rough turn with his car. She slayed all the dreams of her desire, and she would turn them into reality with him. After that day, she would not touch her breasts, nor would she hide under her bed sheets to hide the movement of her hands. She would not dream of a man kissing her neck, inhaling the scent of her lips, touching whatever he wants and wherever she wanted. From that day on, she would make real love that would be far richer than her dreams. It would be violent, magical; sometimes she would invent what to do, and other times he would write it skilfully like a writer whose tools were the words of the body, love, and the soul. He would paint each part of that newly ripe majestic body on a separate sheet of paper.

She recalled that first date with him over and over. Her mother called her for dinner. She did not hear her, and when she came to her room, she had found her lost in thought. She asked if something was wrong.

She answered, "No, I am not hungry, Mum, thank you."

Then she asked her, "At which age did you fall in love, Mum?"

Her mother was surprised by her question, but Yona added, "I meant your first love?"

Her mother answered, laughing, "Oh, a long time ago, at school, I loved someone else. A teenager's love. I kept on falling in love with different boys until I met your father. Why do you ask, love?" Then she added, "Hopefully, it will end well. Take care, I want to see you in your wedding dress."

Her mother warned her of one extremely important thing: she had to choose a man from their religion. Clearly, her mother's warning came out too late; she had already fallen into a love that had all the contradictions there were in the world, and it needed a prophet with his miracles to convince the inhabitants of Earth that these two lovers needed to change all the religious and moral traditions and even change logic. Yona's love was prohibited, even deep within her; she had a kind of rejection against it, but at the same time she wanted to take care of it and protect it, even if she had to take it and run away to the edges of the world.

The first days of love are red, wild, and do not allow anyone to get near them.

Yona came back to her senses. She blamed herself, saying that God would punish them both because of this love, but why would He, when He was the one who had sown this feeling inside of us? She wondered, "Why were we not born into a different time when this love would be accepted? To be able to fearlessly announce it to the world with no one to regard us as criminals. A time where our love is not prohibited by a religion, betrayal, or years, just like his car: it does not follow any traffic rules, it does not even have brakes; it easily jumps over all kinds of contradictions and all the hardships that stand as obstacles in its way. It is the crazy car of love which crosses over all forbidden roads. That love grows within us, and no one has the right to stop it from growing, because it is the only plant the human being brought with him from heaven. He had disobeyed God for it. A holy and consecrated plant."

Yona made a promise to her passionate being to keep her holy plant safe and to water it until it grows. She would never pluck it out because she would be doing so to her heart as well.

Yona was insane for all that she tried to convince herself of; her path required her to fix all the disbelief in the world.

The prophecy of love needs Moses' staff to put an end to the snakes of frustrating charlatans.

Two months had gone by and Samar never missed a day when she wrote her love letter when evening came, and then gave it to Jawad in the morning. He then talked with her about what she had written. They were worriedly loving each other.

Samar tried more than once to hold Jawad's hand, but he always refused cruelly. One time, he almost hurt her hand when he wrenched his hand away from hers. Samar found this behaviour strange, and she almost felt angry at him, but she kept her promise of never losing him whatever the circumstances. She loved him and she would never stop at anything to prove that to him.

When they parted at the end of the day, she blamed herself for that promise, but her love for him was responsible for not letting her think before she acted.

Her love put a stop to any logic and closed all the doors on her pride. Simply, it allowed her to act according to how she truly felt. She could not but wonder at the secret behind his strange and unusual behaviour. That crazy Circassian lover, he was tough like his ancestors who came from the mountains, his reactions were as tough as him as well; he never lied, and perhaps that was why his honesty verged on rudeness. When he was talking to a man or a woman, it was always the same: never changing his talking mannerisms whether it was a man or a woman. That had been the reason behind all the admiration of girls through his way. He never knew how to be embellished, and the most important thing which distinguished him was that he was fearless.

One day, he befriended the Dean after a quarrel which rose between them. Someone complained to the Dean that he took off his under-shirt and played volleyball shirtless and barefoot. The Dean wanted to reprimand him, but Jawad answered that ninety percent of the girls in their faculty wore less than he had been wearing that day, and why was not the Dean reprimanding them as well? Or was it that their bodies were for the taking and men's bodies were not! The Dean did not answer him; instead, he asked him to take a seat and have a cup of tea with him. After that, they became friends.

Jawad, on the other side, was damning his foolish behaviour, which was because of neither religion nor manners.

When he met with Soliman in the evening and he told him of his strange behaviour, Soliman wanted to know the reason.

He answered, "I do not know whether I did it unconsciously, or because I was worried about her. I never touched a girl's hand in my life, I mean a girl whom I loved. When I touched her hand, I believed that it was wrong, because if I did, it would mean that I want her body. When I am with Samar, I do not want a body, I just worry about her. I love her for her soul, for who she really is. It is true that she excites me, but her words and her kindness are the reason for that. She enchants me with her eyes and her bright teeth. I never thought or dreamed of looking at anything else that is more than that."

Soliman interrupted him, saying, "Be honest with me, you never once dreamed of sleeping with her?"

Jawad answered, "What are you saying? I do not have to be honest with you! If you ever tell me that you have slept with any girl, I will never talk to you again. I love for the sake of love, for the sake of love's soul. I do not love a body. Days may change me, and another woman may seduce me, but Samar, Samar is a pure saint. I always see her in my dreams with the halo of the saints around her head. She gives and wants nothing in return. It is not permissible for anyone to touch her. I am even jealous when I see other people looking at her, and I turn into a raging ox; but, until now, I am still able to control myself."

"Girls are flesh and blood," said Soliman, "and no one cares for your perfectionism. I do not know from where you got these kinds of thoughts. I fear that anyone who hears you talk like this may call you rigid or a psychopath. Still, I feel that you have fallen for her. My friend, you are in love. Our friends will be happy when they know that you are that deep in love. You, the one who used to refuse untimely love. You, who is known as the virgin man. Do not be afraid, you will break down the wall of virginity as you have done with the wall of 'never falling in love', because your rule of never touching your girlfriend will be broken by the passing of days. I swear to God, love has turned you into a fool."

Next morning, Jawad stood looking at a young Damask man called Obaid, who had been drawing Samar. He had been insolently drawing her. Jawad snatched the paper from him and violently tore it up. He said, "Do you know that there are people who worship art?" Obaid wondered at his words, which contradicted his actions. Jawad added, "And there are those who consider it blasphemous and a kind of disbelief, and I am one of those. If you do that again, I will do to you what I just did with that paper."

Jawad went back to Samar. He was on the verge of exploding out of anger, because Obaid had not talked back to him, neither did he respond to Jawad's rudeness. He vented it all out on Samar and said, "And you're sitting here happy and exchanging looks with him! Get up and go to your lecture."

Samar did not respond to him. For the first time she felt like she had a man. She tried to smile at his reaction, but the knot between his eyebrows was too serious. A smile would never grace his harsh face, so she preferred not to smile and feign defeat; she won him over when she had him jealous.

It had been an ominous day since it began. They received news that their friend Abeer's father had passed away. Jawad stopped a taxi and took Abeer home. Crying wails were everywhere. Abeer vanished in the black mass in front of her house. Jawad tried to get in with her, but he realised that it would not be suitable to do so since no one knew him, and no one talked to him. He preferred to stand down. For a few moments, he remained standing outside, then he walked away as if he was someone passing through the same street.

He preferred to be by her side because she was his friend. He told all her friends of what had taken place, and the next day they went to her house to pay their condolences, and to be there for their friend. They all tried to make her talk, but her sadness had been heavy and her pain unbearable, and so she did not talk to anyone.

She was the youngest among all her married sisters. She remained lonely in their house with her father, who had always seemed sadder and older than any old man on Earth. He had lost a wife he dearly loved, and she had given birth to his four girls. Now, the mother, the wife, and the lover had gone away and that holy sting tying him to Earth had been severed. Love, however, never ended; it seemed to be digging valleys of pain and stirring up the fire of longing which would never be put down. Lover who went away to the unknown, why would you separate from me now? Do not make haste, wait. That had been the words his face expressed. It was the love that kept on living after death. The love that kept on winding up the tape of memories. Some would stop it because of religion or traditions, but it would always be stronger than death. It would always be a professional killer who would melt down anyone who would hit it. It would kill anyone with the longing for parting.

In less than two weeks after her mother's death, and when Abeer was starting to recover from the shock of her mother's death, Samar told them with her husky, stifled-down voice that Abeer's father died the day before. Faten and Kenda screamed, and with her spontaneity, Faten added that this way Abeer would not finish her school year. Everyone looked at her in bewilderment, but she rephrased her sentence and said that what she meant to say was that Abeer's shock was unmatched, and that was why she would not be able to attend their mid-year exams in one month.

Jawad interfered, saying, "Go to her now, and do not let her fall into an abyss of sadness, because if she did, it would be hard to get her out of it. I will not come with you because I cannot see her like that. I fear her sadness."

They all left, and Jawad remained alone. In tears, he went back home. He could not stop the tears which covered his face. Despite his fatigue, he was restless, so he brought his canvas and colours and started painting. He had no idea what to paint, then he remembered his words to Obaid and his fight with him. He only excused Obaid in his heart because he wanted to draw Samar; she was beautiful, and she had woken up his artistic sense. There he was, talking to his queen. He suddenly remembered that he had a personal picture of Abeer, which he had taken from the students' bureau. Back then, he showed it to Abeer, and had kept it even though she tried to take it from him, but he had insisted on keeping it. As if destiny had meant for that to happen so that he would have it for a day like that. He put the picture at the end of the canvas. Suddenly, an idea, which would be attacked by everyone, occurred to him. However, he would not back down, because he wanted to portray all that Abeer had been through. He drew Abeer's face twice, one in the first half, and the second in the lower one. The second face was hers; it had her hair and all that made her special. The first face had the hair and the details of Christ, as if he wanted to say that Abeer had borne a pain which is like that of the Christ. That she had borne a sadness which is similar to that which people had felt for him. The painting looked like an icon of the church because of its colours and its theme. However, its size negated that feature off it.

For five days, Jawad did not attend his classes, and instead kept on working on his painting day and night.

No one inquired after him, because the only one who would miss him had gone back to his hometown to sit overlooking the sea and be inspired by it for his new poem. He feared letting Jawad know what his poem would say, because it carried within things that Jawad would not like.

Jawad went back to the faculty. Samar met him with her usual tenderness and asked him the reason for his long absence. She missed him and confessed that she had passed by his house more than one time hoping to meet him. He asked her coldly, "If you did, then why didn't you come up?"

She answered, "How would I do that? What would your family say?"

He replied, "My family would not say anything. Ask the girls, all three of them visited me once. No one was at home, and so Kenda and Faten went to explore the house, while Abeer made coffee in the kitchen when my mother came back from the farmers' market. At first, she thought she had gotten into the wrong house, then she saw me and Abeer alone, but then Kenda and Faten showed up and said, hi. My mother laughed so hard and confessed to Abeer that she thought her alone in her house, and that she wanted to hit her with the broomstick. Then she apologised, saying that humans are always too quick to judge."

Samar was surprised at this, and she said, "You want me to be hit by a broomstick?"

"No, don't be scared. When my mother sees you, she will hit me for my choices, not for my doings. When she sees your beautiful face, she will take her coffee with you and tell you all about my faults, then she will pray to God to keep us safe. She will tell you, 'He'll make you happy, don't worry. He is the only one among my children who is loved by God, and He would give him all he prays for. I believe that the door of his beautiful destiny has been opened because of your angelic face.'"

Jawad stopped, then continued, "Why didn't the girls come with you? Abeer is now a friend of my mother." He realised what he had said, so he said, "Did Abeer come back to the university after her tragedy?"

Samar said, "First, I see you're flirting with me, which means you're well. Second, concerning Abeer, she is beautiful, and your mother will not hit you for choosing her. Third, we never left her, we're with her daily because her older sister asked us to do so, and up until yesterday we could not get her out of her silence. They brought her a doctor and it didn't work. She doesn't want to talk with anybody, nor does she want to come out of her room."

Jawad interrupted her, asking, "And when are you going to her today?" But he did not wait for her answer and continued, saying, "Let us meet at her door at eight tonight. I know it is late, but do not worry, I will get you all to your houses safely. Do not laugh, I will get you home first, then I will do the same with the others." Then he poked his tongue out to tease her. He added, "You crazy girl, I only said that Abeer is beautiful so that I could flirt with you."

At eight o'clock, Jawad got there carrying something that was as big as a half door. It had been wrapped up in brown paper bags.

Everyone went into the house, and Abeer's older sister met them, wondering at their late visit and at the disturbing noise the paper bags made. She asked the girls, thinking that they knew, "What is that?"

The girls did not answer her; instead, they looked at Jawad, who was looking at the fireplace, watching the movement of the flame warming the room, as if it was death itself. Just like this flame, we fire up and grow up, then we vanish and disappear, leaving behind the heat of separation in the bodies of others.

Jawad noticed that he needed to answer her questions; instead, he asked, "Where is Abeer?"

She answered, "In her room. She does not want to see anyone, and the doctor said not to force her on anything to avoid worsening her state."

Jawad said to himself, "Those silly doctors with all their restrictions, and we fear those restrictions just because a doctor ordered us, not because they are right or wrong."

Uncaring, Jawad stood up, ignoring those restrictions, carrying his noise with him, and knocked on the door, not to seek permission but so she would know that he would enter her room. When he went in, he closed the door behind him so as not to let anyone else enter. He found Abeer lying down on her bed with her eyes puffed up, miserable and hungry for her parents' affection.

Without any introductions, he said, "Are you challenging God? You want to kill yourself to join your parents? They lived a time that is three times your age. Wait until you are as old as them and do not fear death. Death is a good friend, inseparable from us, and is never bored of staying close to us. It is sincere and friendly and will never abandon us no matter how much we try to disturb it. Do not rush it, it will come when the time is due. However, do not welcome it, because if you do, it will lose its power and tyranny. It loves to come when you are least expecting it. That is the only thing which comes to all of us and makes us all equal. The only thing that makes it distinct is that sometimes it comes early to some of us. As for your father, death was almost his choice: I saw it on his face when I came to console you for the death of your mother. I saw him praying for his death, to be reunited with the one he loved. He loved your mother, and you were the fruit of that love. Let him rest where he wants to rest. No one loves his children more than their mother; some mothers, after some time has passed on their marriage, claim that they love their children more than their husbands, but when they lose them, and their children are out there living their lives, they learn that their love for their partner is what completes them. This is what your mother wanted; she took her lover where she wished to stop life from insulting him after her departure. God wanted them to complete their love story up there in His heavenly kingdom.

"Come on, sit up. Tell them you're hungry and to bring you food immediately. They told me you haven't eaten for days. I will eat with you. By God, I am hungry. Please, Abeer. Your sister outside, she doesn't love me, and I want to tease her. Please."

Hints of a smile were on her face. First, because he was there in her room, sitting on her bed, and not caring that he was in the room of a girl that he almost knew nothing about. Second, because he talked like that about her sister and how he wanted her to join him in teasing her.

She nodded towards the wrapped-up painting, asking, "What is that?"

He replied, "I will tell you if you promise me you will eat." She nodded in agreement. He put the painting in a higher position and removed the wrapping in a quick movement that accompanied her surprise with it.

She asked, "You painted it?"

"You talked?"

"It is beautiful yet scary."

"Ask them for food."

She laughed and stood up to open her bedroom door, and said to her sister, "Bring me food, but first, all of you, come and see this."

All of them went in, wanting to know the reason which had made her talk and ask for food.

Her sister said, while heading out of the room, "This is forbidden; you cannot draw something like that."

He asked, "Why? Is it because I am a Muslim? Or is it because it carries a somewhat religious feeling to it?"

"No, you do not have the right to draw Christ; only saints have the right to do so, and it is also forbidden to draw Abeer's face in the same painting as Christ and in that manner."

He said to her in bewilderment, "No one knows what Christ looked like. In Africa, for instance, they draw him with a black skin. As for Abeer, she lacks nothing which other saints have. We all love her, and she takes care of all of us. She gives and waits for nothing in return. All of you do not know how to…"

She interrupted him, "I will bring food."

Jawad ate far more than Abeer, and he did so to tease her sister, who did not hesitate to call him glutton more than once.

Abeer ate, talked, and promised to go to the university the next day. She got out of her plight and with that achieved, they all left her house. At her door, and before they all left, her sister said to Jawad, "Thank you." As she said that, she put her hand on his shoulder to emphasise her thankfulness.

It had always been a skill of his: to turn those who hated him into good friends.

When they reached Samar's house, she said to him in front of all the girls, "I heard a few days ago someone saying that drawing is viewed by some people as art, but others view it as blasphemy."

Jawad understood her underlying message, but the girls did not. He said to her, "I did not draw a painting, I drew an exit for her sadness."

His answer was curt, but it relayed his message clearly.

Students started to feel the heat of the first semester exams, and they honed their energies for this. At the same time, it got colder in Damascus as January began.

Another kind of coldness described Jawad's relationship with Soliman, especially after the latter confessed what he did while Jawad was busy with Abeer's condolences. He confessed that he took Laila to a room he rented in one of the working-class neighbourhoods. She did not mind; on the contrary, she boldly asked him to do so. Soliman never thought of more than to spend some time alone with her, and to express his love to her by reciting his poetry, and then to just talk. However, once they entered the room, she lay on the bed and asked him to sit by her side. Soliman was concerned because of this boldness, but she said, "Beware, I am still a virgin, and I want to remain so. Everything for the taking except…!"

He did not recall what happened afterwards, but he found himself naked and on top of her naked body. He never believed all that happened between them. He tried to do with her all that he had imagined since he was a teenager. She came five times, and so did he. He kissed her all over her body, her eyes, her mouth, and her toes. He got out all his shyness and threw it away. He killed all his reservations and buried them in her snow-white body. She had been his first trial after a long spell of thirst. That had not been the case for her, though, for she knew what she was doing, and how to do it; she was not shy. She made conservative love with him professionally, like someone longing for something that had been taken from her. It did not seem like a first time after a cruel adolescence. She well knew how to rid him of his virginity, to playfully touch him, and make him get her to her full excitement. He, like an ox, did not care where his ejaculations landed. Everywhere had been permissible except for a few centimetres. He ate her with the lust of a young dreaming boy, who did not see something specific, nor did something he always longed to do, but the monstrosity of his lust had been the one in control. As for her, she enjoyed his passion, which had been harmonious with his confusion. She realised that it had been his first time, and she managed to get out of him all his masculine hidden qualities.

Soliman told Jawad that he did not wish to hide anything from him. Jawad was infuriated with him, especially since he first severed his friendships with all his old friends when he knew that one of them did like what Soliman had done, not because Jawad was religious, but for moral reasons, or perhaps he wanted to show off as someone who was different and unique, like any young man at the start of their lives and how they believe in strange things just to have the attention of others. He became known as the Muslim Priest, but that stance in life took all his friends away, and Soliman had been the last one left.

They remained apart, and even when Soliman went to register for the trip to one of the most important Syrian castles "Kras des Chevaliers", they did not exchange one word, since Jawad had been the one organising the trip.

Yona asked Jawad where he thought their affair was heading, since it had already been two months since they started going out together.

He answered her, "We remain lovers, but we may not consider each other so, and we become just friends!"

Yona did not expect that kind of curt and cold answer from him. She felt as if this was the first time to ever talk to him. During the past few days he showered her with his love without waiting for anything in return; he even used to say that when love entered the heart of the arrogant it turned him into a humble person, and only love could melt the ice of the pole with the warmth of its feelings. Each morning he would call her and say loudly, "It is beautiful to be among the living each morning, and more to it is to start your day with the voice of the woman you love."

Why, then, that harshness today? She felt nervous, then angry. She said, "You cannot be whatever you want each time; I treat you as a lover, then in a few days like a friend. It is not as easy as snapping buttons; there is no grey area in love."

He said, "Stop, do not turn this argument into a river that would separate us." Then he tried to hold her hand.

She refused and said, "Don't touch me. I am only meant for a man who is like Caesar, the rebellious ruler, the man of his word. That who does not fear a religion, nor an age, nor an army. A man who puts on an armour of iron on which all the arrows of doubting his love break. An honest and noble man. I do not want that who castrate oxen only for farming. Choose whomever you want to be, but for me I only want the Caesar."

Before Yona left, they agreed for each of them to think about it, then meet in three days with their final decisions.

It was the kind of love which deprived the fiercest leaders of their victory. All the tricks in the war of love are allowed, except for manipulating the lover.

You may not be a successful leader in love when you are surrounded with hesitation.

What is right could not win over that kind of love, because one always fought for love and not for what is right.

That kind of love was like a snake: it only spoke the language of poisons.

However, it remained a true love; rejecting it was a cinder and accepting it at the same time was a cinder.

That kind of love needed lovers to accept its reality, but all those who surrounded it did not know love.

Who would feel compassion towards Jawad?

For sixteen years, he had been a married man, with three children. He was twenty years older than Yona. He was a Muslim, and she was a Christian.

How would you convince the world of your love?

How would his children accept a father like him?

How would Yona convince her mother, her family, and her friends that she loved that person?

How would she even open such a subject with them?

Who could bet on that love and assure its continuity?

It was a kind of love refused by all on Earth.

It is hard to convince people with a certain situation. It takes years in courts to have the truth revealed.

Was Yona still a teenager to get attached like this to his love?

Why did she only want to fall in love with a Caesar that rebels on everything and everyone? A strong man who said whatever he wanted to say. How could she demand that kind of love when she knew the truth? Who would convince the sensible haters who described this love as madness? Who would take away a husband from his wife and children? The society would never forgive him, nor would the saints of love. They would all curse him. How would you be Caesar when all your subjects are Brutus?

Still, why would Jawad fall into that kind of love?

Why, when he could always stand tall on the rock of survival and challenge the raging winds of sins? He had always been self-composed and never did anything wrong.

Why now? And why this true feeling of love?

He believed that destiny would always get him towards what is best for him, towards a truth that he never thought of. He felt that he had been on the right path while he had been challenging all values and traditions.

Samar began thinking of all the details of Jawad's painting of Abeer. It had a face portraying the face of Christ, and Abeer's sad and skinny face. She had been dressed in a black that was like the colour of her hair. There had also been a part of an old church wall to add the effect of prestige. A small apple in the right corner and a heart, as if Jawad wanted to convey that it had always been the reason for the torment of our hearts. **She feared that this would mean love.**

She wondered whether the tragedy Abeer went through would be an opening for Jawad to change the course of his love.

What did he mean by that heart? And why did he draw it?

Samar replayed all that had happened during the past few days. The love between them had turned cold even before they fully went into it. He stopped caring about her. It seemed as if Samar no longer controlled her thoughts, and that restlessness she felt had been because of what she witnessed the other day. He had been so close and intimate with Abeer. He fed her. As for Abeer, she seemed as if she had been waiting for him to talk. He sat on her bed, and stubbed her older sister, and won her over.

Why did he accuse Abeer's painting of hereditary, and today he worshipped Abeer with his painting?

Was he the only one allowed to paint whatever he wanted and to prohibit others?

But, she did not want to abandon her love story which she no doubt resisted for it, and she would remain hanging on to that love. She calmed herself down and said to herself, **"First rule of love is to make excuses for those we love."**

Next morning, and unusually for her, she put on her beautiful face: a light make-up, then some heavy mascara to her eyelashes, which turned her face into an attraction that would not allow others to look away from her two black diamonds for eyes.

When he saw her, Jawad asked her for the reason she put on make-up; that delighted her, because she had achieved what she wished to.

She answered him, "It's a kind of change and a celebration, since everyone is out of their sadness. Don't you like it?"

He said without his usual bluntness, "You are beautiful without all this. You need nothing, so do not add anything. No matter how you try to make yourself more beautiful, you will not be more beautiful than the way the Creator made you, or at least this is what I think. When you add make-up, you are like the *Mona Lisa*, where someone wants to add to it, thinking that Da Vinci has missed something; however, if you want to do this as a kind of change, then so be it."

She changed the subject and said, "That was a nice painting yesterday. You are always able to do whatever you want. The doctor couldn't get her out of her silence, and you did. I love you because you are determined and always head for your aim no matter what. You do not waste your time with side details. You always achieve victory by the end of the battle with your final hit, and then people would forget the reason for the battle and they would only praise your victory. You know how to place yourself under the lights of fame effortlessly."

"No, they only see the leader of the battle. Do not unclothe me and make the reason of my victory to be a chance or me taking profit from some kind of situation. I knew that she would suffer like that, and I still did not go to her during the first days, but I still did not sit motionless. I thought of what would get her out of a tragedy like that, but I did not have enough, so I thought of drawing her, and I tried as best as I could to make the subject of the painting something that would make everyone intrigued.

"Miss, I planned, thought, decided, studied, executed, got tired, and did my job well, and that was how I achieved victory."

Again, Samar felt disappointed. She no longer knew how to get herself out of that situation. She said, "That was what I wanted to say, but I couldn't convey it to you. I love you…"

Jawad finished her sentence, "Not like the way men love."

"And how do men love?"

"Men love eyes first, they fall under their magic." For a moment he kept looking in her eyes. "Then that magic quickly goes through her eyes and this way a man is able to know her mind. Then, during his first days, he balances all that he has and that she possesses, not as a female but as a being. He scans all she believes in. They most likely separate here if they do not have something to unite them. Some men during that period are mistaken because they only want what is identical to themselves, or because they want someone whom they can shape the way they desire. If that is the case, then the inevitable happens in less than a year, because likes repel as soon as they get close to each other. One year is enough to end any kind of love, because no human being, however weak, would be able to take in the arrogance and enslavement of a man for more than a year, and so they break up.

"There is another type of men who refuse to go on, because, with time, they discover a huge amount of difference in their characters, and that may be in the way they behave or for emancipation or because of traditions, religions, or their social stature."

Samar interrupted him, "Don't you think that religion is the first cause?"

"Some may consider it to be the most important cause, and they have their reasons for that. Islam allows man to marry a Christian woman, but this is not the same for the Muslim woman, despite the fact that Islam did not deem Christianity as heretic; on the contrary, it sanctified it, and that is a kind of contradiction. It seems that this Islamic rule had been for the earlier days of Islam. There is also those who refuse their sons to marry a Christian girl. We are not able to understand those boundaries, because sometimes they are allowed, and other times they are not. It all depends on what one desires and not for reasons of equality. Behind all these divisions of thoughts in religions, even in the same religion, we are stuck. We suffer from rot, we neither tasted civilisation, nor did we accept evolution, and we convinced ourselves that we have indeed become civilised when we upgraded from camels to airplanes. However, we still practise the rituals of the camel-riders when we want to board planes. We do not recognise sophistication and civilisation, but we want the camels and their rituals to remain because they existed when all religions descended upon us. What excites me is that these camels are still there and will continue to be there because they are the only ones capable of resisting the desert of our childless traditions, but we surrendered to them. I know numerous Muslims who are poets, writers, educated people, and scholars. Some of them travelled and learned everything from the West. They lived in their universities and drank from their sciences. Unfortunately, they marry off their sons and daughters without first allowing them to get to know those they are marrying. You will also meet one of those who philosophises, and he will tell you that it is a successful method that our ancestors followed, and this means the era of camels. You ask him in what way is it successful? He answers, because it remained until now. In fact, the young man or young woman did not speak with another young man, and the young man did not even submit to the state of searching for love; he just wants to empty what is in his testicles, even if they marry him to a wall. He wants to stop masturbating because he blames himself after doing it for violating the religious teachings that say that 'his hand will bear witness to what he did'. However, after blaming himself for a week, he does it again. But, after long teenage years, he searches for a complete body, and so his mother would marry him to a girl from the family or the neighbour's daughter, whom he meets only once, in the presence of a Muharram — someone from her family — and then immediately to the marital bed.

I am amazed at how he can have intercourse with a girl when they are not united by love. How can he pounce on her and have sex with her, rip her skin like a predatory animal from the first meeting? I think that such marriage is legal rape. A rape not just of the body, but of the feelings of that girl who is most likely just like him, destroyed by sexual lust. She just wants any bird to drop its wings on her breasts and to build a nest between her thighs. Perhaps she is helpless and forced to accept that man as her husband because marriage is protection as her mother taught her."

"How can marriage be protection?"

"I do not know whether a girl who is in her father's house or who is not married turns into a scandal if she does not move to a house where she turns into someone who cooks and washes and who tries to be beautiful for the Sphinx when he comes from work; then she turns into a prostitute at the end of the night to satisfy the desires of Khufu, Khafre or Menkaure. Is this the kind of protection women need?"

Samar loved this spell of talk from him, but she wanted to go back to her story, to the doubts which invaded her head during the night and reignited the heat of her love.

She said, "I still haven't understood how men love."

Jawad completed what he had started. "After entering the eye socket, man begins to explore the secrets of that woman. Does she really believe that this is the man she wants? This calls for wonder! Women are supposed to decide that thing, but time has proven that women cannot choose or make decisions, and this is not because of a weakness in their personalities. Rather, it is because societies put a woman in demand, and take from her the right to make demands. They always wait, so they fall into the trap of choosing and she practises that even in love; any man who comes may be followed by someone who is better than him, and she may fear that no one will come after him, so she is forced to choose any man. She may also have insatiable sexual desires, and so she wants any husband to extinguish the fire of lust, and that is also a mistake.

"A woman is used to this kind of need with any choice she makes. For example, when she wears a new dress, she asks her family if it is beautiful, and whether it fits with the shoes, and so on and so forth. She likes someone to help her in deciding. She wants the man asking for her hand to help her choose him."

Samar interrupted with a refusing look in her eyes, saying, "Is that because she does not know how to choose or…?"

Before she could complete her question, Jawad interrupted her, continuing, "This case may not apply one hundred percent to all possibilities. It is true that you were the one who pronounced the decision in front of everyone, but in one way or another you were a catalyst for your decision. Let me continue. How does a man discover that this woman will answer yes or no?

"Most women at the beginning of their acquaintance with a man refuse him. Men should not take the first answer seriously. It is in a woman's nature: coquetry, arrogance, reluctance. They like that. Then, man must start the stage of persuasion, so he changes his techniques, himself, how he talks, and how he looks, according to what that woman likes; by doing so, he breaks what he is accustomed to, gives himself freely to her, and stays within her grounds, crawling on his knees to obtain approval or the final answer.

"A man does not love like a woman because he must first get out of her depths safely and then start loving her.

"When men love, they only surrender to victory.

"Men, when in love, they grind rocks with their teeth until they get where they want.

"Men are savages with love, ruthless.

"And if you want to stop loving your man, cut off tenderness for him, and he will gradually subside.

"The most trivial women are the ones who confuse their pride with tenderness."

Samar asked, "And are you that kind of man, then?"

"Yes, unless you want me to be someone I am not."

"You fascinate me at times and frighten me at other times. I do not mean fear of terror or cruelty, but when you attacked me on the day Obaid drew me, I could not answer or defend myself; not because I was afraid, but rather it was a voluntary submission. This voluntary submission, I think, is matched by a raging manliness on your part. Yes, you are my man, and I am proud of that and I love this kind of feeling; it is new to me. I did not feel this way before. When I see you, I drift towards you as if a torrential flood pushes me to you, carrying my feet and planting me near you, and the closer I come to you the more I want more. I like to cling to you and unite with you in one body. I don't want to leave you, and if we part, your soul will remain with me. We walk home and go in together and eat with each other, then go to bed for an afternoon nap and I wake you up for coffee. I am with you as a wife from the first day. All we are missing is to have children. By the way, if we had children together, what would we name them?"

Jawad showed signs of shyness. It was the first time he had heard such words from a girl. He hid his shyness and changed the subject, returning to what Samar originally wanted to convey to him, which is the jealousy that she had from Abeer's painting. He understood that from her question and ignored it to see it in her eyes. Men love women's jealousy, but he wanted to give her an answer so that he could escape from her last question. "Don't think about the painting. Abeer is like a sister to me and nothing more." He wanted with this sentence to comfort Samar's heart, who boldly told him that she wanted to stick to him.

Samar, in turn, acted as if she had forgotten her question and looked into his eyes, then sighed as if she was saying, "I didn't need more than that. He comforted me." He made her happy with his understanding of her jealousy and his unequivocal answer. She almost pounced on him and kissed him or even grabbed his arm, but she did not. She hesitated for a reason she did not know, despite her burning longing to do so, or maybe she was afraid of what his reaction would be if she did that.

Soliman asked Jawad to take his brother with him on that trip. Jawad asked, "Do you mean Nabil?"

"Yes."

Jawad said, "Of course he can come, and I think he does not need approval, but you do!"

Soliman said, "Let's go for a walk. It's been a long time since we did."

Picking up his papers as an expression of his agreement, Jawad said, "Of course we don't walk together any more. You don't have time any more. Siniora Laila and her red nights took all your time and even stole my time with you. Yesterday, sir, my mother told me to bring you home with me because she cooked the beans you like. My mother didn't forget you, but you forgot her."

This sarcasm prompted Soliman to say, "It was a week of voluntary hard work. A week in which I learned all the secrets of women. I knew how to weave sleeves and shoulders, and to sew breasts with magical seams that do not deviate from their fashion by a single hair. I learned how only God can create a body. I knew the secrets of the meeting of lips and bodies and how you can kiss things that you have never accepted and that may be more disgusting than you can imagine, but I kissed them with lust, surprised by the magic of beauty possessed by this creature called a female. I knew how to hold breasts and how your shoulders could satisfyingly lift feet. I knew how the breasts move in all directions like a hammer inside raging bells, but breasts remain silent. I knew, sir, that women scream in pain when they reach their peak, and if you stop what you're doing, the woman will kick you with a stronger blow than a kangaroo. I tell you all this and you still want me to remember beans!

"For a week I have been absent from the world. I even forgot my name. Don't blame me because I saw what no human has seen. But the important thing is that I want to confess something else to you.

"I love her!"

Jawad asked, "What's new about that?"

"You don't get it. I love her and I don't think I will be able to stay away from her. I have become an addict and a lover. Accuse me of madness if you wish to, but I know that she did it with others as well. She told me that. It does not matter to me and I forgave her."

Jawad interrupted him, "What are you saying? Are you in your right mind?"

"Wait." Soliman continued, "But the problem is that she is starting to move away from me and I can't stand this. I love her so much, but every now and then she chooses a man to have fun with, and it seems that my turn is about to end early."

Jawad said, "Thank God she is of this type, and what do you want now?"

"I want to stay with her and marry her, but her family will refuse me."

"Why would they? Sleep with her tomorrow completely, then the story ends and you confront them with the reality of the condition. The law leaves you with two choices: either marry her or be imprisoned. Parents prefer to protect their daughter's reputation, and this is what you want and this way you would eliminate the class differences and sectarian differences in our religion. This is a solution if you like, but a silly one just like you. If you know that your time with her is up, why do you want to marry her?

"And how can you utter the word 'marriage' to a woman like this? I know that you are crazy, but I did not expect you to have reached this dangerous stage, and I even see you as a madman who insists on his madness."

Soliman replied, "I didn't think of it that way."

"Would you think of it any other way?"

"You are a fool. If you were content with the beans and your poetic life and friendships which stop at the limits of logic, your life wouldn't have been better. This is what kept me away from sexual relations, because most likely a girl will enslave you with her body if you love her, or leave you. As for you, you have tried something which you loved and therefore you will go to search for another; then this becomes a habit and you gradually abandon loyalty and become a prostitute?

"Don't think about her too much. Leave her, she is not the one for you, nor are you for her."

Soliman got angry. He said, "There is no obstacle in my story. Why do you want me to leave her? You love a girl who believes in a different religion, and I supported you. I love her and you are the one who sanctifies love. You were the one who was talking about virgin love and fighting for love. Why did you say that even if she was a prostitute, as long as you liked her, ignore her past? Didn't you say that?"

Jawad said, "Yes, I said that, but you said that she no longer wants you and that she is now looking for another man, so you are the one turning into her past. I said ignore the past and do not blame those who carry its burden. Yes, I said marry a prostitute, but on the condition that she confesses to you all she had done before marriage and that she would stop being a prostitute; but you said that she was looking for another man. This is enough of a reason for you to stop now this pursuit and this love.

"I know that love does not stop on demand and does not work on demand. I know that it is a serious disease and spreads at an alarming speed, and the cure for it is hopeless. If you try to get rid of it, it will undoubtedly leave its traces and scars on the lovers.

"I love a girl from a different religion, but this barrier does not concern me. I love her, yes, but I am an idiot lover. I miss her and I hope to never leave her, but every time I see her, I think only of ending the conversation and leaving her because I get excited, and I am afraid that something I say may reveal how much I love her. I adore her. I wish to touch her braid, to catch her laughter. I wake up every morning and find in front of me nothing but her picture that took hold of me, and I am happy with her and I dream every day that I do not leave her. Do you know that every night I stand in front of her house, hoping to catch a glimpse of her? At the same time, I am the one who flees from her when I meet her. I am a coward when I meet her and a legendary hero in my dreams with her. She sees me as her man and she told me that, but I fear her when she attacks me with her frankness. I don't know if my torment is like yours. You don't have it in you to make her yours alone. You are tormented because you cannot surround her and feel that you own her. You love a girl who is like mercury. As for me, what torments me is that she is mine and that I own her, and she seizes the opportunity to pounce on me and possess me. I know that I am like her. I love to be with her, but I fear her. You do not know the extent of my fear of committing to love and its duties, and you want to commit to a girl who knows only the opposite of commitment. Do you want to be a drummer for a dancer?"

Jawad added, "But, my friend, we must admit that what unites us is neither treachery nor sincerity.

"What torments us is that we love faithfully and we are not strong. Today, only those who have money are strong. If you had money, you would have been able to kidnap her and even convince her family and marry her. She would not have abandoned you for another; but she did because you are poor, and the smell of the room where you had sex stinks. What made her ignore that smell was her desire, which was stronger than the smell of your room. You got used to it, but there are other things which she would refuse. Your shared bathroom, the smell of your socks, your clothes, and your legendary narrow shoes, even your breath and your feelings. For all these reasons she will leave you.

"As for me, what kills me is that I cannot equal this enormous love from her because I do not have the elements of a challenge, whether for my family or hers. Imagine that I told her what was in my heart and overwhelmed her with my love and she told me that we should run away and marry and confront our families with this reality. What can I say to her? That I am a man who cannot bear the consequences of such a decision and that I do not have a penny. If I had money, I would snatch her from the fangs of all the beasts and fight for her all the restrictions and build for her a house made of all the treasures of the world and make her a bed of bird feathers and cover her with a blanket that carries my dreams and the warmth of my blood and make her only dream of my days. I will be her guardian and she my queen. I would attend with her every mass, and would crucify myself in front of all the churches of the earth to thank God that I am with her.

"My friend, you love a prostitute and I love a saint. What we lack to obtain them is manliness, and you and I do not possess it.

"Poverty kills the manliness of love.

"So let us dispense with this love, as we are not worthy of it. Do not let us lie to ourselves first and to those we love. Let us for once face the situation with manliness and say to our loved ones: 'No, we are not the men of this love.' We should bow to them and express our regret, then walk away because I believe that the sun of our love is not here yet, and perhaps it will shine some other day in another place. Let's pour vinegar on our wounds and burn our skins, hoping that the roots of love may leave the pores of our skin, then its branches can wither and gradually die, so all the fruits that ripened inside our hearts fall."

When Jawad looked at Soliman, his eyes were overflowing with tears.

Soliman said, "Everything depends on money; it is my enemy who always conquers every challenge to me. It prevented me from flying and prevented me from building a nest, and now it is preventing me from loving. How do I get rid of it? How?"

Jawad wiped his eyes and answered, "Only when we confront it are we able to overcome it.

"Tell her tomorrow that you are not fit to be her lover and I will do the same with Samar. We will be men in front of ourselves if the withdrawal is manliness."

Yona was there preparing the dough, enough for bread that would get her through the upcoming darkness. The first day passed, and the rest of the three days would pass, yet the question never left her mind: what would Jawad choose? Black or white? Would he remain her lover or would he sail into the darkness and part with her?

In the first hours following their break-up, she was barely holding on, like any other female, but her ground gave way bit by bit, and her world started to tremble. What was she supposed to say if Jawad asked her to speak first? Would she remain a faithful lover, despite the obstacles that are in the way of their love? Even if she did, what would come of this love story? she did not even know how to respond and had not made up her mind yet. Because no matter what she chose, it might not affect Jawad's decision. So, she relaxed, and gave up. She convinced herself that it had all been in vain. Her heart, however, skipped a beat imagining that Jawad might end it all with a few calculated words, not with a conversation. The reasons were already there: moral, religious, and social. Every obstacle was spinning its web to suffocate her and her love story, not letting either one of them take at least one breath to stay alive, even for a day. Yet she remembered what Christ said: "If you have faith as a grain of mustard seed, you will tell this mountain, 'Move from here to there', and it will move."

She believed that she was walking into the unknown, but with her sheer faith in this love, she believed that she was not hurting anyone, and that she would not commit a sin. She believed that there was fire in heaven, but it only radiated warmth and love.

Jawad was struggling somewhere else, between what was right and what was wrong. His intuition told him it was wrong, but it was real. A love that was boiling and filling up each crack. It existed. A story started with truth, the frightening truth, but it existed, and it was not made up. A truth must not be denied. This truth had not even been denied in the first place, and no one had the right to neglect it, or else how were we supposed to call ourselves humans? The truth was a public demand, and no one denied it but the minorities, those extremists, fanatics, who benefit from calling it faulty due to religion, customs, and traditions. They never addressed the truth as pure. They stoned it as if it was a whore. They exposed it, then called it a whore who asked for it. No. We could not be selective towards what we accept and defile the rest. The truth was stronger than anything and all religions must acknowledge it. The truth that love ruled and anything other than this had been a lie told by us.

There was a wrong love, but it was love, and love was a fact, and a fact was more powerful than a fault.

Love was the truth they both breathed. Yona hurt him when she said she did not like grey. Yona only acknowledged two possible answers: either they part or maintain this relationship that contradicted the norm.

But, again, Jawad's religion did not forbid this story nor its endings, and again, Jawad found himself against a rite of courage and cowardice, but this time he had no excuse; money was present in the equation, but other variables made their way in. That was what came between Samar, and before her Nora, the girl next door, when he was studying to get his junior certificate, his early teens' crush.

Nora was always standing on her porch waiting for Jawad. They were both fifteen. Nora was an Armenian girl with a fair skin, green eyes, and long hair that was braided most of the time.

Nora used to make him blush with her nodding and small gestures, but he was faking masculinity and ignoring her. His only obstacle was his shyness. Before bed, he used to fantasise about dating her, and telling her stories about his heroism.

When Nora's patience ran out, she managed to get into Jawad's house, when she was struggling with some mathematical problem, and went to Jawad's older sister with another neighbour to help her. Coincidentally, when Jawad opened the door, he stuttered and didn't know what to say. The two girls laughed at Jawad's idiocy, and Nora believed that her message had been delivered to him.

She waved at him again from her porch, telling him that she would be waiting for him downstairs to go out together.

Jawad got her message, and tried to calm his heart for his siblings not to hear it beating. He remembered the acne on his face and tried to remove them, but his face inflamed even more, so he hid them with a concealer which he got from his sister's room. He was running out of time. He went into the bathroom twice and did not do anything. He tried to get a grip of himself, and opened the door and she was already there. She smiled when she saw him and he moved towards her, but he did not stop next to her, and kept walking, ignoring her. He could not even greet her. Nora thought he was an idiot, and he cried all night because he was this shy. He returned after days of crying to his only escape: his fantasies. He lived their story all by himself, until the part when they got married and had kids. His masculinity betrayed him, and he was scared. He was scared of exposing his adolescent self. Back then, he understood that love was a body that needed to be exposed. He had tons of feelings towards the beautiful and premature Nora, but he could not confess to her because this type of feeling could only exist as a scenario of a porn movie and nothing else. He was a sissy teen who was afraid to face Nora, because he could not just walk with her. He wanted to greet her, then make love to her a thousand hundred times in one minute like the lion with his lioness. He was intimidated by her body, and the size of her breasts. Maybe his fear was pointless, because maybe his feelings were reciprocated. She was also a teenager full of desire and maybe even double what he was feeling.

Today, Jawad wished he could sit with his friend Soliman to tell him that, after all these years, he still could not face Yona's problem nor solve it. Masculinity again. It was the price he paid when he lost Nora.

Samar walked around the university close to Jawad and would touch his shoulders with hers, faking spontaneity. She was so happy she could fly and a smile would not leave her lips. It had been a chilly day, and with the spontaneity she stretched her arm and grabbed Jawad's and pulled him close to her shoulder. It was the second time, but she wanted to become his lover. She wanted to add this moment to their relationship's scale. She wanted to probe his response to this act on the scale of his love for her during the past days, intending for an intimate reaction that was not as brutal as the first time.

She didn't know that the same person whom she was passing by yesterday was the same guy who vowed to discard his masculinity in front of her, and admit to her that he was not worthy of her love, but he did not know how to begin. Now, she gave him the reason to do so. Jawad felt her tiny breast pressing against his elbow and he managed to feel her nipple. It was his first time touching a breast and discovering it. Yet he pushed her and said to her, his face darkened, "What are you doing?"

Samar didn't say anything; it even pained her that he drew his arms forcefully, but she got over her pain.

Jawad didn't say anything other than the infamous, "It's over. You're not even a friend," and left. In this disgusting way, he left and hung her love on his wall of cowardice. He was not a man and he did not speak up his mind and did not even discuss it with her as if love was not a common denominator between them. He escaped from himself and from her gaze. He escaped from the love that he thought would weaken him.

Samar stood there for a minute, unable to comprehend Jawad's reaction!

In fact, she did not even tame him, nor knew him well. She had only known him for a short while. She went home and thought about what happened from different perspectives. Did she commit a crime when she tried to hold his hands? She was his lover and she had the right to do so. Was it really that big a deal for him that he ended their blooming love story for this? Is he that uptight? Did her insolence offend his morals?

And why was he so rude?

Samar realised that she could not understand that person she fell in love with, and that satisfying him was an impossible mission, especially that he was her first love; it would take a lot of patience to achieve her goal. She was willing to apologise to him the next day and to turn this page and start a new one with new titles, respecting Jawad's feelings even more.

What he did pleased her because it proved to her that he did not want her femininity to satisfy his needs. He respected her for what she was, unlike the other students.

She would fix everything the next day.

Soliman found Jawad sitting in front of his dorm room waiting for him. Soliman was not surprised when he saw him because they had already agreed to meet up there at the end of the day.

Jawad asked him, "Have you broken up with Laila?"

Soliman answered, and his answer was harmonising with the raindrops tapping on the window. "I asked her to give me a picture of her and she didn't refuse. She gave it to me and I want you to draw a portrait of her for me to look at wherever I go."

And he placed the picture in Jawad's hand.

Jawad said, "If you're not tired, let's go for a walk."

Both Jawad and Soliman's tears got mixed with the rain.

Soliman started talking after around thirty minutes of walking under the light raindrops. He said, "I didn't imagine that one day a beautiful girl would tell me that she loved me, while we're together in the same bed. Even if it was for a short time."

Jawad said, "All girls are beautiful in the eyes of their lovers."

Soliman noticed that Jawad's voice was breaking and that he was almost suffocating on his words, and said, "And you, how did you end your story?"

"I was like an angry bull. We were walking closely and she brushed her shoulder against mine once or twice, and I did, too. I felt like I was holding the keys to Solomon's treasures, and I was mesmerised by the tone of her voice. I swear I never felt such happiness in my life. Then she pulled me against her, wrapping her arm around mine."

Jawad cried loudly for a bit, then went on. Soliman did not try to calm him down.

"In spite of my happiness in this split second, I remembered that I was dragging her into my weakness' swamp, and that I did not deserve to touch. That I'd be damned if I did so, and like an angry bull, I pushed her away. I even hurt her, and told her that she could not even be a friend. She didn't answer and I didn't wait. I left the same as when I ran away five years ago from Nora. I couldn't face her and I was a coward. Today, I was shaken up in addition to my cowardice and lies. I didn't tell her the real reason. I'm ashamed of myself because I made her believe it was because of her kindness and femininity. How am I supposed to tell her that it is poverty and that I love her and I wish I could stay close to her, to hear her voice, and inhale the wind touching her? I love her more than I should. I swear that I love her, and love's the only thing keeping me away from her. She is a dream that transcends time.

"A love which ends with a rich man is a love story, but one that ends with a poor man is a marriage story."

They both took off their wet clothes and hung them and dried themselves when they reached their dorm.

Soliman said, "Laila told me not to share what happened between us with anyone. I wish my story ended like yours, a virgin love story; but how can I forget her love and her curves? She is the first female that ever lay under me. You wouldn't miss Samar because there isn't much to miss, but my pain is doubled. Please draw me the portrait and don't lose it. It might be my only condolence."

The two friends fell asleep, right when the coldness of oppression left their bodies, which seemed as if it would accompany them throughout their trip.

The following day, Abeer told Jawad that Kenda would come and tell him something, and that he should not believe her. She left to catch her test before she could finish her sentence. Jawad did not understand what Abeer said, because he stayed up late thinking about how he could face Samar if they crossed paths.

After their test, Samar appeared calmly with knitted eyebrows, and said, "Good morning, Jawad."

As if nothing happened. Then she told him, "If you want to end our relationship, you don't need this attitude and you don't have to hurt me like this. Because I love you, and swore to spend my life with you, no matter what, and I told you that I'm willing to give up my religion for you. I know what I want, but you don't! Yesterday, you hurt me and I'm willing to forgive you a thousand times, but I want to know one thing before I forgive you.

"Do you want me?

"Do you want to be with me till the end?

"Don't answer me now. I'll wait for your answer tomorrow. Think. I can't force myself on you. If you don't want to maintain this relationship, I'll face my love for you and make it stop. Think and give me an answer tomorrow, and no matter what, you'll always remain dear to me."

Jawad didn't let her finish what she had been preparing all night. What she wanted to say to avenge her dignity. He interrupted her, saying that there was no need to wait until tomorrow. "I don't want this relationship, and you're like a sister to me."

Samar interrupted Jawad, "I don't want to be a sister to my lover! Do you hate me that much, that you can't wait until tomorrow?"

Her eyes teared up. "Why did you make me fall in love with you?"

Jawad replied, "You…"

She didn't let him finish, and said, "How are you going to wake up tomorrow without the presence of our love? How would you face a new day without me? Would you talk with your dreams until you reach what you pray for?

"You're ruining my life, and I don't deserve this. Turning it into ashes and hell. You're unjust. Unjust! I have loved you since the beginning. I've wanted to meet you since then. I've wanted to marry you! I wished for your presence in my upcoming days, and to be able to talk to you every day. To sit with you every morning, everywhere. To talk to you at night. All of this while waiting for you! I've written everything down for you, what's been going through my heart and my brain and couldn't tell you. Now my lips get cold and my eyes are wide open whenever I see you. May God forgive you, and know that my heart won't forget you. I love you, and just like I admitted in front of everyone that I love you, I'll admit to you now that you'll always be my lover no matter what, and I'll never love anyone but you. The days we spent together are enough for me to write our eternal love story, and even if I married another, you'd always be my husband until my soul leaves this body."

Samar cried and sighed, then left.

Jawad finished his sentence all by himself, "You're my dream, but I am poor, and the poor are like armless men on the battlefield. My sweet angel, you deserve someone who'd make you happy, not a pauper whom you slowly kill with your love and patience. I'll wait till the day comes when I'll be able to stand before you, apologise to you, and explain to you why I let you down, and why I was so savage in handling your kind love."

Jawad cried all night. Tears streamed from both his eyes and his heart. He left his house late at night and walked alone, trying to erase her picture from his memory, trying to find an end to this sadness that had started to dry him out like an African elephant when the sun had dried its swamps. The sadness of the break-up that he was forced to want. The sadness of giving up. The sadness of his masculinity that failed him. He walked till the break of dawn, then he said to himself, "Be sad as she wants, there'll come a day when she'll understand the situation better. She'll understand that I couldn't expose myself in front of her. I am a man who isn't capable of taking any step to guarantee us a future together. I don't even have a compass to guide me. I am lost and I don't want her to get lost with me because I love her."

Jawad went to the mosque, prayed, and asked God for forgiveness for what he had done to Samar, and that she could meet a rich, flawless man, and to forget him sooner than she fell in love with him.

The bus moved and Kenda sat happily next to Jawad. She was trying to touch him everywhere. She asked him, "Why are you sad today?"

Jawad answered without hesitation, "Why didn't Samar come today?"

Kenda did not answer, as if the question was not directed at her, and started singing, and Jawad started singing, too, while the bus was on its way to the Citadel on top of the hill where one could see the Valley of the Nassary.

Krak des Chevaliers in Syria was built by Ramesses, then later on renovated multiple times due to an earthquake and being invaded by various armies. It had been captured by Al-Zahir Baybar. It was built of huge white limestone blocks that had been brought from somewhere nearby.

The bus stopped after less than three hours in front of this great historical monument. Everyone was silent because it was their first time seeing it. Jawad had already been there more than ten times, and he was familiar with its entrances. He went to the vast stairs that lead to the gate. Everyone walked in awe, unlike Jawad, who could not hear anything but his heartbeats. He was walking at a faster pace, calling Samar, asking her for forgiveness, admitting that he had been unfair to her, and the fact that he could not live without her. For it had only been a couple of days and there he was hoping he could see her on this trip; but he was paralysed knowing that she was not coming. He wandered around the Citadel and went to the highest wall and started climbing it suicidally. If he fell now, he would die. Kenda called him in a scared tone, asking him to stop, but he did not respond because he could not hear her. He was screaming deep down that he did not want to see anyone. He wanted to hug the sky, to be alone so that no one would see his buried sadness. Students started gathering and raising their voices in warning because he was now in danger. His eyes were tearing up, asking for her forgiveness, and he asked the skies to be the mediator between them to ask for her forgiveness, that he was willing to pay the price for hurting one of its angels. He called her name, but she did not respond, and suddenly a rock that had been in place for so long, slipped under his feet, taking him with it. He somehow managed to push the rock outside the Citadel and his body fell inside from a height of five meters. He fell on his elbow and shoulder. Everyone was shocked and ran towards his body that lay on the floor. His eyes were wide open and his tongue was repeating, "She wouldn't forgive me, and heaven's punished me"; then his eyes welled with tears from his disappointment and not from his pain. Both Soliman and his brother tried to lift Jawad, but he screamed in a way that silenced everyone. Jawad had been saved. He injured his shoulder and his elbow, and most importantly he had lost Samar forever.

Jawad sent a message to Yona saying, "Black or white or grey, I don't care, I just want to be with you."

Yona took a deep breath that filled her lungs. She was sure that it was not a whim for Jawad or an experience to be added to his past ones. At the same time, Yona was the only girl to walk into the fire with ease.

Jawad did not put her in an awkward position. She was willing to destroy everything if his answer was negative in any way. She wasn't willing to give up a love that had been eating her up so easily. She was not too young to make up her mind, but she would have pretended to be young and reckless if Jawad's decision was in her interest and to stay by her side.

She broke her silence and smiled again. She opened her viewless window, just to ask her anxiety to leave. She opened her closet and changed its order. She looked at her phone again and read the text and typed with shaky fingers, "I love you, crazy!"

Jawad called her immediately and shared a call that challenged the universe's laws. It was not bound by any social constructions or morals. They crossed all their limits with this call. The words unified them. They agreed to meet up in front of her house the following day.

Kenda put on strange, delicate shoes and edged towards Jawad, who was sitting with his broken arm raised in a kind of a scarf wrapped around his neck. His eyes were glued to Samar's seat, who did not come.

"Was she that angry? Was it her prayers that did this to my arm? Or is God mad at me for hurting a pure soul in her seventeenth year on earth, who didn't know of human's malice? Was it her charm and anger that ruined me? Let this be my punishment. I deserve it. May God protect her."

Kenda stood in front of Jawad and asked him to support her to sit next him. Jawad extended his other arm and sat her on the edge he was on, but she pressed herself against him in an unusual manner.

Jawad did not move as usual and thought that it was unintentional and that she would sit properly, but she did not. Jawad smiled and edged away from her, but she pressed herself against him again, and when he looked at her, she said, "I want to tell you something. I… I love you."

"What did you say?"

She repeated, "I love you."

Jawad looked away, and edged away from her, then rested his head between his knees and cried, remembering what Abeer said about not believing Kenda. His weeping was so loud that it confused Kenda, but she added quietly, "I'm in love with you."

Jawad raised his head, and his eyes were welled with tears, and he took off a golden necklace that he was wearing. It was a gift from his older sister for graduating high school. He put the necklace around Kenda's neck and said, "Please forgive me. I know how dear it is for a girl to confess her love to a man, but excuse me, I can't love you back. Only because I cannot fulfil such commitment and I don't deserve it."

Jawad left while Kenda was still holding the necklace that has his first letter.

Maybe Kenda, the Maronite, was thinking that maybe if she offered Jawad her love, she'd save her Christian friend from falling in love with a Muslim, and she'd prove to the other girls that he was just a playboy, but she was late.

Yona was racing to reach the spot where Jawad parked his car, like a spring butterfly. She opened the door and grabbed Jawad's hands without a word, and he didn't say anything either and squeezed her hand to calm her nerves and to spread warmth through it. Her hands were shivering, but her longing and yearning lit a fire within her body that would not be easy to put out. Jawad wanted to drive to his country house that was a fair way from the city after asking her, "Would you mind going to my place?"

Yona squeezed his hand as if to say yes.

They reached his country house and Yona kept checking the simple exterior of the house.

She asked, "Were you the one who chose this design?"

Jawad answered, "Yes, and everything else in the house."

Yona went inside the huge reception, which was filled with paintings by famous artists. Apparently, Jawad collected them. The house had a British interior design.

Yona went inside a room filled with books and his painting studio, which showed that a new painting was about to be born. The mess created by the paint sprayed on his desk and the scattered papers were the dream of every girl, a nest in which she could run riot with all her femininity. Her mind was filled with thoughts when Jawad played some loud music that made her thoughts scramble all over the place between reality and dreams. She thought of hugging him and doing everything she had ever wanted, but she maintained her calm after replacing it with another thought.

She imagined herself as the lady of this house. All her dreams boiled down to one big dream that began to climb on the ladder of the mirage of truth. She wanted him and she wanted time to stop here and to remain where Jawad roamed. She wanted to be the queen of this palace. She wandered with her thoughts and started beating the drums of her self-coronation and the thousands of trumpets that played, announcing the Queen's approach to her throne next to Jawad's. For a moment, and before her angelic body sat on the throne, she realised that a thousand nails sprang out of the throne, snarling, "Your religion, your family, your village, your age, our customs, our traditions. Why are you ignoring all that and setting down on that throne?" Yona was frightened and screamed without thinking.

Jawad caught her and asked, "What's wrong with you?"

She answered, "Nothing, nothing, let's leave this place."

He said, "I made you a cup of coffee which you like; come and drink it in the garden and then we'll leave."

Yona returned to her home, not realising what had happened. Why was she afraid? Was it love or lust?

She couldn't hear the sound of her thoughts. Her haste to leave his house worried her. She had been dreaming of a day like this. Was she supposed to do the wrong thing to get to the right one, she asked herself.

Why didn't she have sex with him and go for what she always wanted?

Why did she always have to fly regularly like locusts following what the society ordained was the right thing to do? Why could she not be like a butterfly flying in a chaotic manner, scattered, flying wherever it wanted?

How bad was the day she eagerly waited for?

"Would my kiss remain on my lips for a lifetime so that someone who is right for me according to the religious and traditional rules comes to take my kiss from me and against my will, or would a day come when Jawad would absorb it and I would surrender to him in the path which would end with both our bodies united?"

When Jawad turned several times towards Kenda while she was holding his first letter, he was mumbling that he did not want to lose her as a friend, and she was saying in her heart, "Say what you want, and I will do what I want."

The next morning, Jawad smiled at Kenda while entering the university and then continued walking without stopping, but Kenda followed him and kind of hit him with her body. She said, "I'll wait for you at the end of the day. I want you to walk me home alone so that we can talk."

Jawad did not let her down. They arrived at the gate of her house after a long walk and talk, the last of which was that she knew that he loved Samar, but she could no longer bear to wait and wanted him to choose between them. Jawad said, "I did not expect you to be that trivial. If love is by choice, then I think it is turning into a slave market." Then he surprised her when he added, "It seems that there is something you missed while being busy with this plot of yours."

Kenda thought that he was talking about that plot of confessing her love for him. She did not fathom that Abeer had already warned him.

"I do not even have the option of love, which you are presenting to me now. Leaving Samar and ending my relationship with her is something, and abandoning her is another. I only left her because I love her, and I could not and will not make her happy as I want her to be. I gave up on her because of the intensity of my love for her."

What he said left her dumbfounded. She realised that there was no longer any need for her to stay there with him, but she was the one who proposed her love, and she must prove that he would fall for any girl. Her heart tickled her mind, convincing her to go through with an experiment. She could not deny that she liked him, and she added, "Then you don't have any excuses?"

Jawad laughed and added, "You are a sister and a friend, nothing more."

She said, "Let me be closer to you, then judge yourself."

When the mind and heart focus on the issue of love, backwardness is created.

Their relationship lasted for some cold months, punctuated by some attractions, but they did not go beyond the limits of friendship. He finally made it clear to her as he stood on the pedestrian bridge that he wanted her to understand that he would not keep that relationship with her and that he wished her success and that she would marry a good young man as she wished. They parted quietly, with a smile on their lips. One way or another, she kept him away from Samar and had a little fun for herself. After that day, he would not be friend nor lover. As for him, he stopped the flames of longing for Samar, but he could not stop loving her until he heard that she had married and settled in Venezuela. He wished that one day he would meet her and tell her what should had been said and she would forgive him for what he did to her. He did not meet her, but he met Kenda after more than six years by chance on the street and she was walking, embracing a very well-looking young man. She intimated to him that he was her husband. They did not speak. That had been the last time he saw her. Kenda had been a smart conservative Maronite. She was not beautiful.

Yona and Jawad met again, but with great caution and under a deliberate mechanism of fear that anyone who knew one of them might see them together. This caution would sometimes generate a kind of terror and turn off their thieving romantic music when they used to disappear in the cafe of one of the five-star hotels in the old neighbourhoods of Damascus. The hotel used to be a big house, but it was turned into a hotel (Beit Zaman) without compromising its warm Damascene character, as if it was designed for them with its huge spaces and its permanent emptiness of customers because the security situation in Syria had forced people to stay in their homes, and the incoming tourists had completely disappeared.

All of this did not prevent them from meeting. They sat for a long time under the bitter orange trees and engraved the first letters of their names on their chair like teenagers do.

The sounds of cannons, explosions, and even low-flying warplanes did not mean anything to them. Although they were different in everything, a little love played with their hearts as if it were clown balls, which circulated in a fixed system that never went wrong. But the show might be stopped at any moment when this love would be revealed, and the balls fall scattered.

He asked her one day to come with her car. She was surprised when she saw him take a large painting out of his car and put it in hers and ask her not to look at it until she went back home.

Yona loved the idea, but what would she say to her family? The painting was too big to hide. However, she was not ready to give up this thing, no matter the cost.

Jawad cried that day and Yona cried when she saw him crying without knowing the reason. Then she asked him, "Why all this crying?"

He said, "For the thousands of thoughts mixed in my head.

"First, because I am happy that you now have this painting and that it will be hung in your house, and this means that I entered the house.

"Secondly, because I am afraid of that thing growing up in my heart, and if you ever want to know what it is, then ask the painting, for I have kneaded its colours with my blood, and my feelings, and they are the most precious things that I have and can offer them to be yours."

Yona went back home that day and asked a relative to help her hang the painting and place it so that whenever she went out or entered the house, she would see it. Unfortunately, her room did not have a wall large enough to accommodate it. She fabricated a lie for its source after making sure that the painting was of an ordinary girl who did not look like her but told her story. A tired girl who barely wore any clothes, a bit thin and soft. Her body was slender and her mouth a little bit swollen, her hair long and her eyes sad. The only common thing between her and the girl in the painting was that she had Yona's eyebrows.

The painting was not perfect, but it was like the love that united them. It could be viewed as a painting, but it did not follow the laws of painting. It had been a failure, just like their love. A love which no one heard of or accepted. It was against all human laws. All people should make fun of it. As the main feature of love is its continuity. Their love, however, was cursed by all, and it died even before it began, like the corpse of a pharaoh that was taken out of its coffin in which it lay for thousands of years.

So, it had only been a painting in form, but artistically it had been nothing but stupid lines by which the painter wanted to convince people that it was love.

Two days later, Yona's phone rang at ten in the evening, unlike Jawad's habit of calling. She hurried to talk before he did. "How are you? I was so worried about you today. I don't know why, even though you called me in the morning, but my heart was so heavy with worry. How are you?"

Jawad replied, "I'm at the hospital. I had an accident. I'm a bit broken. I had an operation. I wanted to tell you that I will only be able to see you after several months. I can't move, but the most important thing is that when I entered the operating room and the drug started to overtake me, I surrendered, and you were in my dreams. You were like a dove flying away and I was trying to catch you, and our background was a white space. You were flying and chirping and I was trying to catch you, but you would always touch me, then fly. Eventually, I caught you and held on tightly to you. That's when the doctor woke me up and I asked him why he had revived me, and that I had been in the most beautiful moments of my life. You were with me."

Jawad did not notice while telling the story that Yona was crying and could no longer respond because she knew that when Jawad rushed to narrate something, it meant he was in pain and wanted to delude the listener to convince him or her otherwise.

Jawad continued, "I am still alive and speaking. Why aren't you talking?"

There were vague expressions between her lips. She stuttered, then mumbled, and she repeated one sentence only: "I knew it, I knew something bad had happened to you."

That phrase was enough to ease Jawad's pain and make him cry as well.

There are things or situations in love that are so beautiful that you can only cry in response to them.

"I'm fine, believe me, I'm fine, your djinn is fine."

Yona did not reply, but only cried.

Yona did not sleep that night because the tears kept flowing.

Jawad did not sleep, looking from the hospital window at the rain and the lights that generated a mixture of colours that intertwined and accelerated to form, every second, thousands of abstract paintings that the eye was often unable to follow. Suddenly, all the successive paintings stopped and one painting was mostly painted in black, in which he saw himself struggling with his helplessness to reach Yona, who needed him as much as he needed her.

Six fractures in his leg have separated from the bone in the foot. He needed a long time to recover, so he would not be able to walk or drive his car.

He felt what his friend Soliman had suffered, who had an accident long after they left university. The doctor ordered him to lie down for a year and a half due to many fractures that he sustained. He almost had his leg amputated. He remembered that when he visited him there in his town near the sea, he saw the painting which Jawad painted of Laila.

Soliman's mother said to him that day, "I wish you hadn't drawn this painting for my son. He is crazily attached to it. It became his temple and his gods."

Jawad mocked Soliman that day, but he realised now what was really hurting his friend. Even Jawad could not portray Yona and embody her with his painting as he embodied Laila. Because he was afraid someone would realise his love for her, or perhaps he did not yet have the courage to draw her features, for she was more beautiful to be merely drawn by his hand. Jawad said to Yona one day, "If I drew your face, you would be in danger." Yona did not understand what Jawad meant. He meant that if he drew her, he would do that with his heart and mind first, then with his fingers. She turned into a love that possessed every part of his body, and that could not be abandoned under any influence or reason.

Soliman, who found the sea a friend and a permanent sanctuary he could not leave, did not resemble Laila in anything but in the colour of her eyes. He embraced the sea and loved it, and he tuned in with its waves and told it all the crazy poetry he felt for Laila, who once gave him her body for a week, and, just like a mermaid, left him to return to her sea and to other experiences. No one can catch a mermaid, but many sailors know her and love her.

After years, Soliman married a girl he loved after marriage because she was the mother of his children, but he lived to this day with his story and his first love which possessed him and nestled in every pore of his skin. His body might live with his wife, but his heart remained stuck there where his love had been.

A month had passed since Jawad's accident. He promised Yona to come to her home, when he knew that her mother and sister travelled to their village for two days. He carried his pain and climbed the stairs to the floor where she lived. The electricity was cut off, so he could not use the lift. His crutches took him to the third floor full of his passion for her. Yona was waiting for him. She was terrified when she saw him, but she held him and silenced all her longing and pain by every means she had. After she calmed down, she realised the state he was in and asked him, "Don't your wounds hurt you?"

Jawad laughed and said, "I think my longing for you hurt me more."

Then Yona added, "And my longing for you made me forget your wounds."

Jawad recovered and took his first steps without leaning on his crutch towards Yona, who waited for him near the rock where they used to meet. They always stood there when they met and when they parted. It was a strange rock emerging from an old wall as if it was found to comfort people on its back. Jawad said about it one day that it knew the secrets of all lovers, and that he heard it one day talking to him, so he shut it up because it had been talking about Yona's beauty. Yona laughed that day and said, "Love is starting to make you mad."

Yona's eyes were twinkling, and she was scared and happy at the same time, frozen until Jawad reached her and she hugged him. He said, "I will admit that I was afraid that I would not reach you, then I would fall, but now I am standing in front of you. I owe you that. Thanks to you I have survived the past months in this narrow, dark tunnel which looked like a grave. I will never forget what you offered me after everyone else abandoned me. With absolute tenderness, you kissed my plastered foot. I cried and you wiped away my tears over and over. You rid my heart of all its aches and made me stand again strong, a warrior, who bandaged his wounds, returning me to the battle of life. I will never again accept another defeat, because the land of this love is mine and no one else's."

They sat in Yona's car and Jawad said to her, "I want to tell you a secret. I was afraid to die without letting you know it.

"You may not believe what I say, but I know the place where you were baptised, and I know that you have been stubborn since childhood and that you wore your red sandals with the white dress and was stubborn with everyone on your uncle's wedding day when you were only two years old. I know how you were born, and how you sleep like a ball, covering yourself and your face when you fall asleep; and I know that your body has a strange secret. It changes its colours when you cry or get nervous. How you were on your first day of school, how you excelled without reading, how you changed your baby teeth, and how this crazy out-of-order tooth was born; but it is one of the secrets attracting me to you. I knew everything about you even before I met you, because I was the one who made you more than twenty years before you were born. I am the one who coloured your hair, and changed the size of your forehead, changed the shape of your eyebrows, added the lightening to your eyes and brightened the crescent of your eyelids. I am the one who picked up anemone to colour your lips and your body the colour of spring clouds... transparent.

"I am not flirting with you now. I am the one who hid the features of fascination and beauty from your cheeks so that only I can see them. You are exclusive to me; no one in the world sees you as I see you. I am the one who taught you to speak. I am the first to make you hear and the first to hear you. I created you before you were born. I was your friend and your playmate. You were made from the morning light, and you often slept in my arms. We grew up together and I adored you. You were all truths, all that is honest, and all that could not be accomplished. You were all that I could not find and what I did not achieve. You became my resort. When I fail, or am hurt, when life is stubborn with me, I only see you. I did not see you in the face of any woman. I finally realised that you never complained and did not resort to me. I am the one who always comes to you. I was afraid because I might be crazy, and because I was never a creator and I am not allowed to be. The confusion kept haunting me from the day I first saw you and we met, because then you became real. Am I joking now or did we really meet?

"Today, I decided to end my confusion. Are you a ghost or my Yona? I walked to you and gave up my crutches and said to myself that if I fall, you will be a ghost that does not catch me, and if I stand in your arms and return leaning on you, you will be my love, and with that you will have killed my confusion. You became a truth and from today you will remain a target I seek, because no matter how painful the obstacles are, you are mine."

Yona smiled at Jawad and considered what he said to be a new kind of love. Jawad did not insist on the truth of what he said because the proof was difficult, and he returned his case file to his portfolio of ideas to return to his case when there was sufficient evidence to prove that miraculous event.

After this beautiful day, the two of them thought that clouds had cleared and their skies would remain blue, as the first phase of Picasso's paintings was described, where the lines are clear and mostly pure blue. But, a phone call from Yona, who did not usually call Jawad, asked for an urgent meeting at eight thirty in the morning. In the cafe where they used to meet.

Jawad went to the cafe with worry filling up his being, not knowing what Yona could carry of news, but he was sure that there were unpleasant ones. Yona's voice the night before was painful.

Yona arrived unusually wearing her sunglasses. He walked near her silently with at shake of his head without speaking and she did not answer until they entered the cafe.

Yona said, "I love you, by God I love you." Tears were streaming down her face. Those two eyes were overflowing as if the gods were crying. Jawad thought that she would cry for a lifetime, but eyes would tire and would become unable to cry. This was what stopped Yona from crying after a long time. Jawad did not utter a single word. He was taken aback by Yona's face, whose features were kneaded and its colours multiplied. It was wet as the bark of midwinter trees. A face depicted in it the image of oppression, helplessness, and surrender, crying out of love.

Jawad said, "Rest and drink hot tea and then we will talk."

Yona said, "My older sister knows somehow, and with the help of one of her friends at work, that I love you. I did not deny it." Yona continued, saying, "And my mother was there; they asked me to leave you immediately. They threatened me."

"My sister said, 'He is married, has children, is Muslim and is twenty years older than you.' She was screaming at me as if I had killed someone or that I was a political rebel in front of an investigator. I know all these things, but I also know that I love you sincerely and my love for you is unstoppable. If it stops, I will die. Why don't you talk? Will you leave me? You will leave me, won't you?"

Jawad smiled and said, "When you cry, you cry as if for the dead, but you are getting more beautiful so that you become illegible to describe. You make it hard for those looking at you to describe you. I am in love with this composition. Do you want to stop this as they asked you to?"

"No, no, I don't want to. I can't even think of living without you."

"Then why are you crying?"

"What makes me cry is you, because you will leave me because they now know about us, right?"

Jawad looked into her eyes, which were overflowing with tears and love, which was mainly distinctive with eternity. He said: "I, leave you? Where do you get these ideas from? Have you ever seen a person living without a soul?

"You are the soul that makes me walk and shows me the world and its absolute beauty. You are neither a lover nor a mistress. You are my peace. You are the moments in which a person is alone with himself. You are my purity, and my desire in this world and the hereafter. Sweetheart, do not say that again, even if the whole world knew and our pictures were published in the daily newspapers. It does not concern me and does not make me think of anything else.

"I want to tell you something outside of this argument. I have never thought of how I behave, and I do not care how others evaluate my behaviour. I know that I am a small boat in the sea of this world. I may not mean anything to anyone and the sea may be jealous of me, but I always let my boat sail following the first idea that comes to my head, without discussing its rationale or possibilities. I believe that God is the one who created the world and all that is in it, and He is the ruler of all its actions, and He is the one who beautifies them, and He alone is the one who ends them. He is the owner of all. He does what He wants. Sends some to punish the unjust for many reasons which may be small or big, or maybe for no reasons at all. Rather, He wants to test our faith. We are subject to the rule of the God of all, so we must be satisfied with anything that befalls us. This means that we need to believe in fate and nothing bad comes from it, even if it appears evil. So do not think about things too much and take the first idea that comes to your mind as a decision, because everything in the end is from God and everything that comes from God is good."

The words of Jawad calmed Yona down, who shrank from the severity of her sadness. She said, "I understand that we will stay together no matter what happens?"

Jawad nodded his head and smiled, and she smiled as well.

At that moment, Jawad's phone rang. He pointed the phone at Yona's eyes to see that it was her older sister, 'Detective Kojak', as Jawad referred to her later in his conversations, and who discovered, with her police-like ways, the love of her sister towards a person who she only saw faults in, which were clear like the sun and didn't need to be defined or to be confronted. She basically only knew him from Yona's conversations about him as her manager at work. Jawad asked Yona's permission to answer the phone outside the cafe and went out.

"Listen, Mr Jawad, I am Yona's older sister. I don't want to talk much, but stay away from my younger sister and don't try to justify yourself. You manipulated her and her emotions. She is young and cannot comprehend the consequences of her actions. And if you ever learn what logic is, then logic tells you that this relationship is illogical, especially as Yona is the same age as your children. Be ashamed of yourself and stay away from her. She is a child who does not understand what she is doing. We hope that you will be an advisor and not involve her in a musty swamp." Yona's sister finished her hurtful talk and direct attack.

Jawad said, "I want to tell you two things. Yona is not a young girl and she knows what she is doing, so do not treat her otherwise. Yona is more aware of her situation than you think, and I believe that she is assimilating things better than you. The other thing is, do not use this superior way of talking with her because it worsens the situation more and more. Other than that, I hope you will ease your tension and the hidden threats within your words, because they do not mean anything to me at all. Lastly, since you are Yona's sister, you have the right to speak in any way you want, and I consider myself to have the same right to talk to you. You are a precious sister and you have the right to ask for whatever you want."

She interrupted him, "So, leave her."

"I'll try, but don't hurt her again by attacking her," he replied, and he hung up.

Jawad returned to the sad Yona and told her what happened between them without going into detail.

Yona told him, "Promise me again that we'll stay together."

Jawad said, "Do not ask this question again, because it is directed at you only; as long as you remain, I remain, and you alone have the right to part from me. As for me, I no longer have this option. My heart chose to stay."

Yona added, "And I will not leave you unless I die."

Yona went back with grief and joy, but she was stronger than yesterday. She carried an iron cog made by the hand of a lover who was able to receive the most severe blows. Yona had uprooted fear that day and it no longer had a place in her little body. She became convinced that she had a lover who was not afraid of women's heresies and did not know how to retreat. An assuring lover who did not hesitate to defend her, even if the battle was lost. His manhood did not know how to withdraw or escape, even if it was tactical to do so. A lover who preferred to be a loser than to be a coward. Her sadness began to gradually dissolve, and expressions of joy and a smile graced her lips. She recalled every moment from their date and discovered that he loved her more than she had imagined, and this alone was enough to melt the ice of her sadness, no matter how hard it was. She closed her small fist firmly around the hilt of the sword of her love. Her love contained a mythical energy that emitted a light that blocked her from all sight whenever she wanted.

Her fear of her mother and sister, if they knew that she was in love with such a man, had resolved and they knew everything and even the details of the talk between them. What now?

For her, it became clear, even if she was being watched. But she told them that she would not leave him, and they had to understand that. Now she was relieved of a heavy burden.

She must break the branches in the dense forest to cross into the light.

Jawad remained in his chair, swimming in Yona's face, who remained stuck in his eyes. Tears and pain and a heart pounding like a crazy drum. Lips that only uttered one thing, "I love you." Repeating it and making sure to say, "I swear to God, I love you."

If the knight of love could not know how to dry the tears of the beloved, love would become rusty.

(This majestic scene was later depicted by Jawad with a painting of Yona's face, which he called 'Defeat'.)

Jawad was cohesive throughout the meeting in front of this feminine scene, overwhelmed with the sincerity of her feelings. He admired the composition of that scene and was fascinated by its external appearance. He played only one melody and one tone. Love, only love. He promised himself that he would remain the only listener to this melody and that no one else would be allowed to hear it. And for the world to play whatever it wanted of melodies of hatred, ignorance, customs, and religions, and even the well-known presto of the word 'shame', he will be deaf and will not recognise it.

Two days after this event, Jawad met Yona at her home because her mother and sister had gone to work early. When Jawad entered, he hugged her for a long time. Yona was sighing and her eyes were tearing up. She said, "I was afraid we would never meet again."

He replied, "We will meet as long as we are alive."

At this moment, the doorbell rang, because Yona had locked the door from the inside after Jawad entered. She was confused for a moment. It was her mother's voice from behind the door. She knocked on the door quickly and repeatedly. Jawad hid in the first room of the house. Yona opened the door, asking, "Why did you come back so quickly, mother?"

Her mother answered while getting into her room, "I forgot some work papers."

During these moments, Yona kept the door of the house open, so Jawad got out with his heart almost stopping. He went down the three floors so quickly, as if he was falling down a haystack. He moved away from the building and his heart began to calm down. His presence had almost been revealed, and he would have been in an unprecedented situation, and in front of whom? Yona's mother, the person whom Jawad considered his saint. He never spoke to her. His love and respect for her increased after she discovered their relationship. She dealt with it with much wisdom and did not reprimand her daughter, but merely told her that any human being makes mistakes. "We all sin, but be careful that you do not keep on sinning."

If you see a person suffering doing something, do not interfere with all your skill. Show your helplessness as well so as not to embarrass him.

Jawad opened his phone to check on Yona and found that she had sent him a message containing three words: "Do not leave!"

As soon as he read her message, she called him and said, "Come back, my mum has left."

Jawad smiled and answered, "If I came back, I won't be me, but a terrified person who could not stand on his own two feet."

Yona laughed and quickly added, "I miss you."

He hung up the phone and went back to her, admiring her control over herself, and when he entered the house for the second time, he said, "When I first came to you, you hugged me because I am a man who can protect you; now it seems that you have absorbed my manhood, because I need you to hug me. I feel like I am the weakest man on Earth. I need your courage."

Yona embraced Jawad, calmed his heart, and spent half the day with him at home, with a smile on her face.

Before leaving, Jawad said, "To have a disabled love is possible, but the strange thing is that the beloved is a saint who can heal the disability and not cure you, because as long as you have this disability, she will remain by your side. You were strong today and proved that love is your only engine, and it is your goal, so you were the manliness of love."

Jawad left the house seeing the thousands of values and moral traits he had learned and bragged about one day, pretending before his eyes, wanting to drop him from the list of humanity. He struggled and jostled those things in his mind, trying to push them away, but the screams of the morality crowd did not remain silent. Honesty called him traitor. Virtue called him despicable. Courage stripped him and made him a coward, fallen against all moral values. A married man crossing the streets of teenagers, bragging that he was as reckless as them. Why now, after forty years, are values falling from inside him? Why, with Yona and this family who, when you hear their story, could do nothing but be humble as if you are in a holy place? Why was he in this position?

Crossing the tunnel of life is always fraught with the unknown without any explanations.

Yona told Jawad one day that she dreamed they would walk together in the rain, like all lovers did. Not to meet him only in her house or his or at the cafe. She wanted to walk in the old alleys of Damascus decorated with the bougainvillea and its pink flowers strewn on the walls. She wanted to be among the people, a sweetheart who was proud of the one she loved.

He told her, "Perhaps one day we will be able to do so."

In a few days Yona was holding on to Jawad's hand as she walked in the streets of Damascus with her head on his shoulder and the snow falling on her face and melting faster than usual from the heat radiating out of her joy from every pore in her body. It seemed as if her body was in a state of ecstasy. She came out of herself and became what she wanted. Her happiness was unbelievable. This girl who made the iron of Jawad change with blazing fire and with expressions of love which were like a hammer, warming and cooling him with the water of the melted snow on her cheeks. She formed him as an eternal lover.

Yona shouted, "The Lord has given us more than we wished for, rain and snow." She was disguised with a hat and sunglasses, and so was Jawad. They did not care and continued walking as if the world seemed to draw a path of light for them.

When Yona came home late, she felt the cold, and remembered that she did not feel that while hugging Jawad in all the alleys she crossed. Love was her fireplace and she decided to spread her wings for this love and fly where the wind wanted, since life was short.

Love grew and did not stop. Every day Yona used to say, "I now fear what is between us," and Jawad would answer, "I wish I could hate you or hate anything about you."

Yona asked Jawad if he would not mind it if she introduced him to her best friend after she told her about their relationship.

Jawad replied that he did not mind. Yona lived alone with her complex story that embraced all the misfortunes of the world. She absolutely needed guidance whether to walk or not with that love. She needed someone to complain to. Inside her there were feelings about which she wanted to talk. She wanted to tell the story of her adventure. She needed to break away from her frightening silence with someone else. She needed a different opinion.

We all need a good friend.

Jawad agreed, although Yona started hesitating a bit, not for anything, but for fear of revealing Jawad's identity. But Jawad insisted that she should open up to her friend about their story without telling her his name before she could tell what she thought of their love.

The following day, Yona came to their usual meeting place looking victorious. Jawad took her by surprise and asked her, "You told her, didn't you?" and added, "Ask her to come here right now! I'm excited to see her."

Yona didn't hesitate and called her, and she came. Jawad welcomed her without hesitation or awkwardness, for he was used to being bold and upfront. He wanted to be strong in front of her. He asked her, "Tell me, how did Yona tell you about our story?"

Rama said, "We were sitting near the Umayyad mosque, when Yona started crying. I was worried about her and asked her, 'What's wrong?' But she cried even more. I asked her, 'Is it a love story?' She nodded and I told her that I'm always by her side no matter what, but she didn't stop crying."

Jawad's eyes were watching Yona's and they started tearing up.

Rama kept talking. "Even if you were pregnant I would have supported you. Her tears always got to me, made me cry, too, and I used to scream at her to tell me what was wrong. She started telling me the story from day one. I used to look her in the eyes and notice her sincerity and the love that filled her heart. I interrupted her and told her, 'Why are you crying then?' Yona answered, 'I didn't expect to fall in love like this before, and for that person to fulfil all of my fantasies. His looks and lifestyle. Everything I've ever wanted. I love him and I can't imagine a life without him, and that tortures me, because he is a dream regardless of how real it is. He is a mirage that I can touch. He is a reality and a fantasy. He is a state that never started but it's been fulfilled. He is everything I've ever wanted. He is my sin, yet it's hell without him, because he is me and I have no one else. Do you understand me?'

"I told her, 'It's enough to live a love like this. This feeling that every female yearns for. Why didn't you tell me your story? You've been suffering like this for two years.'"

Rama turned to Jawad. "Isn't my friend unfaithful? I always tell her everything and she didn't tell me about her story."

Jawad said, "I told her a while ago to tell you all about it. I've known you through her and I know you very well, but I haven't heard your voice before. I've seen your face in pictures Yona showed me and I knew how your mind works from different conversations between you and Yona. That's why I was sure that you'd understand a story like ours. One that isn't approved by religion or logic and needs someone to justify its flaws. I'm the happiest today because there's a mutual friend between me and Yona that became like a sister to me from the very first few minutes. And that's very rare nowadays. I'm not going to ask you to take care of Yona because I know how you feel about her, but be more available these days because she has thousands of stories to tell you to empty her crowded heart."

Rama was like the fire that burnt the candles of love for Yona in the following days. The three of them kept meeting up, forming a group that did not know anything but honesty and love.

One day, Yona was awaiting Jawad at her house, and while he was climbing the stairs he saw Yona's mother. For a moment Jawad's heart stopped beating, but he kept climbing the stairs, and when he got closer to her, he said, "Good morning."

She did not answer him and kept watching him. Jawad didn't stop on Yona's floor and kept climbing the stairs because he felt that Yona's mother was watching him, and suspecting him. Jawad had already seen Yona standing next to her apartment's door and motioned to her without making a sound to go back inside. After ten minutes, Jawad decided to face Yona's mother, but he left the building without seeing her. He called Yona immediately and told her that he saw her mother while climbing the stairs.

Yona laughed and told him that he was hallucinating and that her mother left for work early in the morning. Jawad said that he was not joking, and that he greeted her then.

Yona was confused.

He told her, "I won't go near your stairs ever again. My heart almost stopped! Tell her, if she asks you, that I was here to give you a handgun and that I left afterwards, because I was worried about you after the most recent incident and you're all women without a man at home."

Yona's family had been harassed before by gangs that started to spread because of the rising security crisis, and they intended to harass them because Yona's father was a military officer before his death, hence this family was under threat because they supported the system, which bothered the protesters.

Then, he asked her to keep the gun because her house was now targeted, and she agreed for him to bring it to her house. Because she did not want to walk the streets carrying it with all the checkpoints, she agreed especially that she would not be using it unless she had to.

Yona laughed again and asked Jawad to come and give her the gun. Jawad climbed the stairs again filled with terror, and handed her the gun. Before he left, Yona kissed his lips and told him, "I've never seen you this scared before."

He told her, "I'm not scared. I just didn't know how we were supposed to explain ourselves. Who's going to believe that I'm here to give you this damn thing?"

Noble cause under shameful circumstances.

Jawad left. Yona could not believe that he saw her mother, but she grew suspicious when she saw him in this state. She dismissed the idea because if it was true then she was in trouble, which was true.

When Yona's mother got back from work and saw her, she told her quietly, "I saw Jawad heading for our house today. It seems like you're still dating him. Why didn't you end this relationship? It'll only bring shame to this honourable house! How can you be so insolent that you let him in our house? This is unforgivable. I saw him leaving the building ten minutes later and I saw how he pretended to be heading for a different floor when he saw me, thinking that I wouldn't know."

Yona denied everything at first, and was arguing that her mother doesn't even know how he looks. The mother remained calm and didn't argue back with Yona, who was confused that she couldn't hide it, especially from her mother.

Yona waited till morning without a moment of sleep. She called Jawad immediately and asked to meet him urgently. Jawad came and Yona told him about everything and that she had stayed up all night thinking about this crisis and how to get out of it. Finally, she found a solution that required Jawad meeting her mother and talking to her and explaining to her that Yona hid it from her because she was afraid she would refuse Jawad bringing her a handgun to protect her.

Jawad met Yona's mother, who came in all her prestige. Jawad asked her to sit somewhere, but she told him that she preferred walking the streets.

Jawad said, "Do you think that I'd ever bother you, respectful mother?"

Jawad told her why he was at her house and explained why he could not give Yona a weapon in a public place or anywhere else, and added that he wanted to know the family up close, but Yona's sister's accident was what caused this rift and he added that he wouldn't do anything that would harm Yona or her family and that the love story she told her sister about was nothing but a mutual love. Jawad lied in everything he said, because Yona was the one who picked his words for him, to make him look more decent. Jawad had never lied before, but he did today because Yona asked him to. Jawad left Yona's mother while she prayed for him because she was now at ease.

Should we lie for the sake of love? Yes.

Her words were spears piercing Jawad's body, who was never used to deceiving anyone.

He roamed the streets aimlessly for a long time. He got lost in the words of Yona's mother. He despised himself and cried silently. Stopped, then cried again. He cried for himself and for what this sweeping love had got him to do. That love which swept away all the values he had been raised on, and even the way he personalised himself. His silence was interrupted by a message from Yona asking him to call her if he had finished his meeting with her mother. He replied that they should meet at their usual place.

When they met, he told her what had happened, and he could not hide the pain in his chest for what he had done. The weight that the meeting laid upon his shoulders was more than Jawad could bear. Yona left him unsatisfied, saying repeatedly that there was no way out for them; either they lie or they stop seeing each other. She blamed Jawad for not sacrificing for his love and not accepting being a liar, even if for a short time, to continue their relationship.

The relations between Yona and her mother went back to normal, after she told her that she had met Jawad. Her mother asked her to return the gun to him, because it was dangerous and Yona would not be able to use it. Yona refused her mother's request, which led to Yona's mother calling Jawad and asking him to take back his weapon from her.

Thus, the whispers of love between Jawad and Yona were returned to them, and they vowed again to stay together.

During those days, the pace of the raging war all over Syria increased.

(Everyone fights on the homeland, but no one fights for the homeland.)

An external war with internal hands that included all regions, and at times the battles were not fifty meters from their meeting place, but that crazy war did not stop any of their dates. Moments of silence often prevailed after hearing an explosion nearby, and still their love did not stop. The Citrus tree knows all the words and feelings of the love between them. It was that tree under which shadow they always dated.

A love stranger than any love, a strange destiny imposed it on them. Yona's father died in a car bomb explosion before the beginning of the crisis in Syria, which led Yona to be employed at the Prime Ministry in which Jawad was one of the managers. He met her when she worked with him and helped her overcome her grief, as he did with any of his workers. He spent two and a half years with her before he suddenly decided to leave the job. Yona showed love and attachment to him when he was close to quitting his job. This was apparently the main factor that drew Jawad's attention to Yona; before that, he was always busy with his work, trying to be successful in something because he had lost hope in having a successful married life.

His wife was not satisfied with anything at all. She was not even interested in raising their children. She was lost in something that Jawad was not able to understand. He gave her everything, but he could not reach her. She was far away. Jawad used his work to achieve what he could not achieve in his home. He spent more than twenty hours at work, returning home only to sleep and check on his children. Yona's interest in him played a key role in attracting his attention. In the end, he was a man who wanted a female who would complement him and bring out the child inside any man. He wanted a smile or even a simple interest.

Their love was born on the soil of tenderness and doses of femininity. A beautiful love, despite all the differences, but this love was able to challenge the drying up of the social soil and the storms of religions. He began to co-exist with a climate he created for himself and dealt with, and suddenly he established the rise of a huge, strong giant named Love 'Ishq', which he protected with defensive thorn-like spears.

Yona fasted with Jawad during the month of Ramadan and Jawad prayed the Christmas prayer with her. She read to him verses from the Holy Qur'an and he gave her a golden bracelet containing twelve coloured crosses to express the passing of a year since their love began. Their bodies mixed to form fairy-tale paintings repeatedly. They were unable to bear a separation that lasted a day or two. They exchanged millions of emails. Their story became bigger than the mushroom of a nuclear explosion. But, it remained confined between them, and its details were told to Rama only. It was impossible to end their story with separation.

The war was intensifying and the spaces of encounter in which it was possible to move away from the danger of death were narrowing more and more. In every place, massacres unknown to humanity had been recorded, and the atrocities were told every day while drinking the morning coffee, as if they were conversations for entertainment; all Syrians were inside the battlefield.

It had been a strange war, similar to the love of Jawad and Yona. Sometimes it is said that the opponents were radical Islamists, and suddenly they were financed by foreign countries. A thousand factions and legions. Every ten thugs would gather up and call themselves a legion and fight and chant the words "God is great"; then they would kill children and their countrymen. They destroyed everything. They looted anything they could put their hands on and would consider it spoils of war, just like the wars during the times of the Arab tribes before Islam. The same as the Muslim fights between the Umayyads, the Abbasids, and the Fatimids. Everyone was claiming that the fight had been in the name of Islam, and no one cared that the country was collapsing. Suddenly, there were what was called "calls for co-ordination" from Arab or European countries to overthrow the regime. Sometimes because it belonged to an Alawite sect, and sometimes because it was unjust and tyrannical, and suddenly because it sold the Golan to Israel, and after a while you would see those countries meet with Israeli agents, or they would meet them in Israel itself.

The Syrian crisis is so strange.

It did not do anything except that it showed the large amount of backwardness which existed among many Syrian citizens in terms of dealing with the goal they wanted to achieve. All of them dealt brutally with the other who contradicted them; goals were as many as the number of rebel factions and funded parties.

As for the regime, it seemed to have lost control over its units and the way they acted. Especially that it relied on what it called the National Defence Committees, who harassed everything and were a source of nuisance even to the residents of the areas controlled by the regime (the supporters).

All the fighters in Syria lost their humanity and did not realise that the slain is a Syrian, and the stolen goods and spoils belonged to a Syrian brother. Each of them received orders to carry out any operation, and they did not care about the orders or who might be harmed. What was important for any of them had been their personal gains from that operation.

Four years had passed. Yona's face quarrelled with a laughing smile, her teeth veiled and hidden by her lips. She wore the hijab, as the Islamic extremists imposed on all the villages and cities they occupied. She came to meet Jawad as usual, but it was coldness that overcame their dates. She often cried hot rain and repeated a phrase she never got bored with, "What do we expect after all this love? We must end this relationship. This foolish, disabled love buried in two hearts that only we know of its existence."

Four years, and fate did not change anything in their love story, neither negatively nor positively. It was indeed a buried love that did not know life. A Secret love, a handout on how love is a secret. A love with which hands were not intertwined except in the dark. He did not see a light, no one talked about it.

Yona said one day to Jawad, "What hurts me in this love is that you are the man that every female desires. For me, you are complete in all aspects that I wish for the man of my dreams, and even that you are more than I wished, but I am like a princess who has the most beautiful dresses in the world. I wear more than ten of them every day and I try all the colours, but my prince prevents me from seeing any visitor and prevents me from leaving his palace. The princess sits naked today in her palace, just like me. I wish to tell my story to my friends, to tell them all what is happening between you and me, and of what I feel towards you. I want to tell them about the roses you brought in batches one day when we quarrelled, and you wanted to surprise me and reconcile me. I want to do that like every girl does when she tells the details of her love story. To brag about you and everything you surprise me with. To release the fragrance of my love for you in front of everyone after I become a star in the sky of this love."

Being unique and distinguished is what everyone looks for, but returning to your natural state is impossible.

Four years had passed without the two lovers noticing them. They were preoccupied with a rejected love. It was the same state of rejection for the war that was raging all over Syria. Everyone rejected the war, yet they all fought in it. It had been a war in which no one knew who was right. A war in which the regime fought to maintain its adherence to power with all of its joints and its institutions. As for the opposition, it did not have a unified representative. It was scattered and branched. The regime, in an attempt to have support, allowed Russia, Iran, and Hezbollah to interfere. On its side, the opposition was played on by the Arab countries and the United States and several European countries. Huge amounts of money were poured from both sides and the unified goal for them was fighting.

Everyone does not care about Syria, but the chair and the spoils it brings.

Means of life were scarce to the people from all sects. Death had become the guest of every family, displacement and destruction had brought shelter to more than one family in one house. Over-priced food was provided by greedy merchants who exploited the state of war, and lack of control was the same everywhere. In addition were the lack of medical devices and the spread of strange diseases. Another social problem was immigration, which confused most young people fleeing military service in death boats, and the children of the wealthy classes who left in luxurious planes. In any case, most of them were males. The men who were also among many victims in the battles between both sides. Four years marked society with spinsters... lack of men... lack of capabilities and means of livelihood... a future that did not bode well.

The ugliest thing about this war was the fight among its people and that no one acknowledged the fact that the first thing war inflicted had been the sectarian strife between Sunnis and Shiites. A story which was more than one thousand three hundred years old. They were fighting a war motivated by outsiders. This story had been the swing with which the West shook the entity of the Islamic countries to edge them more towards fighting among themselves, and to turn them into a market for the weapons they manufactured over the years and piled up, and just getting rid of these weapons turned into a loss, so it was decided to dispose of them with strategic benefits that would achieve many of their goals.

Syria was one of the countries that embraced the ugliest brutalities of the international conspiracy, and unfortunately its people practised it against themselves.

The story of the fighting in Syria when told to any stranger, would deplore how the people of same country are fighting with this ferocity and brutality.

Do not be sad for a country that incited its people to fight.

In this charged atmosphere, Yona decided to end her love story with Jawad, and to stay as far away from him as possible to end this relationship.

She decided to emigrate and to apply for asylum to a European country. Yona discussed this matter with her mother, who became her only friend after she married her eldest daughter off. Yona's mother refused her idea and said, "I have nothing left in this world but you, and you want to commit suicide by crossing the sea. Every day we hear about hundreds of deaths. No, I will not agree to this. We will stay here and die here. I do not want you to die far from me."

Yona tried to convince her mother by all means and told her that she and her brother-in-law would go, and if they arrived in the country, she would apply for family unification for her mother, and her sister's husband would apply for family unification for his wife, and the family would meet again in a safe place where humanity was respected.

Yona could not convince her mother, who would have agreed if she knew the main reason for Yona's request, because by leaving the country she would get rid of her relationship with this terrifying monster. She turned him into a monster whenever she saw Yona leaving the house.

The next morning, Yona recounted what happened to Jawad, but he did not care much about what Yona said, considering that it was just an idea that was put forward by Yona, knowing in advance that her mother would not agree to such a risk and that Yona was in a state of confusion to find any solution to their love story. For some time, she kept on repeating that this would not stop and dry up its rivers unless they stopped seeing each other.

Jawad jokingly asked Yona, "You will go, then?"

She said, "Yes."

"Where, for example?" he added.

She said, "Sweden; all Syrians go to Sweden."

Jawad said, "Sweden is a beautiful country to which I can go."

"I'm running away from you, and you want to go, too? What is the use of running, then?"

He said, "Who told you that I am going to Sweden for you? No, I will take my children and my wife to live there."

"Choose another country, then."

"No, I love Sweden."

Yona laughed mockingly at Jawad, who was trying to hide his concern about this new proposal, then she left.

In Yona's house, preparations were being made to determine the country to which her brother-in-law would go. He decided to emigrate, because he could no longer bear to live in these conditions in which hoping to have a stable married life had become crazy. He had been an only son, who excelled in his studies and who had worked hard. This groom, who had only been married for a few months. The pharmacist who worked more than fifteen hours a day, and his wife, who worked in a telecommunications company, together, before the outbreak of the war, earned nearly three thousand dollars a month. After the war, what they earned was not worth two hundred dollars.

He finally decided that he would either travel or escape to the Netherlands. The young man started collecting the money. He sold his wife's gold and borrowed from his relatives, in addition to what he could save throughout his life; but the money was not enough. Yona told Jawad these details while they were sitting in the cafe where they always met, and added that both he and her sister were thinking of selling their small apartment which they had bought together. However, her sister cried because she had spent a whole year preparing this small apartment. She rearranged the kitchen. Bought its pieces one by one, but did not complete it because she wanted to do it together with her husband. She postponed a lot of things so that they could choose them together. How could she, after all that, sell a bed that included their long-awaited moments of love? How could she give up her pillow and her fork, or the sofa that she used to sit on when she quarrelled with her beloved husband? How could she give up the house opposite her mother's house? She would have to live with her mother until her husband reached his destination and she joined him, which may take a whole year. How could she see someone entering her house and leaving it? She wept and sighed sadly, but the real fire burning her was that her husband was heading into such danger… a journey of death, as all types of media described it. Despite all that, she did not speak up of all that had been raging inside her, and she agreed to let him go because he had already decided. She did not object to him because he was insistent and indignant at the situation their conditions had reached and the terrorism that floated and exacerbated and brutally investigated every person who was different.

Yes, this country, whose people did not appreciate its beauty, sun, and its seasons, grace, overflowing with tenderness, the walls of its streets, and its tranquillity. The country for which many songs had been written, as well as love songs. The country which gave birth to the great poet Nizar Qabbani, the only poet without rival so far, with his style and light images taken from the diaries of any citizen who wrote about Damascus as if it was a female. He created his amazing poem, 'This is Damascus'. Iraqi poet Muzaffar al-Nawab wrote about it as well after he lived in it. His poem, 'It is Damascus', is a simplified reference for those who do not know Damascus. In it, he describes its goodness and simplicity and how sectarian conflicts have been buried in its graves. Suddenly, this country turned into one which alienated those who were experts in different matters. Its joints were dominated by corrupt and ignorant officials. They cared for their gains only and did not realise that life would never remain the same for them. Their ego was high, the law was absent, and corruption spread in all sectors, even the judiciary.

It is difficult for Syria to recover. Its disease is not war, nor terrorism, nor command, nor state, nor the regime and the opposition. Its disease is that it has a People who were fed with the strange milk of ostentation, superiority, and inequality. It learned to respect those who have money, or the black cars that were allocated to elite officials.

At a certain stage, the citizen was not entitled to own a black car, nor did he have the right to paint his car black, nor did he have the right to own an SUV car, and in the end, the Syrian citizen was prevented from importing a car from abroad. Until this day, fees equal to twice the price of the car are imposed on those who want to import a car from abroad, and this contradicts the principle of tax or fees in terms of its average value.

Favouritism... nepotism... bribery... self-love... lack of sincerity in work... condescension over others... and the ugliest thing is that some of them boast that they are Syrians, when, in reality, they only represent themselves with their dirty and uncivilised behaviours.

Jawad once went on a trip to Egypt, Sharm El-Sheikh in particular, and the plane was fully booked for the benefit of a tourist office. When the plane arrived in Sharm El-Sheikh, the crew of the plane were very annoyed by all the passengers, and what bothered them the most was the presence of one of the elected members of the People's Assembly from the merchant class and a member of the Damascus Chamber of Commerce, who was accompanied by his family.

The captain, who was an Egyptian, said to Jawad, "Please look at the place where the member of the People's Assembly and his sons were sitting." The plane's floor was indescribably dirty.

Jawad was ashamed. He told them that the man and his family did not represent their people, and that he only represented himself. Unfortunately, all the seats were dirty. Yes, we must admit that the majority of Syrians, wherever they go, try to be rude and take everything that is free as a 'gain…'

"Everything that is for free, take more of it."

One day, when Syrians were entitled to enter Turkey without a visa, thousands of them went on tourism to Turkey and booked hotels, but after less than a month a representative from the Turkish Ministry of Tourism came to Syria, imploring the Syrian government not to be disturbed, because Turkey would raise the price of hotel rooms on Syrians only, especially rooms in which the reservation was full or included everything (open). When asked about the reason, the representative said that one day one of the rooms in a large resort was opened. Two Syrians were staying in it. They found inside the room more than fifty cans of Coke and more than fifty unused small bottles of water, and much of the buffet food was crammed into the room for no reason.

Syria is a pure piece of land, but its people are afflicted with a thousand diseases. Their sheikh is an agent, and their merchant is a cheat. Their policeman takes bribes. A People which wants large doses of love, affection, morals, and belief that everyone is human, and everyone is equal in rights. It needs doses of conscience and education on what it means to be a human being and that sovereignty does not mean authoritarianism and strength does not mean respect. The People need a vaccine of loyalty to the homeland and not to people or fear. Every Syrian should know that the homeland without others is a solid block in which he cannot live.

Of course, that does not mean that all Syrians are like that, but the vast majority are. The State did not notice these diseases, but rather helped spread them, intentionally or unintentionally. How do societies develop when the teachers are hungry and looking for extra work to survive the month? University professors sell exam questions to their students. Doctors only care about collecting money. A Customs policeman who is not interested in the homeland, only cares for the bribes, and he can sell anything for money. The word 'teacher' is given to anyone with a fortune or authority, even if he is insignificant and does not understand anything. The People's real self, appeared in this crisis; murder and torture turned into topics people brag about. Everyone wants to become someone who has power.

The armed groups are each headed by a tramp who used to be a drug addict or a drunkard, or the son of a sheikh turned into some kind of the only rooster in his dump.

On the other hand, there are paramilitary elements who did not listen to anyone except their direct officer responsible. He definitely was of a poor-level education, whether he was a truck driver or a retired person who joined the People's Committees, wore a camouflaged uniform, and was appointed to a checkpoint, and who wanted to have revenge for all the days during which he had been looked down upon. He wanted everyone to call him Master "Me'allem", and to pay respects to him. On his side, he was always arrogant and never paid these respects back. He did not submit to any orders. He was the only commander in his area. He often controlled the passing cars loaded with goods. Therefore, the checkpoints inside Damascus were sold or rented to the militants in exchange for millions of Syrian pounds for specific periods. Of course, these checkpoints did not protect Damascus from any detonation of car bombs, because they were only concerned with the levies. As for the security situation, remaining tense had always been in the interest of those controlling the checkpoints.

Everyone had a thirst for domination and power. This was how they learned that a person is not a human being unless he exercised influence and authority and everyone respected him in appearance and spat on him after a few seconds had passed. They knew they were outcasts, but their consciences were sold out, so they did not care how people looked at them.

Those who do not have a conscience, as a rule, cannot feel remorse.

In Syria, thousands of laws were issued and all sectors were meticulously regulated. If they were implemented, we would be a virtuous city. But the laws were issued to only announce that we had laws. All laws can be bypassed, and the organisational and legislative ones can be overruled, even election laws.

Finally, the last thing that was violated had been the constitution.

Will the Syrian people one day judge the committee drafting the new constitution?

The door for candidacy has been opened for the position of the Presidency of the Republic in Syria. Those who applied included Jawad's high school colleague, whom his schoolmates called Zamira: a simple young man who obtained a high school diploma and worked as a sales representative for a company selling medical devices. That day, he was the twenty-first candidate for the presidency. Everyone wanted to be the President in Syria.

It is always a misfortune in Syria to be honourable and responsible, because after that you will become a beggar.

Judgment depends on retards and does not favour decision-makers or thinkers. There is no decision but one. It allows them to plunder from the money of the State and the people, each according to his association and the circle that supports him. A thorny fabric that governs Syria. However, in reality, no official can guarantee the continuity of this state of things.

In Syria, there remain a few of its people who continue to watch the episodes of the series of fighting between the regime and the opposition; each one of them is a mirror of the other… two sides of the same coin. They care for nothing but the chair and the advantages it brings. They shared the lands and looted everything. As for the homeland and patriotism, they were left for those few people who like to drink a cup of morning coffee to the tune of Fayrouz songs on the balcony of the house, in the shop, on the rooftops, or in their offices. They all dream of recovering the homeland from all its calamities, and they do not know that the homeland is infected with a virus that destroys the country because those in it are without conscience.

God afflicted Syria because its people did not fear God when they took away others' right to live.

Yona sat and put her head on Jawad's shoulder. She talked loudly about how she and her mother would survive without her sister.

Was it prescribed for her mother to be separated from all her children, sometimes by death and sometimes by travelling?

Yona cursed the one who caused this crisis and who dared to deprive a mother of her daughter. "If they are quarrelling over the seat of government, then what is the sin that we have committed to pay the price of an issue that we have no control over?" Yona's voice was loud, so Jawad held her to his chest and silenced her indirectly, then they went out. She stood in front of the cafeteria door to say goodbye to Jawad.

He said to her, "No, I will walk you to your car." They walked together and Jawad was telling her not to be afraid. "You won't be alone; I'll stay close to you."

He knew that Yona was resentful of such an argument, because she always answered him, "You were never mine, and you never will be, so do not try to convince yourself that I am part of your priorities."

He knew that every day Yona opened her eyes wanting to take the decision of ending this love and leaving Jawad for his children and wife. She never imagined that she would be in such a situation; to be part of that crime and to love a man who was older than her, who was also married, with children and not of her religion. Every possible reason that would end their relationship was there. If she waited a little, perhaps fate would also make of him a brother to her, and their story would become an Indian movie. Yes, she did not imagine herself to be a girl who would do this and stand in front of her mirror to discover that the mist of love obscured her vision.

Selfish love does not allow any idea to swim in its orbit.

She used to scold herself every day for not finishing this story. Although every day she made the same decision, but when she trained with herself on telling Jawad her decision, her heart would cry, and love would burn with the fires of her love and end her decision.

Yona's phone rang while she was walking with Jawad and before she reached her car. Yona's mother was on the other end. Her face changed. Her answers were very short. She finished the conversation and turned to Jawad, saying, "My mother agreed. I will go with my brother-in-law on that journey of death."

Jawad did not understand what Yona said, and asked, "What did she say to you?"

Yona replied, "Mum told me to hurry back home to go with my sister's husband to make my sister the one responsible for managing all affairs, because the trip may be next Tuesday."

"Why did she agree? Was she afraid?" Jawad asked. "So be it; don't hesitate, go and do what your mother says — but why do you think she suddenly agreed?"

"My mother said to me, 'I do not want to be the reason if something bad happened to you here because of this war, and if God wanted you to survive the journey of death at sea, you would get out of the danger circle that you live in every day. God will grant me patience until I hear you have crossed the sea safely. Only then will there be no other concern for me in this world but your happiness.'"

Yona cried, but Jawad encouraged her and told her, "You were looking for a solution to our story, and it came from God all of a sudden."

Yona interrupted him, saying, "I want to see you every day. I only have four days left. I want to memorise your face again. I want to hear all the words you told me that haven't been spoken yet. I want to hold your hand all the time, because I love your hands more than anything else in you. Promise me that we will meet every day. Four days and our story ends. I won't cry, I promise, I won't hurt your heart."

Jawad opened her car door and said, "Your sister and her husband are waiting for you. Go and wipe your tears. I don't want to promise you, because I will definitely see you every day. This journey will soon make you forget this wild love. Exile will overcome longing and you will start another life in which you fight the world, and you will soon forget. This is what God has planned as a destiny for this story… Go."

Yona turned her car and Jawad turned his head back to where he had come from. His eyes overflowed with tears, and he felt like he was suffocating. The sky closed on every step he took, leaving the place where Yona's car had stopped. He rewound his long tape of memories with her. He could not bear the idea of not seeing her in his life. He crossed the street, crowded with crazy passing cars, without taking notice of anything. One of the drivers shouted at him because he almost hit him. He heard a woman on the other side of the street saying, "Maybe he is deaf."

He stood in front of the old wall of Damascus, then looked at the place he used to lean on each time while waiting for Yona. He said to it, "There will be no more waiting." He walked back to his house and did not feel the distance because the story that this love wrote was long enough to cover more than three hours' walk.

Every month, Yona used to make a name for him: Masu, My Heart, Jussi, Hubby.

Yona was not just a girlfriend; Yona was a creature who loved him first. A classy friend who knew how to act in the right way. She knew her rights and others', too. She knew how to treat people. She knew the meaning of respect for everything. Trustworthy, honest, noble. A gentlewoman, generous, who would sacrifice for others. Qualities that qualified her to enter the heart of everyone who met her. A rare friend at such a time. She excelled in her devotion to Jawad. Then she became his lover, and knew how to play with the cards of tenderness. She always knew how to win. She knew the meaning of love and knew how to get her lover to drink her love. She stopped her wine a little before he lost his mind, because the perfect ecstasy of love creates repetition that leads to boredom. She knew how to pour the glasses of this love and what colour of love wine would suit the moment. She excelled at this, because she had a memory in which she had stored everything she learned from the experiences of her family and relatives. She practised love without any rashness. She achieved what she wanted without committing a sin. Crazy Yona, how could Jawad just forget her?

One day, he said to her, "I turned you into a painting and wrote you as a book, and I won't be satisfied until I make you a statue."

Jawad loved her more than she should.

Every beloved is a messenger from God, structures the conscience of the lover. Regulates the rhythm of his life with one repetitive, but not boring song. A messenger who guides you in the ways of your day and shows you the blessings of God. Then you believe that messenger and believe in God without compulsion, as he or she shows you everything in a positive way. Love is the eternal message that God sends to every person in this world to know that life has another path. For when you fall in love, you see and taste everything in this life differently.

Everyone desires Sex, but sex without love is like the banging of pots in the kitchen that would soon end.

Night is dark and sad without the stars of love. Morning is hopeful with love, but without love it is just a routine of a working day. Without it, Music is stairs that break by the hands of a woodcutter. Food has another taste with the one you love. Everything is moving and beautiful in the world when you are in love.

Next day, Yona came with red, puffy eyes. They sat where they used to. Yona grabbed Jawad's hand and hugged it to her chest after kissing it. Jawad said to her, "God loves you, my love, and here He is taking you out of a story that did not have a happy ending for one day. God answered your request and will end it."

"Do you want to stay in Damascus after I leave it?" Yona asked him.

He replied, "Yes, I want to stay. If you leave, Damascus will remain for me. I embrace the walls of the alleys through which we crossed together. I stand where we always stopped and contemplated the 'Al Majnunah' plant. I buy you the Muhammara [a Syrian dish] with Kashkaval cheese that you love and eat, even when I do not like it. I will live all the daily details that I have lived with you every day as if you are here. You are Damascus and Damascus is you. I hear the ringing of the church bells and the call to prayer of the 'Umayyad' mosque at noon gathered in Bab Sharqi, and you should know that the ordeal we are going through now may be a blessing from God upon us. I will not grieve over a fate that is inevitable for us, because fate is the word of God. He develops the teachings of religions with the ordained destiny, just as science develops through research and experiment. Therefore, we must receive what fate holds as a product of the interaction of the new advanced life equation."

Yona interrupted him, "And will you be happy?"

"Yes, I will be happy. I will do everything we wished for and could not do. I will hold your hand while you are absent on all the roads. I will enter the shops, caress your hair without fear. I will walk in the funerals of the martyrs without fear from all the bullets which I have feared for tens of times stopping me from walking them.

"I will feed you with my hand 'Meshabek' [a Middle-Eastern dessert] that you love every day. I will live in Damascus with you, lacking nothing but you. I won't be able to hold you to my chest like now. Between us there are barbed wires and brains that prevent us from approaching the minefield of ignorance to explode it. I will be happy, do not be afraid. Damascus' heart is big. It will promise me and hug me. She is sympathetic to everyone, although now everyone is stoning her and only caring for its material worth. However, Damascus prays for everyone. It will remain as it is for everyone, and no one owns it. You and Damascus express one word, which is 'love'."

Yona cried with tears that burned her cheeks. Jawad cried with his heart, not his eyes.

They parted that day with their eyelids swollen and faces painted with the most painful and sad expressions. Yona's face was painted with strange details that Jawad had not seen before. She really was like Damascus, strange in all that was happening to it. Strange from what it has gone through since the history of its existence. It was invaded by many. Many of its people were killed at the hands of the invaders. However, that day, it was like Yona's strange face. It was witnessing the separation of its families and its people, fighting over a chair for money for the sake of a sect. Damascus, and Yona's face is Jasmine. A hurried sadness wanting to eat all the spaces of joy.

Damascus is as tender as Yona. Tender because of its people who are affected by the stories of Abu Zaid Al-Hilali and live them as if they are happening now, and they live with Antra in their cafes, and the narrator tells it as if Antra was the son of their neighbourhood. Enthusiasm took them and ignited the fuse of conflicts that only God knows when it will end. The West played on it more than once, as the story of Abu Zaid Al-Hilali, which they hear repeatedly every Ramadan from Al-Hakawati in their cafes. The same sectarian story was carefully planted in the minds of all Syrians. They thought to get more freedom. They entered labyrinths, not realising that things would turn into that. They killed each other. It was strange how all that happened all over the entire Syrian land. People believe what they believe despite the clarity of the truth. They like to remain in their fanaticism. All that happened was strange, the same as the strangeness which coated Yona's face.

They met the next day around one thirty, and Yona's friend Rama came as well.

The traditional orange juice was on the table. The weather was still a bit hot, but maybe Jawad ordered it to cool off the heat of the situation. Sadness completely overtook them. Jawad asked Rama, "We will be alone without Yona, you and I."

Yona interrupted Jawad, "No, she will be alone. She will be, but you won't be!"

Jawad looked at Yona's face, thinking of what she had said, gesturing to repeat what she had said.

Yona confirmed what she said and added, "You will follow me. We cannot do everything with me because my brother-in-law is with me all the time. You will follow the stages that I follow step by step. I will send you each stage in the path that I follow. No, do not try to think of an answer. You will go. You won't stay here. We'll be together even for a few months. Then you bring your family and we part. You'll have no choice. That's what I thought yesterday. Promise me that you'll follow me, please. If it's not for us, then for your children's sake. Don't stay in this country. Choose another country if you want, but do not stay. I cannot bear the fear I have over you in this country, where madness and murder have become its main feature. Without me, I know that you will drift towards danger."

Jawad, with a slight smile disproportionate to the state of sadness that enveloped everyone, said, "I promise you."

His answer came quicker than Yona thought it would. She was dumbfounded when she heard a quick, short answer that extinguished the flames of the final parting. Rama's face showed her surprise as well, who in turn said, "Why travel, then? Why do you want to travel? Didn't you make this travel decision to get away and end this impossible love story?

"Why would you risk this journey of death and ask him to take the same risk?

"Why don't you stay here and that's it, why are you getting revenge on me?

"I am the only one who will be harmed by this foolish decision. I am the only one who will remain without a sister or a brother. I haven't had the time to be content and happy with Jawad's friendship. Why are you choosing this crazy idea to travel? To escape death? Death will come to you wherever you go — it is inevitable."

Jawad intervened to stop Rama's sharp attack and said, "No, Yona loves adventure, nothing more. She does not run away from death or from a bleak situation that hangs over Syria. Yona wanted to stop the routine of the love story that she's living. She did not complain because she would not marry the one she loved. Love walks on its feet after getting tired of sitting long in a wheelchair." Then he turned to Yona and told her, "I will follow you in two weeks, I promise. I have some work to finish here, and I will follow you step by step. Don't be afraid, no matter what fate hides for us. What is important is what we will add to this destiny."

Rama screamed, "Crazy, you both are crazy," and left screaming, "I don't want to see you any more."

Yona embraced Jawad and said, "I took this decision yesterday after I left you. I could not bear the thought of being separated and each of us living in a different country that the other could not reach. I couldn't. I felt that I was being torn from the inside, and for a moment just thinking almost killed me. I started to feel that my heart will stop, but God inspired me with this idea because He loves me, and it revived. Here you are bringing me back to life again when you agreed. Now my enthusiasm for travelling will increase, even if the road is fraught with the danger of death. The important thing is that we will meet again, and this is enough to go through all risks. Oh my beloved, I cannot leave you. This is what I realised, even though I decided to stay away from you and escape."

Jawad said to her coldly, "You did not make this decision. It was made by my heart and yours together. It is just that this decision was known to us today." He added, "Damascus without Yona, a cold body, a face without features. I saw Damascus in you and felt the tenderness of its alleys with you, and I learned that cities speak and love from you and by you. How can I live in a city where you are not one of its residents, nor its smiles, nor the sorrow of its children? How can I live in a city without you where your oxygen is absent? Everyone who lives in Damascus is tied to the love of a girl. A city that has mastered the art of love, so it was easy to incite and lead to an endless fight because all of its residents are in love, and there is nothing in the world easier than to lead a lover, because the lover dedicates all his thoughts and feelings for his lover, so he became empty towards anything else and turned into a person that is easy to be controlled.

"Damascus knows how to distribute its love. It has all the women and the most beautiful women, and all the beauty and most beautiful women in the world are Syrians. Yes, in Damascus, my love, there are all the irregular actions and all the contradictions with this war."

Fanatic love for the idea of a religion and a sect is destruction. Free love is the treasure of the world.

"In Damascus, the jasmine dazzles with its whiteness all those who pass by, and its whiteness comes from your existence in this city. In

Damascus, the jasmine is also black, which grows when you leave. You and all the lovers in Damascus, Homs, Aleppo, and all the provinces, cities and villages. You are the homeland. There is no use for land, stones and trees without lovers. Do not be afraid, I will not leave you."

Jawad walked Yona to her car. Rama was standing near it, apparently still angry. With tears in her eyes, Yona said her goodbyes to Jawad, but unlike those of the day before, because hope of meeting him again had returned, even if they did not know where or when they would meet again. Yona could only hold on to this unknown hope.

Jawad returned and walked in the alleys of old Damascus, pleading with churches and mosques, asking forgiveness for his betrayal of Damascus. He kissed the stones of its walls, he called her from all its doors and implored her, saying that it was love and nothing else. Damascus did not answer him. Damascus is stubborn and right in its stubbornness.

When Damascus loves, she gives. She is the one who opened the dome of the Badr Mosque for him in Laylat al-Qadr to ask for what he wanted from God Almighty. She made the grave of one of her guardians in the Mosque of Al-Shaalan a pillow on which he falls asleep during the days of Ramadan and the sanctity of that grave is a soft moisture which is blown on him to reduce his thirst. Then, he would spend his long summer fasting comfortably. She is what made him a normal human being, opening ways for him to communicate with the Creator in all of her mosques to pray and be answered.

Damascus prayed to God to provide for Jawad to be happy and rich, and God answered her request. Yes, in Damascus and from Damascus, the glory and spirituality are real. It is the city of the forty guardians.

Damascus, which never left Jawad, stood with him and delivered everything he wished for.

Damascus is beloved, may God answer the prayers of those she loved.

Yes, Damascus was angry that Jawad betrayed her. In her lived someone whom God loved in order to deliver God's goodness to His servants.

How could Jawad stab her? Was he feigning all this love for Damascus? He was leaving her for Yona, leaving all the gifts of Damascus and the tenderness of Damascus and the love story that united them and that began from the first day that Damascus knew Jawad. For the forty years he lived, Damascus watered him with the nectar of her jasmine.

His ribs disobeyed. Screams came from all the walls of Damascus. He tried to deafen his ears, but in vain; the cries were too loud for his palms to stop. When Damascus is angry, the sky shakes.

Jawad was unable to withstand her anger. He preferred to quickly leave its alleys to escape her anger. The sound of Damascus's screams kept digging grooves in Jawad's conscience… Traitor. You are a traitor to the sanctity of Damascus. Traitor. You are not trying to untie this collar that Damascus has put on your neck today. And you will not be liberated from it until the last day of your life. As much as Damascus loved, she now branded you with that wrapped collar of forty laps around your neck, "Here is the traitor of Damascus."

Why all that?

Why did Jawad immediately agree to Yona's proposal?

Why didn't he think before committing to a covenant with her?

How could he leave Damascus when he did not like travelling or even tourism? When he used to travel outside Damascus, he would return as soon as possible to Damascus.

Was Yona's love the motive? If so, then she was the one who said to meet him in another country after they requested asylum there. They would meet for two or three months only until he was reunited with his family and then they would be separated. Then, why would he leave for only two months?

Was he unable to make the decision to leave her now and end the situation?

Why, then?

Escape. Yes, escape and avoid confrontation. He found in Yona what he wanted. He really wanted any solution to his obsession that rings alarm bells every day. Since he left work in the Prime Ministry, he had been spending a lot of time at home. He discovered that work obscured his vision of what was happening inside his house.

He gave all his time and effort to work day and night. Now clashes with his wife were anew at home. A wife who did not care for the house… The too-much-troubled wife!

He started watching all the family members. His eldest son, who ignored his lessons. His middle wife's sister, who had become, along with her husband, against the regime. She forgot that one day she was the daughter of a major general in the army and enjoyed the advantages of this position, but now her father has retired, so the benefits are gone, and the loyalty was, too. Her younger sister, who married Jawad's very close friend, was also an opponent. Her husband, who worked in the security services, was also thinking of escaping, but he did not want to leave what reached his hand from the spoils of war. Glory had returned to those who work in security in Syria, so he was torn between dissent and survival, or maybe he just wanted that which paid him more. He sold his friendship with Jawad at the first opportunity he smelled money.

But what occupied Jawad was his wife. He began to feel that there were things that made him aware of the issue of his wife's heresies, and that if he discovered any loophole in her, her punishment would be death for her, and he would not accept anything less than that. That atmosphere that preceded Jawad's quitting his work and after leaving work made him very afraid, as he did not want to watch his wife or follow her for fear of a catastrophe that would be reflected on his children. He buried his still-living doubts, but in their stead a horror grew within him with the passing of the days.

Yona's proposition that he leave the country was as a good way out to escape from all possibilities that were black, even if death itself was the only way out. He wanted to get out of the circle of obsessions that floundered in his head. Yes, he would leave Damascus with all the memories and possessions he had in it… Friends and family. He would leave Syria to escape from a hell that will come.

Yona prepared from the early morning to leave Damascus, to leave the most mad and miserable moments of her life, to leave her childhood and adolescence, to leave the days when she realised that she was a girl when she heard the first word of admiration from a young man who passed by her, and there she was ashamed of the pharmacist because she asked for something only girls asked for. From there, she crossed the roads to reach her university, and there she and her friend walked to buy the hot potato that she liked. Small details which quickly passed in front of her eyes, but the most important thing was that she would leave her mother who was also her friend. She would be leaving the grave of her father and her brothers.

She would be leaving for an unknown place, to a place where you do not know anyone or anything. A new beginning in everything, a difficult path, and at the end, a country in which you are a new, big baby. You have no choice in naming that baby because his name was, naturally, a refugee. A new story would begin. You had to know the laws and the language, and then build a house and start with the lowest kind of work.

The play of the great actor Duraid Lahham, *Al Khorba*, dealt with this issue in accurate details.

But why all this? Escaping from war or death. No. She was certainly leaving with all her conscience, because fate drove her to a place unknown to her, she did not want to know, and she cannot know. The unknown. She was walking towards it hoping she would be able to see behind its mist a ray of light.

"Fate will drive you to where you don't want, and if you are stubborn, it will drive you unconsciously.

And if it does that, all you have to do is enjoy its journey."

One question that kept occupying her mind: "Was Jawad honest in promising to follow her?"

Or was it just an empty promise? So that she would leave with the hope and the security that he would follow her. After that, the story would end, and she would be free in a country from which there is no return. Jawad was never but honest with Yona. Would this be his first lie?

Yona left her house after saying farewell to her mother, who cried her heart out, and her elder sister. It was early morning. She rode bearing the pain of tears and separation for her family and Jawad, who said goodbye to him, promising that they would be together, even if for a short period.

The taxi took off, and with it Yona felt she was dismembered as she left the Syrian border to enter Lebanon, where the trip began from Beirut airport. They arrived in Beirut early and decided to rest in a hotel because their plane took off at eleven p.m. They boarded a minibus to reach the hotel when they landed. Yona discovered then that her mobile phone had been stolen from the pocket of a small bag hanging from her shoulder.

Yona got angry and cried a lot because this phone was the true holder of all her memories. It contained all the messages and all the pictures that Yona meticulously collected in every meeting with them.

Yona was very sad and pessimistic about the trip. Her sister's husband bought her a new cell phone, which forced them to return to the airport because the time allotted for rest went in search of a new device for the angry Yona. As for her sister's husband, he did not know the reason behind all this sadness over a device. He did not understand that this device was basically a gift from Jawad on her birthday. He was surprised at her behaviour and considered it the behaviour of a girl in her late teens.

Their plane took off on time. Yona arrived in the city of Izmir in Turkey and called Jawad, crying over what happened with her. Jawad calmed Yona and urged her to not think of any loss now because whoever leaves their country had already lost everything, even their memories. He asked her to only focus on reaching her goal so as not to stumble midway.

Yona asked him, "What about you? Are you ready to go?"

He told her that he had started the procedures since the morning and that he was now looking for an office to book the ticket.

She asked him to finish his work quickly, and if he could, within one week, not two, because her heart was very worried, and if he hurried, she could meet him in Marmaris, that beautiful coastal city on the western side of Turkey, opposite the Greek maritime borders, from which people are smuggled to Greece via the ferries of death with their large numbers of passengers and its lack of primary safety elements.

After a few days, Jawad went to the cafe. He sat down on his chair and looked at the chair on which Yona used to sit. He remembered her angry and stubborn smile. She sat on it, feeding Jawad with her hands the homemade sandwiches that she prepared and the tarts that her mother made and coconut balls.

She was sitting there when she watched Jawad's eyes shining while presenting him a cake she made, designed in the form of painters' tools on Jawad's birthday. There she used to sit and cried longing for him, even when he was so close to her. There she used to sit and swear she had loved him. There she used to sit and blush while confessing to him that she imagined making love with him before he confessed his love to her. It was there they shared and debated all concerning what is going on in the homeland. There they confessed to each other what the homeland meant to them. There, he felt that he had a sister, a friend, and a girlfriend. There, he felt that he had a female companion for the first time.

Jawad cried for a long time and, like a crazy man, he talked as if she was sitting before him.

The waiter was amazed when he paid the bill, because the first time he asked for two cups of tea, then he repeated the order and asked for two cups of pineapple juice, which Yona liked.

Jawad left after he called Yona and was reassured that she had arrived at her hotel in Marmaris and was waiting for the person responsible for smuggling to speak to them to take them by boat to a Greek island adjacent to the Turkish border.

When Jawad left the cafe, his phone rang. He was surprised to find that it was Yona's mother. He was not afraid because he had been talking to Yona a few minutes ago and she couldn't have left at this time of the day on that sea trip.

Jawad replied proactively, "Hello, welcome mother of all."

She apologised for calling and said to him directly, "I think you know that Yona has taken a dangerous journey."

He replied, "Yes, her co-workers told me."

She said to him, "My heart is burning. Excuse me. I want to talk to anyone about this matter."

Jawad answered, surprised by her call, "I am glad that you thought of me."

Yona's mother continued, "I have not known sleep since Yona travelled, and how does sleep come while my heart is burning for my dear girl? I don't know if I made a mistake in sending her. I was afraid that she would get hurt here, and that I would later blame myself for preventing her from travelling. But the alternative was worse, I think. I'm sorry that I spoke to you, but I know that she is dear to you, and I could only think of you, because you would understand what is in my heart."

"Yes, it is more precious than you can imagine," Jawad replied. "Don't be afraid. Yona is stronger than all danger. She will cross and reach her destination for two reasons. First, because when she insists on something, she achieves it. Second, because she has a mother like you, who does not stop praying for her, and this is enough for God to facilitate her way. Soon you will receive news that will make your heart happy."

"God willing." Yona's mother repeated her apology and ended the call.

Jawad was amazed and surprised by this call! Yona's mother called him; how could that be true? Did she want to make sure that Jawad did not leave with her?

Yes, and perhaps Yona's sister, who was like an investigator, encouraged her to do so. Perhaps they wanted to make sure that Jawad did not leave the country, and now they were assured of what they wanted, and they removed Yona from him and silenced all their fears of a possible relationship.

But if this guess was not true, Yona's mother made it clear that she wanted to talk to someone who had true feelings for her daughter. This meant that she knew what Jawad was thinking, or perhaps what he was hiding!

Mostly, she did this to make sure that Yona was not with Jawad, but perhaps she had put aside all her refusal of him, because now Yona was on the path of death.

A person is content with love no matter how forbidden it is in front of the bill of death.

Jawad had spent forty years here in Damascus, and only left as a tourist or an official delegate. The only love he betrayed Yona for was his love for Damascus. Yona knew Jawad's love for Damascus and was jealous of it, but she knew that Damascus was loved by all its residents. It was loved by its tourists, its refugees. It was loved by the passers-by, the worshippers, and the unbelievers. In Damascus, no one was hungry. Wherever you stand, you can hear its minarets and the bells of its churches. Jawad used to thank God every day that he was one of its residents.

Here in the ancient underground church (Ananias), Yona taught Jawad (Our Father who are in the heavens, hallowed be your name, let your kingdom come, let your will be done as it is in heaven as well as on earth...), and there in the courtyard of the Umayyad Mosque, Yona performed ablution and knelt with Jawad at the beginning of the Holy Night of Qadr.

How would Jawad leave Damascus?

He loved Damascus as a princess that was difficult to reach, and Yona's love was a part of Damascus. He walked in its old lanes. He tried to touch its stones in worship, asking forgiveness for his sin, but she refused. He tried to apologise to her, but Damascus was too big for apology. He stood in front of her white jasmine and said, "O Damascus, for you millions of lovers, and I am one of them, your heart contains us and to you my heart is attached. I leave you not as a traitor, but as a lover who seeks more love. How can I revive love in you when the one containing it has left? I will return with her."

"Do not accept me under your soil unless she is above it living love and its memory."

In a race against time, Jawad completed what could be accomplished in terms of authorising one of his friends to be able to run the affairs of Jawad's property and the affairs of his home and children. Jawad was completely absent-minded from what he was doing. He did not think about anything ten days before. Suddenly, he was in the stage of a radical change for his life. There were many questions within him that needed answers. Would he really leave Damascus, which he loved, for the unknown in Europe? His goal there was Britain, because, as his family members answered, they wanted to settle in a country that did not know chaos and he wanted his children to complete their studies in the best universities.

Or was he fleeing from indignation at what he saw of a hysterical security situation, killing, destruction and backwardness that he could no longer live with?

Or was he angry at the people in power in Damascus because they did not deter the fool who took over as Prime Minister? He was disgusted with his stupidity and his manner of dealing to the point that he did not last more than one year in his position.

Or was there another, intangible reason that pushed him to this decision, leaving three children and a wife who was never but a source of nuisance. He tried throughout his life to find a reason for her rudeness and her way of dealing with the events that Jawad lived as a husband for seventeen years. He was no longer able to endure more from her, and the possibility of his explosion was close, so leaving was an acceptable option.

Was he betraying a homeland which he had always loved? Was he a traitor to leave while the homeland was bleeding?

All were acceptable possibilities, and everything could be treated, but Jawad did not think of anything. It was Yona and the danger surrounding her that possessed him and took sleep from his eyes.

And why was Yona a priority?

Yona, who hugged Jawad in his stumble. The one whose tenderness carried him with her angelic wings and brought him back to drawing and writing. She brought out all his being after he left his work and everyone moved away from him, and when he broke his foot, she was the one who welded his bones with her tears and tenderness. She was the one whom he took his first steps to after he stood on his feet again, and held her hands and said to her for the second time, "Your hand is the one that saves me." Jawad's hand was trembling for fear of falling, and that Yona would be terrified.

Three years in which Yona immersed Jawad with all the meanings of the word love. She brought him back to life as a lover, a brother, a father, a master, and a companion in the path that may be long.

How could he leave her alone now in a strangeness in which she missed everything? How could he lose the first loyal friend he could finally have since he was a child?

Yona, that illusionary girl whom Jawad always played with when he was an only child. She was the one who listened to him and did not disagree with him, but she was the one to whom he used to complain of all his childish worries, always imitating her as if she was embodied in front of him.

Each of us has a loyal friend to whom we tell everything from the first moments we start realising life.

Jawad said to Yona during their first date that he was never as surprised as he was the first time he saw her. For the first time in his life, there in front of him, the fairy of his childhood was embodied. He told her that he knew all the details of her body and what most distinguished her was the redness that took over her chest when she was shy and when she was afraid or sad. He told her that he knew that hundreds of freckles were scattered over her body, condensing on the shoulders and gradually spreading apart as they fell towards the bottom of her back like the stars of the sky, and that there was a large star placed opposite her nape from the left side. All of this surprised Yona, but Jawad was not joking or making up things to have something to enter Yona's heart or impress her with. Jawad was talking about things that were taken for granted which he knew like he knew his name.

News arrived from Rama, Yona's friend, saying that Yona had crossed the sea from Turkey to one of the Greek islands, Symi, and thus had passed the greatest danger. Thirty passengers in a wooden boat intended for three passengers. A trip that exceeded three hours in a state of black terror in the sea which swallowed thousands of Syrians fleeing a war that grew more than expected by those who started it.

Many believe that riding the sea is a trip or some kind of a simple adventure. This may be true when you ride a boat and see that there are many boats surrounding you, or, at the very least, you see a piece of land near you during your trip, or even have someone who knows that you are on that boat. But the matter is completely different when you are in the hands of smugglers who are real mafias. For them, you are just a commodity or a box that must be delivered any way possible, no matter how dangerous the risk; and if it does not arrive, there is no compensation for the damage, and, most importantly, you may be thrown into the sea when the mafias are surrounded by any danger. To ride the sea for the first time in your life in a rubber or wooden boat that does not contain any means of safety and enter the sea at night with infernal blackness surrounding you and the crashing waves, it is all as if you have been taken by the jaws of a hungry whale that never knows satiety. The issue here is completely different, as the circumstances of your riding that rickety boat in the middle of the night and the way you are driven as a slave to ride it is like the experience of entering a cemetery at night alone and sleeping in an open grave, and being told that the dead will pet you at night, so do not be afraid, the night will pass quickly. It takes more than courage and masculinity. Those moments were passed by thousands of Syrians, including women and children.

The Syrians are able to do anything to escape the fever of war, for their escape from a burning death to enter a cold death road is in itself a strange simulation in which the possibilities are not differentiable. They fought a cold death because their path seemed to give them the hope that there is a small possibility of survival, after which a respectable life would start, even if it was marked with the term refugee.

So, Yona crossed the sea, despite her small body and weak strength, because she had a beating heart and a destiny charting a new path for her.

It was happy news, but it seemed to Jawad like a strong blow to the head. One phrase he repeated in his head, "She went further than I expected. Yes, kind Yona crossed the sea, and this means that coming back has become almost impossible."

Jawad took a leave from his work and bade farewell to his father, who was over eighty-four years old. He did not tell him that he would leave the country. It was a one-sided farewell. His father lived alone in the family home after his sons left him to establish their families and Jawad's mother died.

A person might try to hide what is inside him from people, but when it comes to your parents, a person is stupid when he or she tries to hide something from them. They are the ones who know you well. They raised you. They know your formation more than you do.

His father, who sensed something strange about Jawad's farewell this time, said to him, "I hope my son will be close to me when I die."

Surprised with what his father said, Jawad replied, "I am always close to you, but do not do it in the near future." Jawad said it jokingly, but his father was serious.

(Two years after this farewell, Jawad was told that his father had passed away, and Jawad was not close to him, so he did not fulfil his father's wish.)

Life is hard on you at its end, when a father needs his children just to help him eat or even to bring him food. It is a kind of an end to your abilities, and therefore time accelerates to end your ability to do the things you used to do normally. Your old age strips you of your manhood and strength and even your thinking ability. It robs you of the dress of wellness, carries your medicine bag, and makes you a burden on everyone around you, so you return once again into a child. This is the amount of time that a person lives between his birth certificate and his death certificate with which he builds himself, and then he quickly rests from the journey of his misery. Time begins to put barriers in front of him to vanquish him and throw him into that hole. During this period in our lives, we only remember our moments of happiness, but only if our memory helps us do that.

A Human's life is as long as years, but its happiness is as short as minutes.

Yona's mother called Jawad and told him that her heart was now at ease because Yona crossed the sea safely. Jawad deluded her and said that he did not know that, and that he was happy for her joy. He thanked God with her for the good news. That was the last call that Jawad received on his mobile phone. He comforted Yona's mother's heart because she was probably reassured that Jawad was still in Syria. She also wanted to tell him that he was a friend from now on.

Jawad left his house, bidding farewell to his children and his wife, who did not ask Jawad about anything. On the contrary, she was absolutely satisfied with his decision. She wished for it more than he did!

Nine security checkpoints separated the Syrian border from the Lebanese border. Jawad sat alone in the taxi crossing these checkpoints without being subjected to any harassment, because the taxi driver paid the needed cash to each checkpoint. They differed in terms of their dependence, but they did not differ in the manner of their use and performance. All these checkpoints followed a single system, which was 'pay and pass'. No one cared who you were and why you were travelling. It is a taken-for-granted culture in Syria. No one could deny the spread of bribery to the extent that it had become frighteningly public. A culture which parents raise their children to accept, the same as Jawad was raised. His father, who worked in Customs for thirty-five years, was able to bring Jawad's two brothers to work there as well. Both of them were professionals in taking bribes, and they proved to all relatives that a simple Customs employee can own so much from his simple salary, which was not enough for many employees to live on for more than five days. A Customs officer could buy real estate and cars, and more than fifty times the monthly salary could be saved.

This is not a rare case in Syria, but it can be generalised to more than ninety percent of workers in all sectors, including the head of the government where Jawad used to work. Everyone there was a copy of his bribed brothers. Even the judges, everything. Yes, everything is subject to bribery. All laws and decrees can be bypassed by bribery. Syria is the

Cambridge in teaching the art of bribery, as it is most probably the same in most Arab countries.

The Syrian crisis has opened new doors for bribery and widened the open doors. You are a fool in Syria if you are honest. Everyone argues with honour and convinces you that he is a saint. He criticises the bribed and calls for reform, but he takes bribes. Even the sheikhs and priests issue a fatwa against you that contradicts their creed if you pay.

Jawad arrived in Beirut and rested in a hotel near the airport because his plane would take off for Izmir in the early morning. He called Yona, who was resting from the journey of death and relieving her head of the possibilities of the truth of Jawad's promise because he started his journey and did not let her down. Jawad laughed a lot when Yona told him that she did not feel the dangerous sea voyage because she was exhausted and tense and was affected by the Faisal Syndrome.

(Faisal Syndrome is related to Yona's uncle, who liked to sleep after lunch no matter the circumstances, just like Yona, who falls asleep wherever she is when she is exhausted.)

She slept on her brother-in-law's shoulder more than half the time, and she was dreaming of the day when Jawad would book her a room in a hotel, and ask one of the workers to put candles in the corridor leading to the room and in the room as well. He would also ask the hotel manager to hire someone to play the violin for them while they were sitting around the table on which the cake was placed with dozens of gifts, which he carefully selected. The room would also be full of red flowers. They were celebrating their first Valentine's Day. Yona was taken to the room by the worker, and when she entered, as usual, to meet Jawad in the cafeteria belonging to the hotel, the waiter asked her to follow him because Jawad was waiting for her somewhere else. She was astonished when she entered the room and the music started playing. A smile pushed Yona's cheeks to the top, expressing joy in her eyes. It was a happy day for her and it made her forget everything.

Yona wished that Jawad would arrive in Greece before she left it; she wanted to meet him, because the fire of longing had begun to burn her. Jawad promised her that he would do his best to meet her as soon as possible.

At five in the morning, Jawad was in the passenger terminal at Beirut airport, waiting for the gate to open to set off for Izmir. He reviewed all the information that Yona gave him and the phone numbers of people who smuggle Syrians and non-Syrians to Greece, the first stop to enter Europe.

Like a forest fire during Summer, Jawad burned everything he had in Syria: his memories, his friends, his family, his work, his wealth — everything. His new birth will be a faltering Caesarean section from his Syrian mother, from whose womb he had come out faltering, exhausted by the fight towards the new world. A birth marred by many questions.

Syria, which was attacked by the monsters of the world and which were helped by its ignorant people, was destroyed. A new global catastrophe. No one was spared from its curse. Many died, others kidnapped, those who lost everything, and the many who were forced to leave his city and become internally displaced, or became a means of receiving dollars under the pretext of humanitarian aid in the camps of the neighbouring countries as refugees. Many of its wealthy people who hold other nationalities left until the war ends, as they did in the eighties, following the events of the so-called Muslim Brotherhood.

As for the likes of Jawad, they were many. Lots of them were unemployed from the youth category, and some of them were tired of the revolutionary tales and rotten heroism of both sides, and among them were the youth who fled military service so that they would not die in a war in which neither side would win. As for the families who left and faced the danger of the sea, they were looking for a livelihood, because the government had become unable — or its inability increased in this crisis — to secure the most important necessities for living: water, electricity, fuel, and bread. Whoever heard of the Syrian crisis from abroad could not imagine the tragedy of the daily lives of the Syrian citizen. Economic atrocities swept through Syria.

Just because you live in Syria, you are undoubtedly a superhuman because you co-exist with the madness of the ego.

Many programmes on European channels ask their citizens to donate to help children in Syria and Africa, some of them to support food and some to deliver drinking water. You are surprised when you see these programmes presented daily as if the governments of those countries are not concerned, nor are they the mastermind of the ongoing wars that cause these crises in those areas. The West has mastered the art of lying to its people and used the media professionally to stir feelings. In fact, the majority of the people in Europe donate to help. The question which no European who has sincere human feelings has asked himself is, does any African country have a factory to manufacture warplanes or even gunpowder?

Poor European citizens, most of them learned human values and believed that no one would lie. Man does not need to lie because he is free to do what he does, and no one questions him, and he has forgotten that his government is the biggest liar and that the beneficiaries in their countries are the thieves of power. They are just as in the Arab countries; they exercise the same authoritarianism, and they rob the State, but in a different way from the Arab countries. In the Arab countries, they steal openly. In Europe, the lords share wealth in an artistic way. The only difference between Syria and any European country is that the government there has secured the basic means of livelihood for the citizens, and the rest is equally divided among the ones in power.

In Syria, theft and corruption have led the country to a state of inability to secure the basic needs of the citizen, such as water, electricity, and bread.

The most beautiful thing that the Syrian tragedy has done is the stripping of entities and principles that were well-established in the minds of many and are considered red lines. In the Sunni doctrine, the Sunnah meant the hadiths that were narrated from the Prophet (Muhammad), peace and blessings be upon him, and whoever touches or doubts any of them is a disbeliever according to what was stated in the Holy Qur'an. However, during the crisis in Syria, it became clear that the most famous hadith writer in Islamic history (Al-Bukhari) had written about six hundred thousand hadiths and later said that he believed only in four thousand hadiths. He had been from Bukhara and not of Arabic origin.

'Alawites' was a word that was not allowed to be circulated in the Syrian streets, and it has now become one of the words you hear daily. Shiites have announced what they feel and what they hold against all who were not like them.

The Christian sects of all kinds openly knew what was in the bellies of those who thought they were infidels, and they knew what was worse than that, when the heads of their churches abandoned them in adversity. What the Cardinal claimed of protecting them was an illusion, and in the end, the whole matter had only been about money. If you have it, the church takes you and brings you out of death to European countries. "Donate and we will be with you." There was no one on Syrian soil who carried the concern of the human being.

The Syrian crisis exposed all beliefs, religions, and even morals. Even God Almighty did not respond to either the minarets or to the churches in which the religious ones prayed during the years of the war, prostrating and crucified. The game of death continued in which all Syrian sects paid their dearest possessions and the best of their youth.

God was tired of their flattery and deceit. God forgave them for their ingratitude. God gave the Syrians gifts that no country in the world had.

Syria has everything; even its sun is good, its land is good, but many of its people have been afflicted by God with this war; there is none among them that God listens to their prayers or begging. A hypocritical sheikh, a priest collecting donations, a greedy and responsible merchant who cares only for himself, a student who buys his success, and a policeman who even sells his slogan, "The police is the servant of the people". The poor and the oppressed cry out, "O God, take revenge on everyone who did that to us," so God responded to the oppressed and the poor. But God's wrath afflicted most of the population of Syria; all of them are concerned with this prayer and this response, and everyone who was afflicted by God's curse in this war grew ungrateful and considered the death of his son a kind of heroism, whether that son was from the regime or the opposition.

In wars in which a person defends his homeland against an external invasion, whoever dies can be considered a hero or, in another sense, a martyr. As for whoever fights his countrymen and reaches the point of brutal bloodshed and mutilation of corpses, this is considered human madness and is not permissible, and who boasts of such an act is a brute and should be classified as an animal. A predator.

(God will punish all the Syrians for this war. He will make the earth swallow them up because they have overpowered each other and all of them have lost their minds and are only concerned with the spoils from the other.)

When American soldiers went to Vietnam and fought, American films portrayed the American soldiers as heroes. They were, in fact, invaders who killed and attacked other countries and peoples as they did in Iraq and

Afghanistan. They deluded their people that what their soldiers did was heroism and they were rewarded with medals for killing other peoples.

We in Syria have departed from the reprehensible norm. We didn't defend our country, nor did we attack another one, and yet we were heroes. What had been portrayed as an international conspiracy and terrorism, was nothing but the impurities of some citizens who sold their conscience and brought strangers to the homeland to kill their own people. What happened in Syria is the ultimate Ignorance, and the State did not take notice of its aggravation. Also, the injustice that was practised on a segment of the intellectuals. The State did not pay attention to the people in power who unjustly treated citizens, and there were many laws that harassed the rights of many citizens. Backwardness and the lack of human awareness by the majority resulted in a situation that you could not just tell to any sane person. How would you tell them that the demonstrations called for freedom, but at the same time broke into libraries, public buildings, railways, and wheat stores, and blew up all infrastructure? Since this category of freedom-demanders was so brutal, the State dealt with them with greater brutality. It bombed them with planes and artillery. The freedom-seekers demanded support from all those who hate Syria. Then, when all haters pressured the State, it asked for help from allies with hidden interests, and others who had known interests, and foreign fighters were more than Syrian in the country.

Syria was colonised and the occupation army was mostly Syrians. Unfortunately, both sides were the stupid Laila who believed the wolf and it ate her.

Whoever hears this story asks you, "Isn't everyone Syrian?"

You answer, "Yes, they are Syrians geographically and with official documents, but in reality, they are demons who practise crime and drink blood and do not care about human dignity. They do not recognise anyone's rights. They do not want to be civilised or learn. The problem is that most of them are university graduates and are classified as intellectuals. Studying is one thing and urbanisation is quite another."

Ignorant intellectuals, you are asked, "Why are they like this?"

"The government's neglect and the State's lack of interest in teaching the subject of love and respect for the other and holding accountable those who violate the rights of another human being. The State neglected this type of education; rather, it practised with all its organs during many years the disregard for the feelings of the citizen and practised insult and humiliation as a custom between the State employee and the citizen. Many people accepted this kind of abnormal custom because they are beneficiaries, but there were also those who did not want their dignity to be offended, so they turned into time bombs wanting to explode at the first opportunity to avenge the violence of a government employee somewhere one day. All of them blamed the head of the State and did not realise that whoever did the shameful act is perhaps a relative of them in a responsible place. The blame is certainly not only on the president, but on a culture that has become generalised among the people."

The most difficult type of injustice is systematic injustice.

But let us not philosophise matters and cause this brutality taking place in Syria, and then say, as we always do, that it is a test from God. Yes, it is a test, because people considered themselves at some point to be civilised, but only a smart part of them was. That small part only knew how to live life according to a specific lifestyle. It only cared for its own life, and never cared that others were dying. This was not being civilised, but backwardness.

The selfishness of a people does not create a nation, but rather destroys values and civilisations.

Jawad's plane took off, heading to Istanbul as a first stop, and then to Izmir, where Jawad spent his first night without closing his eyes for a moment. In the early morning he set out to take the bus to Marmaris, that picturesque city with its scenery, nature, and climate. After he booked his hotel, he spoke to the smuggler — the one whose name Yona sent — and Jawad told him that he was ready to go at any moment he wanted.

Yona called Jawad and reassured him that she had moved from the small island that she reached and had left for Athens to prepare to set out for her main destination, Britain.

Yona arrived at Omonia Square in Athens, which was a major gathering place for all those wishing to be smuggled to other European countries. She rented a room at a hotel near the square.

Yona said, "It's been fifteen days since I last saw you. Try to come as fast as you can because longing is starting to dig trenches for its defences and is preventing me from continuing this."

Yona and her brother-in-law met the person responsible for their smuggling. He was an Iraqi.

Abu Saja was a first-class philosopher who turned himself into a hero. At every opportune moment, he claimed to understand everything, when in reality he was an idiot. Destiny put him in this profession when the Iraqi regiments were leaving Iraq, whether during the era of Saddam Hussein, who pressured the Shiites and the Kurds and subdued them by the edge of the sword, or after the occupation of Iraq by the American forces. Abu Saja became one of the main pillars for escaping to Europe from Greece. He had a lot of money. He smuggled about ten people every day to Athens airport and other airports. Half of them would manage to escape, and the other half would be arrested, and thus he would receive fifteen thousand Euros to smuggle only five people. This had been the case for more than ten years. As for the price of leaving to Britain, it was higher, because the possibility of arresting the departing person was much greater, so eight thousand euros must be paid, not three thousand like other European countries.

He promised Yona that her forged travel document would be ready in a short period not exceeding a week. As for her brother-in-law, he was supposed to stay until Yona left and reached her destination, because if they travelled together, Yona might be arrested. However, her brother-in-law could not let her stay alone with a smuggler, who did not know any law, either made by humans or my God. Anyway, they both agreed to what the smuggler proposed because they had no other choice. He asked Yona to ensure the amount of eight thousand euros and leave it with Mr Naji, a nice Coptic Egyptian who was the link between them. The amount would not be handed over to the smuggler until after making sure of Yona's arrival in Britain. Arrival in Britain needed a stolen travel document, not a forged one, which meant that it must pass through the forgery detection devices in the controls imposed by Britain when you enter the planes heading to it. Naji would take his fees after making sure of the arrival of the person. They were a commission of fifty euros.

Jawad walked the streets of Marmaris and the market, had his dinner and decided to return to the hotel to rest. He walked by the sea. Only this sea separated him from Yona. Sadness tried to wear him down, but he quickly woke up from it, saying to himself that it was just a sea. "I will cross it tomorrow or the day after tomorrow, with God's blessings."

At the hotel gate, his smuggler called him and asked him to come to a specific address and not to cancel the hotel reservation so that no one would get hint of what was going on. Jawad hurried to his room and collected his needs. He called Yona in a hurry and headed to the gathering place and met a respectful young Palestinian man. They arrived at a very far one-star hotel. About twenty young men and women were gathered in its hall. They all sat down, and in the eyes of each of them there was a story that only God knew. The majority were Syrian, but some of them were Palestinian-Syrians, who left their homes in Damascus after the Islamic groups had seized them and after Hamas — spoiled and loved by the Syrian regime — had betrayed them. In other words, it turned to those who paid more, because it could see that the regime in Syria had begun to crack and would eventually fall.

Syria supported Hamas for many years, funded and maintained it with weapons. The head of its political bureau lived as a minister in it, allowing him to deliver sermons in the mosques of Damascus. Both Syrians and the government loved him, but he sold his loyalty despite the warnings Assad received from officials in the Palestine Liberation Organisation, the party in power inside Palestine, and whose relationship with Damascus was marred by a coldness of silence. Its delegate said that Hamas could not be trusted, but Assad did not respond to what they said because the position of the Palestine Liberation Organisation was clear after its late president, Yasser Arafat, accepted negotiations with the Israeli side in the Oslo Accords in 1993.

Jawad and the rest of the group prepared themselves to leave the hotel and head out to the sea. They were taken to the city of Bodrum, which was about two hours away from Marmaris, then everyone was transported by a Syrian boy from Aleppo city in a very small van to the seaside. The boy asked them to go down immediately and hide by the side of the road and not take any luggage with them. Everyone did what he asked them to and gave up their bags, but Jawad did not give in to this request and insisted on keeping a small bag with him. Suddenly, a Turkish gendarme appeared from a tourist car, took out his weapon and asked the driver and the young man to raise their hands and to not make any move.

The boy insisted that he had nothing to do with him and that he was only one of those who wanted to escape to Greece, but the gunman was wary of any movement, so he surprised him with a strong slap and soon reinforcements arrived and everyone was taken to the police station. The investigation continued for three hours, no more, after which the chief ordered everyone to get out, including the driver of the car and the quarrelsome boy, and he said to Jawad in a whisper, "Continue what you came for."

Everyone, including Jawad, returned to Marmaris, joking with joy at their unexpected release. It was an opportunity for everyone to get to know each other.

However, Jawad was puzzled at the reason for their release without any problems; even though the accusation was ready and one of the smuggling gang members and the driver were arrested, the case was complete and the charge of human trafficking was punishable by Turkish law and even international legislation. Jawad was well aware of this. He studied law at Damascus University, and the college was a stage for him and his ideas. One day, he stood before his professor, objecting to what he said that the death penalty was not applied to the mother who killed her son because a mother would not do this heinous act unless she was exposed to harsh factors. Jawad objected to what the professor said because he believed in the exact opposite. The mother who killed her son should receive the penalty because she had the emotions of motherhood, and if she could overcome that emotion for any reason and kill her son, then the most severe punishment should be inflicted upon her. The professor replied that the laws applied in Syria were mostly inspired by French law, and that was what the French legislator deemed right, just to end the discussion.

Yes, they were released without any accountability. International mafias follow the issue of refugees, and Turkish politicians are undoubtedly involved. Huge sums of money had been collected from the suffering of the Syrian people. Crime is legitimate and is now practised as a legal and systematic act. Humanitarian organisations were the only market in which the products are collected to be resold in retail to all countries, according to demand.

Jawad called Yona to tell her what happened.

Yona was sad again. She did not hear that anyone had been arrested by the Turkish authorities, but it seemed that Jawad's luck was undoubtedly very bad. She repressed how she felt and said to him, "I hope you will arrive in Athens soon to be with me." She said it hoping to motivate Jawad for the second attempt that may begin any time. "I will wait for you, and you may have another try tomorrow. Don't be sad. Go back to your hotel and sleep well, because the next night may be tough, too."

The following night was the most shining night for the two lovers.

Yona boarded her steamer and travelled to the island of Crete, which is about eleven hours away from Athens by sea, and from there she would try to set off from the airport to Britain, using a forged passport bearing a picture of a British girl who looked like her. She sent a picture to him. The similarity between them was great. The possibility of Yona crossing was great, because she knew the language, as well as the passport she had. Hopefully, no one would have reported on that lost passport. Her brother-in-law took her to the island, where they arrived in the morning. Yona did not sleep well. She was tense, and after three hours between the start of her flight, she entered the airport. This was her first attempt. Hundreds of people try to get into Europe every day from all the airports of Greece.

Yona, with her small body, childish face, European whiteness, sad eyes and resemblance to the owner of her fake passport, was able to cross the most scrutiny of the security centres, which is the gate for planes leaving to Britain. Few smugglers gambled to smuggle people to Britain because the departure gates to Britain in European airports were mostly controlled by the British themselves, but Yona simply crossed. She did not know that she had an invisibility robe within her eyes, which by looking at them, one could not help but sympathise with her.

Her plane took off. She did not believe that she had accomplished her mission. She got rid of her forged passport and threw it in the plane's toilet. It cost eight thousand euros. She threw it and did not care about this amount because happiness overwhelmed her quick achievement and it was just around the corner from her landing at London Airport to apply for asylum and start the first moments of her new life.

Jawad left his hotel in Marmaris in a hurry on the evening of the second day. He got into a taxi and headed towards Bodrum for the second time. He and his new friend, the joker from Homs, Abu Nazih, whom he met in the previous attempt, arrived.

Fifty people gathered, including twenty-five African girls, who all slept on a forest floor near the sea for about five hours until they were called one by one. Jawad was the last one to arrive, but he was happy and excited. He did not feel afraid. Perhaps the main reason was Yona's eyes, to which longing was huge. Since the boat taking them was a yacht from the Onassis yachts, led by Ukrainians raising the American flag, Jawad knew that he was in the hands of professionals. The boat sailed at sunrise, and after about three, it stopped, and all its passengers got off quietly on the bank of one of the Greek islands. Jawad reached safety.

The trip on board that yacht was like a dream. Jawad was not afraid for one moment. He was looking at the sky and watching the stars. He knew that he was getting closer and closer to Yona with every wave the boat split.

This journey was the journey of death. He passed it with complete ease. Even for a moment, he was enjoying sitting on that chair while watching the breaking waves. One of the sailors told him, "Take off the life jacket you are wearing. You are safe." He was the only one sitting on the deck of that yacht. They took out a girl who did not exceed twenty. They told him that she was pregnant and suffering from shortness of breath. Jawad sat her in his chair and stood on the edge of the yacht with an easy feeling in his chest. Only now was he able to tell Yona that he was on a safe road and to inform his three waiting children of the news that he had crossed the gate of death in peace.

Yona's plane landed at Heathrow Airport in London. Until this moment, she thought she was dreaming. She did not believe that she had arrived in Britain until she read what was written in large letters on the airport wall: 'Welcome to Britain'. She told the authorities that she wanted to apply for asylum. She was placed in the detention room, which she later told Jawad about, that it was a five-star reservation. She was comfortable with everything and was treated with respect. After spending one night, she was transferred to the city of Birmingham to wait there in the camp until she was sent to a city in which she would spend the waiting period for her temporary residency of five years. The place was a bit bad, but Yona tried to get used to it, especially that it was temporary. Just a few days and it would pass. Everything became easier after crossing the cunning sea which devoured the bodies in seconds and then extinguished the romance on its shores after it wrecked the corpses of the dead.

On a huge rocky edge of a small Greek island, the migrants were disembarked at lightning speed because a Greek coastguard boat was approaching. Jawad climbed to the top of the hill while holding the hand of a third-month pregnant girl. A Palestinian woman named Rend. Her husband was carrying their bags. A young man as well.

Rend had a story that would make even the stone cry. She was working for UNESCO inside the Palestinian-Syrian camps, and with the beginning of the crisis, the Palestinian parties operating on the Syrian land or incubated by the Syrian government began to pretend that they sympathised with the cause of the people against the regime, when, in reality, its leaders had different agendas, so a friction occurred between the Palestinian parties. The Popular Front was nothing but a wing of the regime, and Fatah remained silent. Hamas bet that Assad would fall as the Tunisian, Egyptian, and Libyan presidents fell. So, it decided to find an alternative, claiming that it knew the future.

Hamas is a religious organisation and it has religiously and ideologically extremist followers, but what the followers do not know is that the leaders of the organisation are tools in the hands of the party that pays more, and since the regime supporting them will fall, the leaders decided to go to other countries.

The strange thing is that the Palestinian supporters of Hamas in Syria, immediately after the outbreak of the crisis, changed their direction from the liberation of Palestine to the liberation of Syria from its rulers. They sympathised, of course, with all the factions that followed the religious approach and rejected the regime and made the issue in Syria look like it required jihad. It was a hellish plan to make them ignore the Palestinian issue, and unfortunately, their minds were empty, and they were led towards a conspiracy which was only meant to weaken them and change their orientation. The Syrians will never forgive them for this blind drift.

Rend, this good girl, tried to help the wounded after the Palestinian camps began to suffer from the fever of the Syrian crisis. Her husband's family travelled to Turkey and she decided to join them, but the camps were surrounded by the Syrian security, and somehow she managed to escape from the siege and head to northern Syria to enter Turkey by land and join her husband and his family. However, she was arrested by an extremist Islamic organisation and imprisoned in Syria as a war-prisoner. Because of her pregnancy, she was not handed over to a man who would marry her. On the eighth day of captivity, she was able to escape towards the Turkish border without any shoes. She walked for more than thirty kilometres, after which she encountered a large trench on the border, and she was able to enter it, but she could not get out of it, because it was higher than her ability to climb. After more than thirty-six hours alone inside the trench, God sent her help. She came out almost collapsed from a lonely night that almost caused her to have a nervous breakdown, but she was the daughter of Palestine and a natural fighter.

Jawad, Rand, and the rest of the crew arrived in Athens after spending two nights on the island. Everyone's faces were relieved after they took off their masks of fear. The journey of death was over.

Yona, who received the news of Jawad's safe arrival in Greece, had spent two whole weeks in a refugee camp in Birmingham. The name of a prison could easily be given to it. On the first night, she cried silently on her pillow, as she was shocked by this place. She feared that she would make a sound. There were three girls of different nationalities with her in the room, two huge Africans and an Indian. Yona, a small and innocent figure, was not used to talking to them. She was afraid of this new situation. Many people think that asylum in a European country is your access to heaven, but it is the opposite. No matter what your previous life was, in this new life you are looking for yourself in the midst of a strange huge mass surrounding you, and at the end of each day you spend the night looking for your parts which started to change their colours. You hate that new self of yours, but it is imposed on you. Colours would be mixed, and what you used to love would be lost, and you will not be able to preserve the new colours, because you are no longer the same person you used to be; nor are you what they want you to be. Everyone after his asylum longs for his village, even if it was in the desert. Everyone dreams of returning to the details of their previous life, no matter how trivial. They want to go back home to their families, to their homeland, to the geography they are used to, to their language, and, most importantly, to themselves.

In Britain every day, hundreds of asylum applications are submitted, Syrians making up only a very small percentage of this number. There are Indians, Pakistanis, Afghans, Iranians, Africans, Kurds, with all their components: Kuwaitis, Sudanese, Moroccans, Egyptians, and Thais. The list goes on for every country in which there is an ethnic conflict or war on its borders. All those come to Britain as refugees, in addition to all the European Union nationals from the countries that were under the umbrella of the socialist camp. They come to work in it according to the rules governed by the European Union, from which Britain has left because of the losses it incurs as a result of entering this union. A person who sets foot on British soil will by definition receive all the benefits of a British citizen, except for voting or the elections of the parties. This is a matter governed by other conditions.

Yona was sorted to Coventry to live with four girls in a house where she would wait until it was time for her meeting to get temporary residence. In this house, every girl had a room, but unfortunately for Yona her room was also shared with another girl.

In any case, the house was better than the camp and close to the city centre. She received subsidies from the government — five pounds a day — to provide herself with food and simple necessities. It was certainly sufficient for Yona, the careful mastermind, who astonished you with her ability to knead and conquer the most difficult circumstances and bear every difficulty. A sister of men, as they say, but at the same time, a butterfly. She learned to cry away from everyone's eyes to maintain her balance.

Yona was now waiting for her brother-in-law or Jawad to arrive in Britain. She thought that the matter would not take more than a week, considering that she was the weak girl who could easily pass.

Her brother-in-law's first attempt was a month later, after a forged passport was secured for him; but he was easily arrested at Athens airport.

As for Jawad, he tried after fifteen days from the same island from which Yona had started, Crete. He was also arrested and transferred to a prison that lacked dozens of requirements just to be suitable for animals. It was like Arab prisons. Jawad spent his first night without speaking to anyone, because everyone seemed to be a professional criminal. On the second day he was able to speak with a young man from Afghanistan and asked him, "How many days do those like me spend in prison?"

He said to him, "Don't worry, two or three days, then the prosecution and the judge and you are free."

Jawad knew that it was not possible to arrest someone who tried to escape and sought asylum because he was fleeing from war and danger as stipulated in international conventions, the most important of which is the Dublin Convention. On the second day, Jawad was standing before a judge, handcuffed. He stood before a beautiful young judge with an interpreter. The judge asked him, "What is your name?"

He did not answer and she repeated the question again. He did not answer again. She asked him, "Why don't you answer? I can imprison you if you don't."

He said to her, "I am a law school graduate and I know that no accused can appear before the judge handcuffed, even if he is a dangerous criminal. A prisoner is placed in a cage, but with his hands free, because he is accused of committing a crime and has not yet been judged as one."

The judge apologised that she had not paid attention, and asked him, "You are accused of forging a passport and trying to cross from Crete's airport with it. What do you say about that?"

He replied that the first part of the accusation was incorrect, but the second was. "I did not forge a passport, but I used a forged one to leave from Crete airport."

After an hour of trial, the investigation was completed by postponing the issuance of the judgment until after three months, and he was free to go. The judge whispered something to the translator, then left. The translator told him that the judge sympathised with him and advised him to leave Greece within the next three months, otherwise he would be sentenced to three months in prison, according to the law in Crete, because it differed from the rest of Greece; but the ruling is generalised to all of Greece.

Jawad got out of prison and boarded the ship all night long back to Athens to start his second attempt. Indeed, an incredibly similar British passport was secured for him within a week and then he would leave from Thessaloniki, which is about eight hours away by train from Athens.

Jawad and a friend of his left; he wanted to travel to Sweden to join his sister, and Jawad was leaving on another plane to London. The two boarded the train from Athens, and after the train had moved a quarter of an hour, Jawad wanted to review his passport information and for his friend to see if the picture did resemble him; but, unfortunately, he did not find his passport or plane ticket!

They were lost or stolen from him while he was boarding the train. Jawad continued the journey with his friend and took him to the airport, and his friend crossed the plane to France with success, from which he would continue to Sweden by land.

Jawad returned after spending two hours at the airport because he had to stay there or the smuggler would fine him with the money of the passport and the ticket, for Jawad claimed that he was discovered by the airport security officers and he was released. One of the smuggling gang members was outside the airport waiting to make sure that the customer had left, so they could demand the money from the third party.

Fate did not want Jawad to leave, and he did not grieve, for he was used to the fact that his first attempt at any work and perhaps the second would not be successful. He was more accustomed to striving towards his goal than anyone who walked towards the same goal. He was never lucky to cross any obstacle easily.

Every person wishes to reach his goal easily, but most of those who fail later discover that their delay has been for good reasons.

He believed that God was with him, and he must strive to reach his goal, because if life granted him his wishes easily, he would lose the joy of it. He thought like this to try and get out the nails of failure from inside his head.

Another week in Athens, a third passport was secured for him, holding Icelandic citizenship, and this was one of the rare things to obtain. In fact, a ticket was booked from Athens to Switzerland, and at Zurich airport, the plane would go within a quarter of an hour to London. Jawad was finally able to miraculously get out of the Athens airport. He was smiling at everyone. He had lost hope because the possibility of discovering him was great, because his photo was placed on the passport, which meant that it was forged in a way that was easy to detect. He was used to wrestling with critical situations, but fate desired this time that he succeed. He crossed the first barrier and then the inspection of luggage and then the door of the plane. He did not believe that he crossed and got inside the plane. It took off and Jawad dreamed of surprising Yona with the news of his arrival in London. He repeated the sentence that he would say to her dozens of times. However, he did not tell her that he still had one more escape attempt to make.

But fate intervened negatively during the change of the plane, and it was discovered by the Swiss authorities that the passport was forged, and Jawad was taken again to prison. He was interrogated for the second time, but this time he was in a prison that was more like a five-star hotel and he was treated with more respect than anyone could imagine. Yes, the criminal in this country is a human being who gets his rights. Rights that even the free person does not get in the Arab countries.

The policemen's respect for him and his appreciation of his situation and respect for his humanity was something that could not be described.

A judge was immediately assigned to look into his case in the presence of the translator, and after making sure of everything, he told him, "No one can stop you in Switzerland for more than twenty-four hours without a trial. Therefore, you have been detained for twenty hours, and I have no right to interrogate you; but if you want to close your file, you have to pay a fine of one thousand four hundred euros."

"What if I don't carry the money?"

"But you carry eight thousand euros," she said.

He told her, "Yes, but it is the money with which I am trying to get to a safe country."

She said, "And you arrived safely, and I can tell you that if you want to apply for asylum in Switzerland, there is nothing to prevent your acceptance of asylum here, although the government does not give this offer to everyone who arrives in Switzerland."

Jawad thought for a while and then said to her, "I wished all my life to wear a Swiss-made watch and not a fake. Today you are offering me asylum, and this means that I will become a Swiss citizen after a few years, and this is bigger than my dream; but I face two problems. The first is that Switzerland speaks two languages of which I do not know a single word, nor my children. The second is that you delay the family unification procedures, and it may not take place at all. So, thank you and I prefer to pay the amount and continue my trip to Britain, whatever the cost."

Jawad was released and given permission to ask for asylum at any time he returned to Switzerland.

The prison door was opened, and he got out. It was eight in the evening. He saw the outskirts of the city of Zurich and did not know where to go. He froze, because the temperature was four degrees below zero. He walked for about an hour to reach the city and was finally able to find a hotel and book a room. He started looking for a solution. He was like a wanderer in this city. He did not know anyone in it and did not know what awaited him. It was stupid for the Swiss authorities to leave him like that when he did not know the directions of the city or the language of its people, nor did he carry any papers that would allow him to stay in it.

He called Yona, who cried when she heard his voice because she was nervous, and Jawad did not tell her that he would try a third time. If he told her that there was a change in the plane, she would not have agreed for him to board it. Suddenly, Jawad remembered that he knew a friend in Germany whom he would call and ask for help.

Yona said, "Don't go to Germany, because Germany takes your fingerprints and if you do that, you will not be able to come to Britain."

Jawad told her that he knew that, and he was afraid that the Swiss authorities would do the same, but thank God he was safe now.

Jawad phoned his friend Abu Muhzab, who answered him immediately. "Give me your address. I will reach you within eight hours," said Jawad. This good friend from Homs saved Jawad from the greatest ordeal and ended all his worries. After he calmed down, he noticed that he was inside a very luxurious hotel room. He moved the curtains hiding the glass walls of his room. Even the bathroom was looking over the glowing city of Zurich. He took his bath and decided to rest until morning. His friend might arrive at seven in the morning. He told Yona that help was coming, so that she would not worry. Then he relaxed on a plush pillow and imagined that he was hugging her.

At three thirty in the morning, his friend called and informed him that he was standing at the gate of his hotel. Jawad packed his bag and left the hotel immediately. Within four hours, he and his friend left the Swiss border, entering France at the risk of his friend. If he was arrested, he would have been sentenced to ten years in prison under the charge of human trafficking. He was arrested once while helping his Syrian friends from Homs, and he was released after he proved his kinship with one of them, but in the event of a repeated offence, punishment is inevitable. Jawad did not know that, but Abu Muhzab told him about it after they crossed the border. If Jawad knew that, he would not have put his friend's life at risk.

They reached the French city of Calais, the place from which everyone who wanted to reach Britain crossed. Thousands of Africans slept on the land, and many Syrians as well. But his friend, after several contacts, concluded that he would take a truck from Belgium, then to France, and then leave for Britain by sea was the best way.

Jawad and his friend left for Brussels after they spent a night in Calais. It was the beginning of December of 2014, and the temperature was minus four degrees in this city, where Jawad was left alone. His friend took him there and left for Germany because his wife was undergoing a surgical operation.

All Jawad knew was that he had the number of a smuggler named Osama and he also knew the name of his hotel and that he had booked for two nights only, since the cost of one night was more than a hundred euros. He did not know anything else except that he was hungry, and that fear began to creep into him. What if any policeman stopped him? Would he be forced to submit to asylum in Belgium? Or be returned to Switzerland or to Turkey? He had no answer. He called Osama, whose accent was Lebanese or closer to the Palestinian-Lebanese. He promised him that he would come at nine o'clock at night.

Jawad woke up frightened by the sound of the phone alarm, and in a hurry, he got dressed and went down to meet the smuggler.

With cautious fear, they met each other and there was a third stranger sitting in the back seat of the car. Jawad feared that he and Osama might have another purpose, as he was sitting in the back seat of the car from the beginning, but the fear quickly dissipated when this person spoke, as his dialect was Damascene. He was short and small in size, and he also wanted to leave for Britain.

They all agreed that Osama would meet with them on the second day at ten o'clock at night, to accompany them to a company outside the city of Brussels that would fill trucks with goods that go to Britain through the

French port of Calais; but the way to enter the company was somewhat strange. They needed to enter the company without anyone noticing.

On the second day, when they reached the door of the company, Osama informed them that he would drop them near the trucks that were standing outside the company and wait until it was time to load them, provided that the two would hide under the truck without anyone seeing them. It was raining heavily and the possibility of anyone seeing them might be limited. But Jawad asked Osama, who seemed very afraid, "What is your job then as a smuggler if we have to do everything?"

Osama told them that inside the company there was a friend of his who informed him which trucks were going to Britain. Jawad and the other person got out of the car and headed towards the wanted truck. Jawad was able to hide on top of the truck's spare tyre carrier, but there was no place left for the other person. Jawad tried to help him, but in vain. The truck was very slippery, so they could not hide. After ten minutes, they got out from under the truck and called Osama, who was angry because they had to stay until the truck moved; but Jawad told him that his method was a failure and that he could not escape from the company's guards and that there was a great danger to their lives and another way must be found. Osama tried to calm him down to win the situation and told them that within two days he would find another way, and thus the first attempt to cross from Belgium to Britain failed.

The smuggler brought them to the city centre.

Jawad asked the other person, "What is your name?"

He replied, "Yaman, from Damascus, and I live in Masrou' Dumar."

"But you look young?"

"Yes, I am twenty-one years old."

Jawad said, "So, did you leave Damascus in order not to perform the compulsory military service under these conditions?"

"Yes."

The two agreed to find a cheaper hotel, and Jawad asked Yaman to stay with him that night, because Yaman was going to go to a church that sheltered refugees. Indeed, Jawad rented a room for two in a hotel in the centre of Brussels that was a little cheaper than the first one, and asked Yaman to stay with him without having to pay anything. They also agreed to find another smuggler.

Having the help of a friend in exile is a new ammunition for your empty weapon.

After two days, Yaman reached another smuggler named Adam. Of course, all the names were fake. He was one of the Iraqi or Iranian Kurdish brothers who spoke Arabic, but with difficulty.

However, Jawad liked him from the beginning because he seemed to be a dangerous and fearless man.

Jawad asked him, "Are you not afraid of the police if you are arrested?"

Adam replied, "Of course I am afraid, because the penalty for human trafficking is imprisonment for fifteen years, but this prevents fear." Then, he took out a pack of tobacco from his pocket and put a piece of hashish in it. This was their second attempt with Adam because the first failed before it began.

They arrived at one in the morning at one of the guarded bus stations. Adam took them to a truck and opened it within seconds and told them to be safe and not to forget to tell the owner of the money insurance office when they arrived to pay him. Adam was terribly confident.

The two entered the truck. The temperature was minus two, and they were not allowed to make any movement inside it so that the truck would not shake. If the driver knew that there was someone inside, he would inform the authorities. The two did not utter a word. Their veins froze and their heartbeats accelerated to try to warm their bodies. Six hours in the cold of a Belgian winter's night. In the morning, the truck, loaded with four large rolls of paper, moved. The two sighed and each of them started moving to restore energy to his body. Yaman took out a bag of black pepper and sprayed it inside the truck so that the dogs would not smell them. Then he took out an empty bottle and urinated in it, and the two ate a piece of chocolate. But the cold air entering the truck made them hug until their bodies warmed up. The road trip took about three hours.

After two hours, Yaman took out his phone to try to learn where they were, and to their surprise, the truck was heading to the south of France and not to the north of it. Yaman tried to find a way out to make the truck owner stop, but the noise did not help. Jawad laughed, and Yaman was surprised by him!

Jawad said before he asked him, "I was amazed at myself when it became so easy for me. From the second time we get in the truck and leave!

Usually, my affairs are not that easy. Do not be afraid, I am not jinxed, but I need some suffering in order to reach what I seek. Stop banging the truck; he will not hear you until the truck stops. Come and let me tell you a story.

"I failed high school exams for the first time and the reason was my failure in the Arabic language, although the total was acceptable. Anyway, I succeeded the next year. After that I wanted to study at the Faculty of Law, which was my dream since I was a child, and I do not know why I chose that faculty except I remember that I once asked my father what university the President of the Republic graduated from, and at that time the President of the Republic was Nour El-Din Al-Atassi, as I remember. My father answered me, the Faculty of Law, and since that time it became a dream to enter that college, and all I thought when I was young was that just graduating from that college was enough to be a president and help people.

"Childhood dreams came true and I entered college, and in the third year I failed, so I decided not to waste more years of my life, and I applied with an urgent request to join the compulsory military service, to complete my university studies during military service. I finished the military service, which was two and a half years after I graduated from the university. My happiness back then was like it is now with the easiness we climbed into this truck quietly.

"I began to prepare to enter the fray of working life and to collect money and marry the woman I love. While I was busy wondering which way to start — to be a lawyer or do a government job or travel abroad — the postman knocked on our door and handed me a letter with my name on it. That was a rare thing to happen in Syria. He said that it was a registered mail and he asked me to sign. I opened the letter and found it was from Damascus University, Faculty of Law. The dean of the faculty wanted to meet me on such and such a day. I said to myself, it seems that fate has a different path for me, and perhaps they would send me on a scholarship to complete my studies — but why? I am among thousands of students and my graduation rate did not allow me to do that at all. I went to the dean of the college at the appointed hour. I introduced myself and found that the secretary had my name. I entered the dean's office; he was a professor of penal law and a brilliant lawyer in Damascus. He smiled and told me to sit down and asked me whether I brought the graduation document that he mentioned I should bring in the letter. He took it from me and put it in his desk drawer and told me there was an error in my graduation certificate. 'There are two subjects that you did not take the exams for, so you have to take another exam in the first month of the next year.'

"I was astonished, and when I inquired about the two subjects, I knew that they were the subjects of the fourth year, so I told him, 'Excuse me, professor. It seems that you are wrong. You say that I did not take the exam for both subjects?'

"He said, 'Yes.'

"I told him that I have proof that I applied, and therefore I need my exam paper, even if the mark is zero.

"He said, 'And where is your evidence?'

"I said to him, 'In order for me to obtain a leave from the military unit in which I serve, I must submit my examination programme, then prove the attendance of the subjects by submitting the examination papers with my name on them. They should also be stamped with the seal of the Deanship of the College from inside the examination hall, confirming that I attended the exam. I still have those papers since I have not submitted them yet, because my chief in the military unit did not ask for them and he was confident of me. This material evidence suppresses the accusation levelled against me and accordingly I proved with conclusive evidence that I took the exams and what you say is not true, with all due respect to you.' Then I added philosophically, 'And you should be proud of me because I successfully practised my first plea and won the case as one of your students in this college that you preside over.'

"The dean of the college answered me that he could not accept any evidence and that what he said was the final decision and that I must retake the exams for the two subjects. I stood in his office and tried to control myself, but I could not, so I told him, 'Excuse me, if you are the dean of the college of law, and a famous lawyer who does not do justice to people, then who would?'

"He said to me, 'You only take exams, and I promise you that you will succeed.'

"I said, 'You will help me cheat! I think that you should throw yourself out of this window. What I see now is a disgrace to the Faculty of Law.' Then I attacked him with all kinds of vulgar curses and added threateningly, 'I will make you regret that God created you.'

"But he only answered me with these words, 'You will take the exams.' In fact, I was thankful to him, because he endured the curses I had thrown.

"And that was the beginning of how I learned not to rush into something, even if I got it, and was not happy about it. My life has moved since that time, with many of those situations to which I got used to because, after a while, my life would return to normal."

Yaman asked, "You did not graduate from college?"

Jawad said, "Yes, I graduated after I repeated the exams. Until today, I don't know what happened, but it was good, I think, because my graduation was late — it opened for me another gate that I did not intend to enter."

The truck was stopping in the far south of northern France near the Swiss city of Geneva. The doors opened and the two of them jumped on a factory floor in a remote area near the Autostrade. The truck driver saw them, but he did not make any movement. The two stood outside the factory and looked at each other, wondering which direction to take. There was no creature and no clear trace of the proximity of any city. They followed their hunch and agreed to walk. After about an hour and a half, the outline of a small village appeared in front of them. The rain was falling, and they were totally wet, but walking in quick steps warmed their bodies. They immediately went to the train station and booked two tickets to Paris (Nord station), but the train due to take them would not arrive until three hours later. They looked for a place to eat some food and dry their clothes. There was only a small bar near the station; when they entered it, old men looked at them with surprise. Jawad nodded that they needed food and they had money to pay. They ate small pieces of croissants and drank orange juice. They returned to the station and then to Paris and from Paris they walked to the Mughrabi neighbourhood and took a taxi that crossed the French-Belgian border to Brussels, driven by a Moroccan refugee driver.

There will come a day when you will be saved from what you might previously think is an anomaly or a crime, so do not rush with your judgments.

They arrived in Brussels at night and called their smuggler and told him what had happened. He told them that this happened all the time and that he regretted this mistake. Then he told them to rest and tomorrow night they may have another attempt.

Jawad called Yona and told her what had happened. She said to him, "Do not despair. The important thing is that you are fine, and you will arrive, and I am waiting for you. I want you to promise me that you will come no matter what, because I will not be able to live without you."

Jawad swore to her that he would come, and apologised for the short phone call, but he needed the rest because it was dawn, and he might try again that night.

Jawad did not sleep because someone was waiting for news, too. He called his children, who were under the fire of the crazy war in Damascus, and told them what had happened. They were too young to comprehend what Jawad had suffered. They were not like Yona, who understood but showed nothing but a stimulus. She injected him with a love that ignited his energies with her tender words. She rode with him on a horse and put in his hollow heart of Hulagu Khan.

Children always look at the father as if he was a superhero who could do anything. And if he did not accomplish what he sought, he must be stoned and should not be called a father. They were children, and this was a logical reasoning because everything they asked for, he got for them. Since Jawad chose to go to another country — and he told them that it was Britain and promised to make them study in the best universities — they were waiting to see this country that everyone wished to visit, and they would not accept anything less than that.

London was the city of imagination. The symbolic clock tower. The flag with beautiful and elegant colours, the Queen's guard. They were things drawn in the minds of all boys.

Jawad's eldest son, who finished secondary school and had started his first steps towards high school, spent a lot of time on the street with his friends. He did not study his lessons, saying, "My father will take us to Britain," as if his father was the ambassador to the United Kingdom.

As for his middle daughter, who excelled in her studies, she would show you that she did not care, but it was preferable that you did not bet her on anything that belonged to her, because you would always be a losing judge. She always acted as if she was strong, but she had a tender heart. The last year of secondary school was about to begin, and it was a year of tension for Syrian families, because the law stated that the student must obtain approximately seventy percent of the general average in order to be entitled to continue and move to high school. She always asked Jawad, "Should I study hard if the school year begins, or shouldn't I care since I will go to Britain? Please tell me, Father."

But Jawad had no answer, because only God knew the future.

As for the younger one, she did not care for anything and did not neglect anything. She finished the primary school and started secondary school. She did what she had to do calmly and never rushed into anything. She used to be nervous about any obligations such as her school duties, and this caused her a lot of pain in her childhood, but she learned to control everything. She studied and did her homework and had time to take care of her hair and made some things out of coloured papers. She tried to learn music, but she had not devoted herself to it yet. She was born with the coldness of the British and deserved to live with them because her mood was a British mood.

Jawad said to his children, "One day you will be as you wish, not because I am a father and motivate you, but because you were created and bear the mark of respecting others and fulfilling your obligations, and this is an essential feature for success. Whoever deals politely with people reaches what he wants."

Yona turned off her phone, hugged her pillow, and cried in desperation, complaining, praying to God for Jawad to succeed. Yona asked herself if fate wanted Jawad to get to Britain, then what next?

Would she continue the story of oppression which she had lived in Damascus?

Jawad was married with three children. After his arrival, he would conduct a family unification transaction, to bring his wife and children, and continue his life again. Jawad only needed to settle in a place to start a comfortable life, as he already had the necessary money and did not even need a stable job, and his children had only a few years left, and they would start universities, then work. What would be Yona's role in this new scenario? Would she go back to being the fearful secret mistress?

But she remembered what Jawad once said to her while they were sitting in his car in the evening near his father's house.

He said that a little before he left his job, he had despaired of satisfying his wife, as he worked day and night to make his family stable, not needing anything, and he even started to secure his children's futures, so he bought a small house for each of them, since that had been the main problem facing young people in Syria, especially in the city of Damascus. He did not deprive his wife of anything. He had registered for her a house in her name and bought her everything that women desired, but she was only present just to fill her role as a wife and a mother. She was lost, absent, not interested in anything. She was with everyone against Jawad. She was hostile towards him and yet she was the one who said that she loved him. A strange contradiction after all those years of marriage.

Jawad's story with her started a little strangely. He did not ask her for marriage, nor did he think of her as a wife or girlfriend, because she was the sister of his close friend, and according to Circassian customs, to which he belonged, no young man should marry the sister of his close friend. But she was the one who told Jawad that she loved him and she even asked him out for a date. Jawad was loyal to the family of his close friend, so he did not agree, but respected her desire and told her that he could not engage in such a relationship because he was still a student in the third year at the Faculty of Law, so he had a long way to graduate and then join the compulsory military service two and a half years later. He still had a journey to find his way, and here was the calamity, because many young men remain unemployed for long periods after their graduation. Private work required capital and government work required favouritism or valuable bribes. Both were not available to Jawad.

Jawad decided to meet her older sister and tell her of the situation. If she accepted, the relationship would continue. Otherwise, he did not want to be a thief or a traitor to his friend, who had lived in his house for more than three years as one of the family members. But the older sister agreed in a somewhat artificial way. The relationship continued for six years, then they got married. Those years included many sad and joyous moments, but after the end of his military service and two years before their marriage, her behaviour changed a lot and Jawad asked why the sudden change? He did not get an answer. He was saying to himself, perhaps because he was too late to establish a house and secure the requirements for marriage, so Jawad rushed to work at anything. He worked as a porter, a waiter, and a smuggler. Eventually, in a short time, he was able to buy a house in the countryside of Damascus and a car. He was young and bought everything she desired and booked a wedding hall for her in a five-star hotel, but that did not change her ingratitude, and she continued in her sullen manner despite the fulfilment of all the dreams they had previously agreed upon.

During this period, Jawad's work was transferred to the presidency of the government and he was appointed as a director in it. Despite that, he continued to work after the end of his official working hours as a porter at the Customs. He was known there as Abu Arab. He did this work so that his house would not miss anything. He had three children and with each one of them, he used to say to himself that she will change, despite the dissatisfaction that continued to control the mother of his children.

Here, Yona, who was listening to the story eagerly, interrupted him, and asked, "Why was your wife not satisfied for all these years, even though you are a dream of many girls?"

And here the tears he was trying hard to keep from falling, overflowed Jawad's eyes, and he said, "I don't know, but I will say what I feel for the first time, and I don't know if it is true. It is just a feeling, and I don't know why I am saying it to you, but it seems that I trust you a lot and I can only tell you.

"I think she was in a relationship with someone before our marriage and at some point she wanted to break up with me because she loved him and her feelings towards me had changed!"

Yona interrupted him again, "But now she is the mother of your children."

Jawad continued, "You are right, the mother of my children — but she was not a wife."

Do not accept the half of something because it is nothing.

Yona remembered how much Jawad was feeling oppressed back then, and that if it was not for this feeling that he hid even from himself, he would not have been sitting with her in his car and telling this story to her. Yona grieved for him a lot and knew for sure that he was not playing with her, because he needed a friend far from his family to whom he could speak of everything, even his secrets. She was happy because she was trusted by Jawad, and that just revealing these things to her enhanced her position with him.

She loved him, but it was more of a forbidden love.

It was hard to look at him and imagine him as her husband.

In the evening, Jawad set out for a new attempt to cross from Belgium to Britain in the rainy weather of December. He crossed a field of mud with his friend, Yaman, and an Iranian family consisting of a couple and two children under the age of six. The smuggler took them to the parked truck, after waiting in the forest for two hours. It was two o'clock in the morning. The truck moved at eight in the morning. They all remained motionless for six hours, in a temperature of three degrees below zero. Yaman told Jawad, "If the truck had not moved, I would have frozen."

The truck arrived at the crossing of the French port of Calais, crossed the French checkpoint in less than ten minutes, and crossed the apartments made for drivers and the policemen who walked with dogs. But when Jawad and Yaman tried to leave the truck, they found the British policemen over their heads. The Iranian man, his wife and the two children were asleep and did not know that they had been discovered, and the policemen were trying to wake them up quietly, as if they were working in a five-star hotel.

The questions that the investigator asked Jawad were, "Did any of the policemen bother you?"

"Do you want food?"

"Do you complain of anything? Do you need a doctor?"

Before that, they had been put in a room and given blankets and hot soup. Before bringing the meal, the policeman asked, "What kind of meal do you want?" He added, "It is better that you take the fish meal, because the rest of the meals have meat in them, and it is not halal." What kind of people were these policemen? They were like a rare kind of humans that had a high sense of humanity.

It is impossible for dolphins to live in water full of tears.

They knew without questioning that you were a Muslim and did not eat meat that was not slaughtered according to Islamic law. Without showing any hostility, they quietly offered what you should eat or not according to your faith. In Arab countries, if you were arrested in such a condition, you would only eat one meal: hot slaps on your neck, five kicks, and ten paws as everyone's opening meal.

There is no room for comparison, but I think that if the security men dealt in this way with the citizens of Syria and with this generosity, many would have preferred to go to prison and endure as long as they were treated like this.

It is the strange nature of the Arab man that he deals violently with the other to show his superiority. All the security and police agencies in the Arab countries are determined to spread terror in dealing with situations related to civilians or citizens to dominate and create a citizen who is submissive to orders, although experiences have proven that the path of violence only leads to violent reaction or intransigence, accompanied by hatred and seizing the moment of revenge. Thus, states lose their citizens and the circle of discontent against the government and dissonance expands. This generates a state of hostility between the citizen and the security services which extends to all workers in the government sector and then to the head of the government, and cases of revolutions and oppositions appear. Then, these movements use violence as a weapon to reach their goals, because from the beginning that violence was practised against them.

The Arab regimes were not convinced that the weapon of endearment and showing respect even to the criminal and treating him according to the regulations and laws and giving him his rights leads to a better way. Rather, all of them are violating the laws by assuming power. Therefore, they do not like to open the way to law, to deal with it and apply it to everyone, because if it is applied to them first, they will not be rulers in the first place. Therefore, one should not be surprised by what is happening in the Arab countries.

With this politeness, Jawad and the others were interrogated, and within less than three hours they were taken to the main square of Calais. They were saluted and the police car left. Jawad said to his friend Yaman, "I wish they had kept us in their custody tonight. We were warm and eating better than we did in our hotel in Brussels."

The two went back by train to Paris and then the Moroccans' Quarter and by taxi to Brussels, and they informed their smuggler that they had returned to make a third attempt for them again.

Jawad called Yona and told her what had happened with controlled emotion because he knew what awaited him when he was arrested at the Calais crossing. He was no longer afraid, except that returning to Brussels after the trouble of riding at night and waiting for the truck to go was the tiring thing. Yona answered him, "Do not despair. You have to cross.

Hundreds of people pass through this gate. I will give you the phone number of someone I met. He will tell you what you should do when you get on the truck again so that the British do not find out about you. He tried more than eight times and finally arrived. He told me how you should bury yourself under the goods loaded in the truck. In any case, call him, he is a good man."

Indeed, Jawad called the man, who told him about his experience and what Jawad should do. He focused on the issue of hiding under the goods, muting himself and remaining immobilised in the last stage of the inspection. "Because the French might know about your presence and not move a finger. They prefer you to cross to Britain. Yes, the French do not want any refugees because they have enough from Morocco.

Immigrants or refugees from all Arab countries were distributed in European countries, America and Canada, and many of them were creative. I think that what made Lebanon a somewhat civilised country is the large number of returning immigrants. Many Arab citizens in all countries resent when the expatriate returns to them, so to speak, and they say, "He was a refugee and came back." But, in fact, we must admit that the difference between the Arab world, including the Arab Gulf states and European countries, and I do not mean the countries of the former Soviet Union, there is a vast difference in the feeling of your humanity. You learn in Europe the meaning of the word 'human' from the first moment you enter it. If what any human being needs to develop and be civilised is to feel that he is a human being, and if he feels that he deals humanly with everything and everyone, and this is what we lack as Arab societies which need to develop.

"Through oppression and repression, you can only raise an ignorant herd and limit its movement. But bear in mind that the herd's rage will uproot the barriers of eternal republics and stupid kingdoms."

Yona was in the Church of Coventry, which had embraced her, with a heart that did not know how to open a connection with heaven. A girl who no longer had a brother or father. She carried the concerns of her mother and sister, who were still in Damascus. She had been waiting for her brother-in-law to cross. He had been stuck in Greece for more than a month and a half. And a lover who had all the faults of the earth was waiting to reach her with trucks of hope. She did not know anyone in this country, and no one knew her. "What saint are you, little girl?" The walls of the church called her and said to her, "None ever stood between the walls of the church and carried this huge amount of worry and pain, oppression, alienation, homelessness, poverty, and love, and above all, vague waiting." The walls cried and waited for Yona to start her prayers.

Where to start from and what to ask for? Yona was of herself in front of the Lord.

All her requests were indivisible and had no priorities.

Should she pray to the Lord for Jawad her lover, who would sooner or later turn into a temporary lover, and come for a few months then work to have his family with him? His wife would come to conquer all the love that Yona carried and scatter her dreams like Summer clouds.

She dreamed and lied to herself about these dreams. She was now only holding on to her loyalty to him. Or was she holding on to some magical ropes because logic deemed it was a lame love that could participate in a running competition towards the future that any female on earth desired?

Despite that, she could not rule out starting to pray to the Lord for Jawad to come and hug her, even if for five minutes only. She also pleaded with the Lord that her papers would be facilitated and her asylum request approved, and then she would follow up on her mother's reunification papers without resorting to the path of death that Yona crossed.

She also prayed to the Lord for her brother-in-law to arrive and start helping her, or at least to rid her of her insomnia, because of the fear of loneliness surrounding her in her room, in the house, in the city and in the whole kingdom.

Yona was alone in everything. The frost of fear in her heart amazed Britain's coldness because of its severity.

She prayed in the church, often raising her head, pleading with the Lord, sometimes with her eyes only. She prayed with all her power and begged while kneeling in front of the body of Christ crucified on the cross, hanging at the top of the wall, surrounded by windows covered by coloured glass with light filtered through it reflected on the cross. She wanted him to rise even for a moment and send his miracles to carry Jawad, who was still there beyond the English Channel. She knew that she would violate the rules of supplication in prayer if she raised her head, but she wanted to see even a small gesture or a sign that God would not refuse her prayers.

She used to always end her calls with Jawad with one phrase, "May the Lord bring us together and never separate us."

A question always crossed her mind, "Will everyone fail, and I end up going back and becoming a laughing stock of my big family and friends?" There was one answer, "Yes, if everyone fails, I will return because Jawad will be there."

Jawad called Yona and told her, "Pray for us. I will try again in an hour. The smuggler called and asked us to be there at ten o'clock tonight." Jawad's voice was strong.

She encouraged him and said, "I will pray that the morning light will carry you tomorrow for me to hug you and sow my body and soul within you."

At twelve o'clock in the morning, a truck parked in one of the stations to pick up Jawad, Yaman, and two young men from Lebanon, who wanted to apply for asylum in Britain as Syrians. The smuggler quietly closed the truck and left. Silence and cold fell again for seven hours. The driver finally woke up and started the engine of the truck and set off towards Calais. Two hours and forty-five minutes aer enough for Yaman to scatter a bag of spices and peppers in the truck to hide the smell of their bodies from the dogs, and for each of them to dig a place inside the carry-on goods (parts for Range Rover cars, and among the pieces were headrests made from luxurious leather, including small screens). These were the loaded goods. Yaman shouted at the two young men, who were throwing the pieces after tearing the cartons, saying, "Fear God, guys. Each piece costs more than a thousand dollars." He was an expert in this field; he used to work with cars.

Each one of them dug their own places and the truck arrived a quarter of an hour before its time and entered the inspection platform and they were arrested and this time by the French authorities. The inspection official was opening the truck and calling out, "Hello, hello." Then he heard Yaman's voice saying in Arabic, "May God take you and your hello, they've discovered us."

Jawad called Yona after they were released and told her, "Do not be sad. God did not want this day to be the date of our meeting." Yona did not motivate Jawad this time and did not console him. She remained silent and hung up the phone.

Jawad thought that she was crying, but she was inside the church praying, and she did not want to make any sound. She came to the front, kneeled and lowered her head, and tears streamed from her eyes. She addressed the Lord with her small heart throbbing with pain, saying, "There are only five days left for your birthday, Jesus. May your will to carry Jawad be fulfilled so that we may pray together, giving thanks for your blessings on your birthday."

Bad news comes when you are the happiest, and vice versa.

Jawad did not tell Yona that on the second day and after resting for only a few hours, he tried again. This urgency in setting out was justified by the fact that the trucks might stop transporting goods to Britain because the festive season was close at hand. The trucks may stop as of the twenty-fifth of the month, which was in four days. It was Christmas and no one worked during the holidays. All work would resume after the New Year's Day celebrations.

Of course, Jawad did not tell Yona about the story the smuggler told them, so as not to put additional pressure on her. Another reason was that she would worry all night, especially since she had stayed up the night before.

The smuggler drove his Mercedes this time with only Jawad and Yaman. He was smoking and, barely speaking Arabic, he said, "If you don't leave today, you will be late for a week or ten days!"

The smuggler got out of his car and went to a nearby truck station. He was gone for about twenty minutes and came back saying there was no British truck. After that he went to another place an hour further and also did not find a truck. He said, "This is what I was talking about. There are fewer trucks. We must go to a third place, but if we don't find a truck there, please excuse me, you will have to wait for the beginning of next year."

Anxiety overtook Jawad. He knew that he did not have strong luck, but he held on, convincing himself that the man would return and tell them that he had found a truck. It was three in the morning.

The smuggler came back and got into the car and set off. He shook his head that he had not found anything. Yaman seemed at his limits, but he tried to convince the smuggler to return again the second day, because accommodation in Brussels for a week was going to be extremely expensive.

Jawad looked at the sky and said, "Praise be to God." It seemed that God did not want them to spend the whole night in a truck and get caught in the end. He thought how he would tell Yona that he would not try again until about a week later.

Jawad dared to open the car window a little to let in fresh air and reduce the smell of hashish. He remembered that the day before, he had called his father and told him for the first time that he was in Brussels and that he had arrived there by smuggling and intended to go to Britain. Jawad's father cried on the phone, but in the end he said to him, "I will pray for you today to reach what you want."

Meanwhile, the car entered a gas station. The smuggler got out and filled the fuel tank. They were about to leave the gas station, but he suddenly stopped, and told them, "Don't move. Lower your heads." Then he got out of the car for two minutes. He opened the car door and asked them to follow him. He got Jawad and Yaman in a truck which was parked inside the gas station, and he silently locked them in. Jawad looked into Yaman's astonished eyes, and they did not make any sound. Less than four hours later the truck took off.

Jawad said, "I think the smuggler threw us into this truck to get rid of your insistence that he should try tomorrow."

Yaman interrupted Jawad and told him, "Let's dig a place for us and lie down to get some rest, because we need it. If we are arrested, we will need half a day to go back to Brussels."

The truck entered the French checkpoint and crossed it, despite the opening of the truck's door and the entry of a security officer who stopped over the boxes under which Jawad and Yaman were hiding, but he did not see them. After a while, the two of them felt that the truck had crossed the British point, but it stopped, and the engine was turned off.

Jawad said, "We have been discovered."

Yaman asked him to calm down a little bit. Ten minutes passed and Jawad began to fidget. Yaman begged him to be patient and calm down.

The driver turned the engine on and drove for about fifty metres, then stopped again and turned off the engine.

Jawad said, "The truck is in the inspection hangar. Let's get out of this grave before our necks are broken." Yaman did not respond to Jawad's request and signalled to him to shut up.

Moments later, the sound of the loudspeaker began to speak French and buzzed in the place as if it was an airport lounge. Then the sound of a ship's horn followed. Their eyes flashed. The ship sailed. Jawad jumped out of their hiding place and threw off the boxes. He looked out of the truck hatch and saw that they were inside the transport ship crossing the English Channel and it would arrive on British shores in two hours unless they were discovered inside the ship.

Yaman asked Jawad to calm down again and told him to sleep a little and rest, but what sleep would come in such an hour of victory?

Thousands of pictures were drawn inside Jawad's head. He wanted to tell Yona, but he was afraid he might reveal themselves. Perhaps he was dreaming!

When your imagination is wide and your dreams are big, you must at every stage make sure that you are not within the circle of imagination.

Two hours and the truck would get out of the ferry. If it landed inside the port, everything would be over. The Dublin Convention on refugees was in accordance with the state of both of them: "Anyone who sets foot on British soil has the right to seek asylum."

The most beautiful thing about it was that Yona did not know that Jawad was that close to reaching her. Only one hour remained for the dream to come true. The roar of the ship was like a melody which their loving hearts played. Perhaps it was the longing for a companion, a sister, a house of secrets, and a loyal girlfriend he had not been near for nearly three years. She was the only one who remained loyal to him, doing her best to restore Jawad's walls that were beginning to fall apart. Her small hands would hold his face and bring him to her chest at every ordeal. She threw her heartbeats like sharpened daggers at all his worries. Then she sprayed stars with her hands over him. She wanted Jawad to remain full of positive energy, so that he, in turn, would forget the sadness that had surrounded her so early.

Yona did not possess any femininity worth mentioning, or masculinity. She was a peaceful angel who was afraid, but stubborn at the same time. She fought with prayers that ashamed fate into answering them. She was too tender for anyone to be angry with her. The sadness in her eyes filled most of the spaces, and it was her terrible weapon that forced you to surrender to what she wanted.

Only two hours, and the ship would reach the other side. It was enough for Jawad to remember all the moments of his life during which he never once thought of leaving Syria.

Every human being has a homeland, and it is the most precious spot on earth, no matter how barren it is to his dreams.

Homeland is the word that means sincerity, faith, sacrifice, tenderness, and stability.

Jawad never thought of leaving his country, for the war was never a reason for his departure. Perhaps he did not think about the decision to leave, even for a moment. If he did, he might have stayed.

But destiny had another saying in the matter!

A wound sustained by his wife's family, whose scheme he began to discover. Perhaps he was able to confront them and break all the dirty boards with which they blocked his eyes from the real face of his wife. That feeling had never left Jawad's head. He sensed that they all knew the story of their daughter before marriage and only married her to Jawad to keep her away from someone she could not marry. All of that was just a feeling, but it was strong, and it was the only justification for his wife's actions. Her strange behaviour was sometimes a justification for his irrational relationship with Yona. Sometimes, he felt a kind of astonishment for the duality of his wife. She had been the one to ask for his love; suddenly, she could not bear to live with him.

Jawad left Damascus because he was shocked and helpless. In fact, his wife's family was the only card he held on to and belonged to. He loved them all, but what he started to feel was a great shock. Fate forced him to leave because he did not want to think about dealing with a topic that had no solution. The only solution was amputation.

Jawad spent two full months reaching Britain. Two months of anxiety, during which he was arrested eight times and put in different prisons. Two months in which he took all kinds of risks: the sea, mafias, hiding, cold, staying awake, hunger, and humiliation. He was not young to bear all that and he was not obliged to, but it was a written destiny. Jawad said to many of those he met after that arduous journey, "If they asked me whether I would do it all over again, I would say yes."

By nature, Jawad loved adventure. He loved irrationality and hated the routine of life. He loved change, even if it was for the worse. He always said that many Europeans leave their green landscapes and their seas to come visit the arid sandy city of Palmyra to see its traces and enjoy them, while the people of Palmyra dream of going to Europe. "So, we must try everything, even the worst, because it might be what we want."

The ship started to stop, and the truck driver started its engine. The truck moved and within ten minutes it was running fast on the highway.

Yaman turned on the GPS. They were on British soil. The sound of their screams was like a woman giving birth. They danced over the loaded goods. They embraced. Each cried separately from the other. The tears poured down all the oppression buried in Jawad's heart and over all the intrigues and all the fear of never reaching his destination.

He went through the experience of illegal immigration with all its negative sides. But his experience was like the ugly things in nature which appear beautiful when we look at them under the light of the full moon. Likewise, love was the magician who beautified Jawad's thorny path.

After an hour, the truck stopped in London. Both Jawad and Yaman jumped out of the truck after the driver had talked to them in a loud voice in a strange language. Perhaps Polish. Jawad did not respond to him and shouted at him as well. They ran off as fast as horses in battle, without knowing which direction to take. Finally, they headed towards a petrol station to buy some new SIM-cards.

Nothing is better than arriving.

Jawad called Yona, who did not believe what he said at first, then she cried, too, but this time they were happy tears. They wetted the roots of love which boredom and fear of Jawad's failure to arrive had long plagued them.

She said to him, "Take any train and come to Birmingham and I will meet you there."

He told her, "I am standing in front of a sign that says 'Birmingham 90 miles'. I will reach you as soon as possible by any means possible, even if on foot." The two walked on the highway towards Birmingham, hoping to find a train station in any small town. But, in less than five minutes they were surrounded by the police.

All public roads in Britain are monitored by cameras, and no one has the right to walk on the edge of the motorways.

Jawad was taken to be interrogated. Then he was placed in solitary confinement, but without any disturbance or insult. After less than two hours, they were taken to stay in a detention centre that was very large and had all the means of entertainment. Each of them was given a cell phone to call whomever they wanted for ten minutes.

He called Yona and told her to go back to Coventry because the police had caught him. "Don't be sad. I'll see you on Christmas Eve by God's willing."

On the morning of the second day, they were returned to London and placed in a hostel with two free meals a day, and they could go anywhere. They would stay there for one week only, after which each of them would be sent to the city in which it was decided for them to stay until they obtained the residence permit, and their asylum was accepted.

Jawad slept his first night after he called Yona and asked her about how to book a train ticket and the name of the station he should go to. He wrote everything on a piece of paper, as he only knew the words yes and no in English. He struggled a lot in his life to learn the language, but to no avail. Finally, he gave up learning it.

Yona did not sleep. She was busy all night booking a room in a hotel for them, because Jawad would not be able to sleep there since the house was not intended for receiving guests. It was also forbidden to host males because the house had three girls. This was what the instructions stipulated when they were handed their keys.

She booked a room at the Ibis Hotel, which cost per night about sixty pounds. Yona got thirty-five pounds per week to secure her food during the week. She went to the train station two hours before the arrival of Jawad, moving from one platform to another. Looking at all faces. Watching the movements of the trains. She climbed stairs. Her heart was beating so fast that she could hear its beats in her ears.

She wanted to find her strength, the bosom of her father, who passed away early. She was the pampered one, always riding on his shoulders while he walked the streets of their village. She wanted to find her two brothers who passed away before she could take shelter in their shadow. She wanted to find safety in the manager friend who hugged her one day and made her accept life even if it was cruel, who made death seem ridiculous and told her that it was the worst guest a person might have, that it was a path all of us would take one day. Each of us had his own way which led to the gate through which he would leave this world. She wanted to find her best friend; the distorted lover. She wanted to find anyone, whomever he was. She wanted someone because she was afraid of her loneliness in this strange, cold, and distant country. She wanted to throw her delicate femininity into a circle of masculinity with which she could finally end her anxiety and fear of alienation that almost made her autistic.

Although she knew that train times were very accurate in Britain and she also knew the platform number he would arrive at, she still doubted everything.

Was she afraid that she would lose Jawad and all the hopes he came bearing to her?

Or had her eagerness for a lover made all the shocking facts accept change, thus allowing all taboos?

What was the value of your life without a lover? He was the world to her. No one left for you, no brother, sister, son, father, or mother, except the lover who is the sum of those numbers.

The beloved is the sum of those numbers. He fears for you more than himself like a father. He yearns for you like a mother. You are like a sister to him before marriage. He is the son who does not reach the age of puberty.

Jawad was what she desired from life. Yona was waiting for that lump of masses, a wave drifting towards her city, sweeping away all her fears and dampening the dryness of her waiting.

Jawad arrived at Coventry station and got off the train. He stood on the platform. There were many people coming and going. He no longer thought of anything. Even his heart almost stopped. All his energies were harnessed to the sense of sight, searching faces.

Not more than two minutes. He raised his eyes to the stairs leading down to the station platform. There was a body flying, throwing itself over the stairs. He rushed up the stairs, pushing anyone who was in his way. Yona saw him from the top of the stairs and ran towards him, fearing that he was a mirage that would disappear. She wanted to hold him. They were a few steps, but she felt as if they were much more than that. Jawad did not have enough time to smile when she pounced on him like a spider and surrounded him with her arms and feet, throwing away all the bags and negative thoughts she carried. She decided to be blind to everything which might distort or even disturb this moment. She wanted to spend days without fear of anyone, not even of ridiculous traditions. Here, in this country, far from all eyes and fear. Here, in the middle of a crowded station, she had removed the mould of customs and fanaticism, and she knew that the Lord was with her and had answered her prayer. This was enough for her to throw anything behind her back. If what she was doing was wrong, the Lord would not have answered her prayers.

If you feel that God is with you, stop all constitutions and laws and go with what God facilitates for you.

Here, hanging to Jawad's shoulder, she regained what she had lost in the streets of Damascus. She embraced him and did not fear anyone. Jawad felt the heat of her tears. She whispered in his ear, "Let me hug you. I am afraid to let you go and discover that I am in a dream and wake up to return to the nightmare of waiting."

He replied, "Don't be afraid, do whatever you want, but I want to see your face."

Yona, who was still holding onto him, did not respond. People stopped to watch this hug, which they had only seen in war movies when their loved ones came back alive. The smiles of the passers-by and those who stopped adorned that moment of joy. Their pure hearts saw the truth, the reality of this amount and the longing between these two.

Jawad walked with her holding on to him for a few steps to sit down, then he took her hands in his and looked into her eyes. He said to her, "Finally, I arrived before Christmas Eve. I was afraid that you would spend it alone. I don't want to tell you how much I miss you. I think it is obvious, but reaching you has almost turned into a dream. I am overjoyed at my arrival in Britain because my goal was to reach you. I brought you a gift."

He reached out his hand and handed her a small Unicorn, and said, **"This horse is one of the fiercest of animals. But, when he sees a charming virgin like you, he gets rid of all his wild and fierce manners and puts his head in her lap and sleeps."** He added, **"It is true that it carries a terrifying horn that can kill whoever it stabs, but inside this horn there is a substance that cures any disease. Even poison."**

"Take him and be sure that he will fall asleep in your arms for the rest of his life, and he will be a faithful guard and will heal you from all evil and even the sorrows that have been surrounding you for years. He will work to remove them and restore to your eyes the sparkle of joy. Now let's go. I am tired, and I want to sleep peacefully, knowing that you are with me at last."

Yona did not utter a word. She only smiled. She picked up all the things that she had dropped on the ground and held Jawad's hand, then they walked together, stuck together, stunned by what they were in… Victorious at the end of the terrifying wait that ended with a gift from destiny; the most beautiful love scene.

A reception and a hug at the train station is the dream of every two lovers.

When they reached the hotel, Jawad took a shower and hugged Yona and kissed her and emptied his mind of any thought. He grabbed her little shoulder and rested his head on her chest. With his other hand, he closed her eyes as usual when she slept. The two slept for two hours, with thousands of tons of love and longing flying like roses above them.

In the main square of Coventry, to which Jawad came, there was a monument of a naked girl riding a horse.

Jawad asked about that girl, whether it was just a statue or if it had a story.

Yona said, "No, it is a symbol of the city's past. There is a legend of a real girl who was very beautiful. Her name was Godiva and the ruler of the city was an unrighteous, unjust, and greedy man who imposed incredibly high taxes on the villagers. One day he sent his men to collect the taxes, and those who couldn't pay were imprisoned, flogged, and their houses taken from them. This girl stood in the face of his soldiers and prevented them from taking what they wanted. So, the ruler asked for her, and when he saw that she was beautiful and young, he said to her, 'I will forgive your rebellion, and I will not take taxes from you this year, but on one condition.' She said to him, 'Do what you want with me, but leave the people of the village.' He told her, 'I want you to ride a horse completely naked and to walk in the streets of the village for a whole day. If you do that, I will carry out my promise.' The girl agreed and set the day for her to go out naked and informed the villagers of what happened. At the appointed hour, the girl came out riding her horse completely naked, but the people of the village decided not to leave their homes on this day and closed their windows until the day passed so that no one would see her. But there was a man from the village whom everyone hated. He tried to open the window and look at the naked Godiva. It is said that he was immediately blinded and therefore Godiva turned into a saint and a symbol of the British city of Coventry. Every day at twelve in the afternoon behind the Godiva statue there is a figure that emits music and brings out a horse walking around the window from which this hateful man came out, and when the window is opened, you see him sticking his head out and screaming in pain from what happened to him."

(In another narration, it is said that she was the daughter of the ruler.)

Jawad said, "What a beautiful heroic story. When the war in Syria ends, there will be thousands of statues of heroic tales and stories that are stranger than fiction."

Yona interrupted Jawad, saying, "I had vowed to pray together in the church if you arrived here safely." The two entered the church. Yona bent down on her knees in front of the cross and lowered her head and thanked the Lord for answering her prayers.

Jawad fell near her on his knees and began to recite verses from the Noble Qur'an. They thanked God that they had finally met, and when they finished they looked at each other and tears streamed down their cheeks, and their lips painted a smile that hid a thousand questions behind it; most importantly, what next?

Was it really tears of joy of arrival or tears of a new kind of loss?

Despite all the differences between them, Yona only saw Jawad as a lover who could be reprogrammed to be hers, or even to spend the longest time with him. She loved that kind of man, but her heart froze when she realised the fact that Jawad had a wife who would come one day and take him away. Thoughts clashed at that moment inside Yona's head in front of the crucified body of Christ. How could she ask him to save her from such an ordeal? She was the one who prayed days ago and from this place that Jawad would arrive safely, and the Lord had answered her prayers. She was near him and her eyes were raining tears of bewilderment. Did she make a mistake in asking for that? Jawad arrived and this meant that sooner or later his children and his wife would follow. She did not want to repeat that forbidden love. She ran away from it, but she could not escape from Jawad. Tears were still flowing. Jawad looked at her and understood everything that was going on in her heart and her floundering thoughts. What kind of love was it that lived in front of the eyes of everyone who knew it, defying the eyelashes of their eyes, which turned into deadly poisoned spears?

Jawad also longed for his children. He had not seen them for two months. He left them in Damascus, where death was being given away for free. Damascus, which no longer recognised sadness since it had become one of its main features. When someone died, the news of their death was announced just so everybody would know.

So-and-so will not come tomorrow because he died in yesterday's terrorist bombing or because of a missile.

This was how the news was simply told to others.

The atrocities of the war were not only caused by the fighting of the combatants and their operations. No, it was more brutal in many cases than the fighting itself. For example, there was a friend of Jawad's son in high school, an orphan and a polite youngster. He never knew his parents and his name was given to him in the orphanage he grew up in. When this young man turned eighteen years old during the crisis in Syria, they gave him a new identity card other than the one he was carrying, and he was told that they had proven in the papers that he had a hypothetical brother. He was no longer 'lonely'; according to Syrian law, an only son was not allowed to enrol in compulsory military service of two and a half years, but was exempted from the compulsory military service imposed on all young people in Syria. This procedure, which the government took brazenly, was because it wanted someone to fight on the frontlines. After the state lost hundreds of thousands of young people who died for the ruler's survival, why not change the rules? Change is nothing but that it is not what was. The State continues and life continues. The one who ruled was never changed, it was normal everywhere else for him to be changed, to have elections and bring someone different, but no. It was easier to change the laws. On the other hand, many of the children of officials who stole from the people's capabilities were exempted from military services, even though they were subject to the compulsory service law, as did Yona's uncle, who was able to exempt six of the family's children from joining compulsory service at the height of the ongoing battles. He who considered himself the trumpet of reform and a fighter against corruption, an honourable man and a patriot, loyal to the authority that appointed him a minister one day, even though he did not know anything about how to govern, because he worked all his life in the security field. No wonder everyone called for idealism, but none of them wanted to look back and see their mistakes tailing them.

How could an orphan child without a family who had spent his whole life in an orphanage suddenly get a hypothetical brother, then it was compulsory for him to go to the army and fight in the first ranks in a battle in which he had no interest whatsoever? But who suggested the idea of having children join the military and fight?

The one who took such a decision must be a son of a whore, and the one who agreed to it was like him as well.

This is a small scene from the mechanism of action of officials and how they handle different situations in Syria.

Another question is, if there was no president in Syria, no government, no army, and no security, what would have happened?

The answer is that Syria would be occupied by armed groups or from another country. It would be a subjugated country. It would depart from the steadfast resistance line that defends Arab rights. The repeated tone, the boring tone of speech, which usually ends with a string of lies. Any answer can be said and no matter how pessimistic it is, it will never be worse than the way Syria is now.

Today, Syria is occupied by America in the northeast, from Russia in the coast and the capital. Turkey in the north. From the south, the extremist organisations in Daraa. From the north, south and centre, the Kurds, and from the southwest Israel. So, today Syria is occupied. What is worse than that is that we Syrians still believe that we have a government, a president and a State, and the funny thing is that if we were occupied by a country, we would have lived a better life as citizens in an occupied country, and the occupation would have provided us with means of livelihoods so that we would not revolt.

The important fact is that Syria is neither a supporter of the Palestinian cause nor is against it. Syria is a global and local investment zone whose general manager's goal is to make profits, even if all the employees die. To remain a ruler is linked to the goals he achieves for its global board of directors.

A statue of the ruler of Syria should be made and placed in the capital of every country hostile to Syria.

The story of Yona and Jawad is like the Syrian crisis.

There is religious fanaticism. There is a huge gap that prevents understanding between the people and those in authority, which is represented by the age difference between Jawad and Yona, and the acceptance needed from other parties. It contains the people themselves who were lost between the struggle of the two fronts and represented by the children of Jawad, and the fear of saying what you want or you do, because you are not what you want, because there is an authority that determines your rights for you, and this authority does not apply laws to everyone, for its laws are like a spider's web which only catches small flies; as for wasps, they are not subject to the laws as is the case with Jawad's wife. She is like the law; imposes that Jawad be loyal and submissive to her, and, in fact, she is a wasp who broke all laws before she married Jawad, even though she was the one who told Jawad "I love you", and Jawad never thought of her as a wife or even a girlfriend. As for Yona's sister and her mother, they are examples of democracy, liberation and openness, but like most of the fanatical extremists, they call for liberation and freedom, but they do not want anything of that to do with them. They are liberated in form, but in substance they are statues of the stubbornness of the inherent backwardness.

Jawad wiped Yona's tears with his hand, and she, in turn, wiped Jawad's tears. When they left the church, Yona said to him, "Why were you crying?"

He told her, "I don't think that any of us has a definitive answer, but the days will answer this question. The Lord that you and I were conversing with, needs from us deeper faith, longer prayer, and prophetic reverence to achieve what we prayed for. He alone knows what is inside us. But do not despair. God restored Zulaikha's eyesight and made her once more a young girl, the same as her husband, Yusef, because of her continuous prayers and du'a, because God knew the size and sincerity of the love that was inside her.

"We have that sincere love and we do not need a miracle to reconstruct our physiological composition.

"What we need is only patience and waiting for fate. The minds around us find it difficult to understand this love or even the idea of this love. It is difficult for your mother, sister, and my children to accept it. So how can you expect a wife to accept it, even if she was my wife in name only? There is also your friends, your big family, and the society. But time is the key to the solution of all these obstacles. Let us be with God only. We are together now, and I think most that he did not bring us together just to separate us again."

The two spent the glorious Christmas Eve together. It was already a birthday night for them, for their story that started slowly, and only fate would know if it would continue with steady steps. But for them, today it was better than before, because their love returned after difficult days of longing.

Jawad returned to London, and two weeks later, his temporary residence was located in Liverpool, but for some reason he was placed in Manchester. He was a little sad because he preferred Liverpool because it overlooked the sea, which Jawad loved more than anything. In all the days he spent during his military service in the city of Lattakia, the sea was the friend to which he resorted whenever he felt that the world was bearing down on him.

He lived in a house of nine rooms which was an hour and a half away by walking from the city centre of Manchester. Jawad settled in a room with a bed and a closet. The lady responsible for the house said to him, "You can receive a friend, but he cannot sleep over. You will get thirty-five pounds a week for food." The house was dirty, and its bathrooms were filthy simply because nine young men were living in it, waiting for their asylum requests to be approved. Each of them was from a different country. Four from Africa, two from Iran and three from Syria. One of them did not like to be called Syrian, even though he was from the Syrian city of Ras al-Ain. He would reply that he was from Kobani, that he was Kurdish and waiting for his state to be established on Syrian soil. In his view, the state or the regime, as the opposition called it, would inevitably fall. The revolution had started, as he claimed, since 2011, and we were now at the end of 2014 and the regime would not be able to bear more than that. The reason for his hatred of the regime in Syria was that he graduated from the Faculty of English Literature, and the government did not offer him a job opportunity, so he worked as a driver for a refrigerator company.

As for the other Syrian, his story represented the majority of the armed Syrian opposition. He did not complete his secondary education. He completed primary school because it was compulsory, and success in it required only attendance. Then, when he became of a legal age, he was asked to perform compulsory military service. He went to one of the Gulf countries in order not to enrol in the armed forces, and to pay for not fulfilling his military duties. He worked in the United Arab Emirates, enslaved by its heat, for four years, and when the revolution began, he decided once again to escape from paying the cash allowance of ten thousand dollars and from the harshness of working in the Arabian Gulf, which he used to brag about in front of his friends when he came back on summer vacations, driving with the car he bought. Cars in the UAE are cheap in comparison to Syria. The Syrian government imposed a percentage of two hundred and fifty percent of the value of the car as fees, and no one knew why this sterile financial measure that deprived many citizens of having good cars sold at the international market prices, as well as the neighbouring Lebanon and Iraq, was introduced.

He came to Europe, which gave rights, and in which you obtain citizenship after a reasonable period, not like the Gulf states that did not grant their residents citizenship because they were often afraid of many things; like if they grant it to Bengalis, for example, they will become a majority and control the government. If those countries followed the democratic system and got rid of the so-called kingdoms and emirates, all would have been different.

He left the United Arab Emirates, and after suffering for more than a year, he was able to reach Britain. He was from Damascus and his brothers had preceded him to Britain and they encouraged him to come. Jawad was optimistic about his presence because he gave him a kind of an outlet during the next six months that he must spend to obtain residency.

Jawad liked it on the first day there, when they went to get some things from the market and he bought a luxury perfume for sixty pounds. He made a good impression on Jawad, that he was a young man who loved life, although through conversation it became clear that he was a No. 1 enthusiast of the opposition in Syria. Jawad asked him, "What is the main reason for your opposition to the regime?"

He said that he had no reason, but he did not want the current system and wanted to change it.

Jawad said to him, "You told me that you worked in the United Arab Emirates in a bar and a night club. Does that mean that you are not a fanatic?"

He replied, "Yes, I am not a fanatic."

Jawad said to him, "But those who want change in Syria today are groups that want an Islamic state that applies the provisions of Sharia. Do you want this change?"

He said, "No."

Jawad asked him, "What do you want, then?"

He replied, "I don't know, but I want to change it."

In the evening, he came to Jawad's room to stay up with him. Jawad prepared two cups of tea, and the guest took out a roll of smoke and put a piece of hashish in it and presented it to Jawad. Jawad asked him, "What is this?"

The boy replied, "Let's forget our worries and pass the days quickly, my friend."

Jawad rose up, opened the door of the room and threw him outside and told him not to come back again. This kind of atmosphere made Jawad leave Manchester every week for three days, which he spent with Yona in Coventry.

But why, then, did Jawad and Yona come to Britain and apply for asylum?

Yona thought one day that the way out of the torment of this love would be to get away from Jawad geographically and as far as possible. But when the procedures began to take a serious route, and only a few days separated her from her trip, she told Jawad, "Promise me that you will follow me, or else I will not travel."

So, what was the need for her to take this deadly road?

Was it an escape from death?

Or even just fear of death?

It was neither this nor that, because the family had lost half of its number in various accidents. Death was the desire of some of those who remained alive, grieving for the death of the brothers and the father.

So, was it ambition to achieve material goals because the situation had become difficult in the country?

Yona's family was able to continue its affairs despite all circumstances, as it owned a house in Damascus and another in her village, and everyone worked at different jobs and positions.

Was Yona opposed to the system, as it was said?

This possibility was also out of the question. Her father was an officer at the rank of a brigadier general who was martyred in an explosion of which he was not the target, but fate decided that he and his son would be at the site of the explosion. The family ideologically belonged to the regime.

The remaining question would be, if Yona decided to take this unknown road of death to meet Jawad outside Syria, regardless of what was happening in the country, and regardless of whether this period that she spent with him was temporary, until Jawad started the procedures of family reunification, then she would return to what she was in Damascus, a mistress of a married man. She detested that name, as all the women of the universe did.

So, what is the motive for this adventure in which many people have lost their lives by drowning, kidnapping, or people being robbed of their organs, and those who might be called survivors were forced to work in brothels until they could no longer do that?

The main reason for her escape was mostly to do something… anything, just for change… Sheer madness. Maybe her belief that fate was hiding something for her and pushed her to such an adventure towards an unknown change, maybe worse than what she was in now. Successive signs that did not allow her to think seriously. A destiny which generated obsessions inside her that called her, controlled her thinking, and pushed her to move because persistence did not help with anything.

Yes, persistence is the sterility of creativity.

As for Jawad, he was one of those who generally hated travelling, and if he had to travel, it would not be more than a week. He worked as a director in the Syrian Prime Ministry and was very close to the Prime Minister and was able, through his work, to gain the trust and love of the Prime Minister. He worked for more than ten years until he became bored with this kind of work, as it consumed most of his time. He loved to draw and to listen to music. He loved to walk. God did not deprive him of anything, so he was never in need of anything. He was financially sufficient and had everything he wished for. He never knew how much money he had. He was able to obtain all the aspirations of young people with his work before he reached thirty-four years of age. He was assigned many critical and secret files and was able to carry out everything that was asked of him. He loved his workers and they loved him. He was close to the drivers and other people, and he loved sitting with them, because he loved their simplicity.

When the government resigned following the beginning of the events in Syria, Jawad could not complete the path with the new Prime Minister. He was more than stupid and could only be described as an idiot. A shaky personality who was nominated to be the Prime Minister for special reasons by another idiot. In fact, he did not complete a year until he was dismissed. Stupidity was his main feature that no one disclosed during the ten years that this deranged person spent as minister of the most important ministry in Syria, the Ministry of Agriculture.

In this crowd of stupid human disasters, Jawad submitted a request to be moved to a place where he would be by himself and search for a solution to two important issues in his life… His wife, who lived with him for seventeen years, without him comprehending what was wrong with her except that she was never a wife and was not satisfied, no matter how many requests of her he granted, and she was not a good mother to his children, who feared her more than they loved her. She hated them and treated them with restlessness.

Jawad repeatedly tried to understand the reason for his wife's imbalance, and he thought of all the possibilities, but he was still perplexed because she was the one who told him that she loved him. He convinced himself that it was her nature, that she was not a good woman, as they say… but he was tired of this mood. When a man lacks the feeling of man safety in his house, he is strained, and his house is shaken with the uncertainty.

This issue needed to be resolved no matter what the results were. It had become impossible to live like that.

The second issue was Yona, the soul that must go and stay at the same time. She was stuck and needed to be resolved, but dare he resolve it? A thousand issues were related to her: religion, the difference in age, his wife, his children, and her family. Dazzling lights that prevented him from looking at the measure of one step forward with such a love story.

Jawad was summoned to the Presidency of the Republic and offered to be transferred to the Ministry of Foreign Affairs with the rank of ambassador and to be assigned with administrative tasks in the ministry until he was transferred to an embassy. The necessary decree was prepared in secret in the Prime Ministry and handed over to Jawad, to be carried to the Presidency of the Republic. Jawad arrived at the office of the President's secretary, but something stopped Jawad from handing over the decree. The manager of the office asked him, "What is wrong with you?"

Jawad replied, "Nothing, but I do not want to go to the Ministry of Foreign Affairs. Can I postpone the matter?"

"But it is a good opportunity; do not let it fall from your hands."

Jawad insisted on accepting his request to postpone the position, and the office manager agreed, surprised at Jawad's request!

Jawad left the building wondering at himself: why did he give up this position which many aspire to? But he did not find an answer other than that he was feeling a little bit of happiness.

In many cases, sudden decisions stem from a person who did not study them, nor planned to take them, and did not think of them as a possibility.

His decision can be defined as destiny, where fate intervenes in a tangible way and changes the course of your life suddenly. When you go back to what happened, you know that you were only obedient; therefore, it becomes very clear to you that it is not your choice. This matter may be repeated several times during the course of your life, and if it is repeated, you must believe that God is with you.

Before Jawad's journey of death, following Yona, a security agency sent him a delegate requesting to meet him urgently. During the meeting, Jawad understood that he was a candidate to be a governor for one of the provinces, and he had the option to be the governor of the Damascus countryside or Latakia. It was a position he would have liked, because it was completely independent, and from it he could help and provide his services to the citizens. But Jawad was separated from Yona, and now the only thing he knew was that he had to go after her, whatever the cost. He promised her. He did not know why now all the doors were opening for him in vain.

Jawad did not leave Syria because he was afraid of death or was looking for money or a future or a position, or because he was against the regime or because he was with the regime. No, he was one of the sons of Syria who could only be loyal to their country. In Syria, everyone had gone crazy and was bragging about killing each other. A battle in which everyone lost. Jawad used to say to everyone who discussed the issue of the conflict in Syria, "First, no person has the right to attack the sovereignty of the State, which is represented by elements of the police, the army, or even the piece of cloth that is called the flag. If a policeman is killed in a state of the United States, the emergency law is imposed immediately until the perpetrator is arrested, then this policeman is the state. Expressing an opinion against any of the officials, this is the right of everyone, whatever the opinion.

"Secondly, anyone who sought help from a stranger to fight with him against the sons of Syria is a traitor, and everyone who takes up arms to kill a Syrian citizen is a traitor to his patriotism, whether he was a member of the army or one who claimed to be revolutionary."

So, why did Jawad leave Syria?

Jawad left to find himself… to follow his feelings before his mind. He left everything he had earned in his life and left with an arrow in his compass always pointing to love. Was it really love, or was he escaping from a wife who did not have any quality as a wife? A woman lost in the cursed swamp of her family. He began to smell their rotten stench. For seventeen years, he suffered because of her for the sake of their children. He did not know why a mother who gave birth to them would act like that.

Yona and Jawad were not like anyone else who immigrated and applied for asylum in European countries. They were in a rather good economic situation. They were not afraid of crazy death. They used to live in the relatively stable Damascus. Their financial conditions were good. The crisis came and was a way out for them to be together in a strange destiny that made their story go on and on.

Yona called Jawad and told him that she had obtained asylum approval, so she became a resident, not an asylum seeker, and that she must leave her home and search for the city in which she wanted to stay in order to obtain a permanent home, and then start the five years which would qualify her to obtain a British citizenship, after which she had the right to visit her homeland as stipulated by British laws or the Dublin Convention, which regulated the affairs of refugees in Europe.

"For how many days can you stay in Coventry before leaving?" Jawad asked.

She told him, "About ten days."

He said to her, "Book a hotel room, and I will come to you the day after tomorrow to spend the remaining week together until your departure time."

Yona interrupted him. "No, I will not book a room. You will stay with me in my room at the home."

Jawad asked, "But how, as the rules do not allow this?"

She said, "You will stay in the room all the time and only go out to the bathroom. We will spend most of the day outside the house together, and if the inspector comes, I will hide you in the wardrobe. The money you have is little and you will not be able to move after that if all the money runs out. With what will remain with you, you may need to travel to the city that I will move to. The costs of travelling are expensive, because the city I am moving to is in the north of Britain, in Scotland. Mostly, you will also get the residency and you will need some money because you will not be charged any amount until you settle in the city you want, so you will remain about two or three weeks without any support."

Jawad agreed and asked her to make sure that she would not be held accountable if he stayed in her room.

Jawad arrived in Coventry.

When Yona saw him, she asked, "What's wrong with you?"

He replied, "I received a message from the Immigration Department saying that my asylum application has not been decided on and that they will delay their response up to three working months. This means that they will study the application more thoroughly and that I will stay in this dirty house for another three months, and the application may be declined. This would call for an objection and a court case that may last a year."

Yona calmed Jawad down and took him to her room, where she prepared hot food for him.

On the morning of the second day, the two of them went to the garden and took lunch with them. Jawad said to her, "There is something which has been occupying my mind for some time now." Yona was surprised by what he said, but she let him continue. She just nodded her head inquiring what this thing was. Jawad continued, "I got married nearly seventeen years ago. She has a thousand faces, and it is difficult to know what she is thinking of. It's not only her, but all her family are secretive. There is a matter that they keep in complete secrecy. You treat them as parents, but they do not allow you to get too close to them. They are ready like snakes if you approach their secrets.

"I took a long time to tell you what I wanted to say, but first I wanted to make it clear to you that it was my wife who confessed her love to me. I realised later that it was a careful decision. I have to admit that when she confessed her love to me, I decided to continue with our relationship out of respect for her and for myself as well. But now, I realise that it has all been a scheme by her family.

"I joined the compulsory military service immediately to finish it with my university studies. I went and finished two and a half years of military service, during which a nice, interesting, and somewhat crazy love story began. My main goal was to be a man who fulfils his promises.

"But her requests suddenly began to be so much. She wanted a separate house and a big wedding celebration. We started to quarrel and decided many times to end everything. She had been employed in a hospital as an administrative worker and totally changed afterwards. I started working day and night, not in my field of study, and I also worked as a porter, a servant, and a smuggler to reach my goal, which was to get her whatever she wanted; but nothing was ever to her satisfaction. I repeatedly thought that I fell short in some matters, so I tried hard to make up for that, but she was never satisfied.

"We decided to break up and stop this love, as it had become controlled by demands that were fulfilled, albeit slowly, but without absolute consent from her side. Indeed, we broke up for a month, but she returned after her older sister intervened and she called me again. She returned only in form, but in substance she did not. She returned to me because they made her do it. She went back to a cage of love that was invented for her and she no longer desired. Of course, I did not understand this equation before. Now I say it, but in the past, I considered her a woman who wanted to make a family which are living in a golden palace and meet all what was needed and required. I liked that and considered it an incentive for me to be what she wanted me to be; but, unfortunately, she did not know what she wanted.

"I was able to buy a house, a car, and the required gold, and we decided to get married. Every time, she would postpone the marriage for strange reasons. Once because of the dress and another because of the number of guests. Finally, the marriage took place. She did not give birth in the first year, and it was a hell of a year for both of us. She was still working in the hospital. After two years, she gave birth to our first son. I asked her then to leave her job and stay at home to devote herself to raising our son, but she refused, and we quarrelled a lot. Then I made the decision, and my answer was that either she raises our son in this house or goes back to her parents' house and I raise our son. She hesitatingly gave in to the decision, but on lots and lots of conditions. I did not understand her insistence on this work, as she was a part-time worker in the hospital. I convinced myself that her insistence was just because of her friends and because she wanted something different to break the routine, but her job did not go with what she had studied at the university.

"In the meantime, I was appointed to the Ministry of Finance. A year later, she gave birth to our first daughter, and I was transferred to the Prime Ministry. However, she was never satisfied or thankful. She wanted to buy a house in Damascus because our house was in the countryside of Damascus. It would be easier for her if we moved, and closer to her family's house and her friends and the market. She considered it her right to demand, although buying a house in Damascus was not an easy thing. I bought the house and received a car from work, which I gave to her to be able to go anywhere. After she gave birth to our second daughter, I thought we were on the right track. I was able to build a family and buy a house in Damascus.

"The years passed and I worked day and night in government. I was not bound by the official working hours, and you know the amount of work that was placed on my shoulders during those years. You were with me for the last two years. My main concern was to work and succeed and achieve my dream of being something of importance in Syria, and for my children and my wife to be happy. My children grew up quickly. I only saw them in the morning, as when I came back late they were asleep.

"I gave her everything that a woman could wish for, but she was never satisfied. She was never with me. On the contrary, she was seizing opportunities to be an enemy and to always discourage me. When I wondered at the reason for all this meanness, I said to myself that she did this because I did not let her work. Perhaps she also had ambitions like me, so depriving her of work built a barrier between us."

Yona interrupted Jawad, saying, "You did not say yet the thing that's making you think so much."

"As you know, after I quit my job in the Prime Ministry and moved to another place, I was not assigned any work, and that happened to be the same time as the beginning of the crisis in Syria and the beginning of my relationship with you. I had free time which I used to get closer to my children and I stayed at home for long periods of time due to the crisis that caused a bad security situation.

"I began to notice all that had been going around the house more than before. She never changed, but increased in her ferocity and her dissatisfaction with anything. I decided to talk to her and end our marital relationship. Indeed, I told her that I was tired of continuing this relationship, as she tried repeatedly and failed to be a wife. That she failed to support her husband like all wives do. At first she agreed and started preparing her bag to leave the house. I told her, 'Don't worry, I will get you a house in the same neighbourhood so that the children can live next to you, but they will live here because of their schools.' Suddenly, she collapsed, crying, so I told her, 'Don't try to beg for my affection. We have known each other for more than twenty years and have been married for more than sixteen years. The decision has been made.'

"She cried, 'Please, I know I have not been a good wife to you, and I know that you have put up with me too much, but please, I do not want to be away from my children.'

"I told her, 'Please, I want to live a life that is empty of misery. I want to live like all men. I want to live with a person who, if she does not love me, then will at least respect me, because I provide you with everything you wish for. The relationship that unites us is ended.'

"She said, 'Please, for the sake of our children let me serve them and live with them.'

"I told her, after hours of arguing, 'So be it, but for the sake of the children only, and you will not be a wife as of this day. You are just a mother to them, but I have nothing to do with you and prepare to leave my life the moment I ask you to do so. From today I am free, and you are free.'

"Today, I'm here in the UK, sitting next to you, but my mind will not stop thinking of the reasons why, all of a sudden, she entered my life.

"Was she in love with someone else and her family wanted to keep her away?

"Why didn't she tell me the truth and make me live all these years like a short circuit?

"Was the one she loved from another religion?

"Why me? Why did her family choose me to be subjected to such misery and unhappiness?

"I think, if they told me about the matter and treated me like a son to them, I would have proceeded with the matter, either to achieve what she wanted, or to get married after she had told me the truth."

Yona, who was listening very carefully, said to him, "You once told me something similar when we were in Damascus, but you weren't that clear. Do you want to say that your wife is having an affair with someone else?"

Jawad replied, "I don't know; maybe her heart only!"

Yona said, "Do you want to be sure, or will you dig a grave and bury this feeling in it after bringing your wife here and consider that her relationship has ended geographically, at the very least?"

Jawad said, "This is exactly what's making my mind explode. I don't know what to do. Even more to my distress is that you will leave to the North and I to the South."

After a silence that went on for a few minutes, Yona said, "What if what you doubted all along was true? After she comes here? You won't be able to do anything, and she will have the right to take the children, and you will lose everything."

Jawad replied, "If this is the loss, then I am satisfied. But if she comes and lives with me while I am in doubt and I do not discover anything, my life will be completely turbulent. I don't really have a wife and the children are lost and I am lost. I want a truth that comforts me, whatever the results. Do you understand?"

"How do you verify such an issue when you are thousands of miles away from her?" Yona added, then began to lay down their food. She placed a rug on a green meadow under a giant tree that was as old as Britain. Jawad took a few bites and then laid his head on Yona's lap. Tears began with a rapid flow, hurrying to escape the heat of the flames in his head.

When Yona saw Jawad's red eyes, she cried, too, but her pain was confused between what had happened to Jawad and what she was in at that moment. After five days, she would leave Jawad forever and lose the man she loved. The only one she trusted in this country. The only one she was trying to incarnate as a father, a brother, and a lover. Jawad became everything in her life. He was the one she had been waiting for. She was content to leave Jawad and bear her wounds and let time heal them, but now Jawad was making the task more and more difficult. If he left, he might not be comfortable and would not live happily, and perhaps this pressure would make him think of looking again for Yona, and he would end up reopening her wound, which would not have had enough time to heal. She cried for leaving Jawad and going to a far-off place, and also for his sadness. Other times, she cried because of a love that carried a thousand impossibilities within her that did not want to be extinguished before it burned everything.

In the evening, Yona put two cups of Nescafe on the edge of the huge window in her room, and asked him, "What is your decision?"

Jawad said, "I have reached what can lead me to a point through which I can express a truth, or perhaps the consequences may be greater, and as the common saying goes, 'If it grow, it gets smaller.' Tomorrow morning, we will try something, and I will use everything I have learned in my life to reach the truth. Tomorrow we will start trying the shock method that makes the recipient unable to focus so that we can get definitive answers. Don't ask about anything now and let's enjoy drinking these cups."

In the morning, Jawad asked Yona to extract some old photos of them that were taken in the Beit Zaman cafe, located in the warm old Damascus alleys, where they used to meet. Yona opened the pictures on her cell phone and started showing them to Jawad. Jawad picked a few of them and said, "But they are not enough. I must prepare a letter to prove a relationship between you and me." He had written a letter already and asked Yona to send those pictures and a copy of the letter to his wife!

Yona was perplexed, and asked, "What do you want to do?"

He replied, "I told her more than a year ago that she was free and that I was, too, with my life, and that she stayed in my house just to take care of our children. Accordingly, I am able to admit that I am in a relationship with you and to be frank with her about this thing that I think she is aware of. She may or may not recognise you, even if this causes you trouble. Once she learns the truth through you, she will be happy and ecstatic that she caught something that she can use either to humiliate me or to admit in return of what she is up to as a kind of revenge and pride, and so as not to appear that she was a naive victim."

Yona immediately answered, "Yes, I will do it no matter what."

Yona also wanted to put her foot on solid ground, no matter what. If Jawad discovered the truth about what his wife really wanted, Yona would reach a path to choose between two things: the first was that his wife would choose to not just go on as someone who would take care of their children, and then Yona would have a lover without a partner. The second was that his wife would stay for the sake of her children no matter what. Then Yona would return to her life and filter what was left of Jawad in her memory and heart, and turn him into a memory that would motivate her to struggle with a life in which she was strong, and not drawn into a love that did not contain the logic of life and was not opposed by a mother, family, traditions, and religions.

She would not lose anything. She was ready for a final adventure in which she would make sure of Jawad's vision on things. He might have been through the experience of love with her just because of a whim or a wrong reaction that she misunderstood from his wife. He wanted to get away to where he could break all concepts and habits. Soaring over the world of contradictions as if he was alone, not caring for anyone's opinion. He wanted to get drunk with the wine of a sincere and tender love. Maybe he was a fake lover, even though he gave Yona what any girl would wish: he gave her attention and crowned her the queen of his kingdom. He swam with her in romantic moments and surrounded her with a silk cocoon. She rebelled against everything to be with him.

She sent the pictures, and two days later, Jawad's wife replied to her, asking, "What do you have other than those pictures? They do not prove anything. They are in a public place, and you might be the one who wrote the message and know his writing style. What do you want exactly?"

Yona did not answer his wife's questions, but she told Jawad of what had happened.

Jawad received a call from his wife, inquiring about what Yona had sent. Jawad asked her, "First, why haven't you asked me about it immediately, as any jealous wife would do? How could you wait for two days to do so?"

His wife replied, "I was preparing a careful answer for you." She continued, "I envy her for this much love. The one you shower her with, and I also envy you for this love that makes you like a bird in the sky. I watched you for some time. I know that for a year or more you fell in love with a girl and that you were no longer with me."

Jawad interrupted her, "Since before we got married, you weren't with me!"

"Yes, this is true, and I must confess to you, because recently I suffered a lot of torment regarding this thing, and I was trying to get out of this disaster by any means possible. Now, you have made it easier for me. Yes, my heart is with someone else, and it has been so even before I married you. He was doctor who came into my life during your military service."

Jawad interrupted her, saying, "I think you met him before that. He is the doctor who used to treat your aunt and your father. I think his name is Ibrahim?"

His wife continued, "It doesn't matter when the relationship started, but this is the truth. I wanted to confess everything to you, but I couldn't, and now, do what you want to do because I want to rest from this life."

"Why did you marry me then? Was I a plaything for you? Did your family know about that and I was the scapegoat to save the situation because the doctor was from another religion and the situation had to be saved, so you suddenly entered my life and imposed yourself as someone who loved me? All of this and your whole family knew?

"Is this how things have been going on so brazenly all these years?

"I used to consider myself a son of your family before you confessed to me that you loved me. How did your family accept this farce?

"Your brother was my loyal friend. Your older sister pretended to accept me as a brother-in-law when I went to her and asked for her consent to start a relationship with you which she had openly opposed from the beginning. All these episodes of drama which your family participated in perfectly.

"All of you are impure, perfectly practising the art of lowliness, damn you."

She said, "I confessed everything to you. There is nothing I want to hide from you any more. Believe me, and I deserve anything you do to me, but I hope you will save our children and take them out of this war."

Jawad persisted and added, "Listen carefully. When I send applications for family reunification and entry to Britain during the coming period, including your own approval, you follow the necessary procedures at the embassy to obtain the visa for you and the children. But I advise you to send the children only and stay in Damascus, because if you come to Britain with them, you will undoubtedly be racing against fate till the end of your life. So stay where you are and wait for your divorce documents and pray to God that the boiling blood in my veins will cool down until I return to the country. I will take my revenge from the whole family, not only from you."

Jawad hung up the phone without waiting for an answer and began to replay his memory tape from the first day his wife confessed her love until today. He got many answers to questions that had long puzzled him.

He tried to restrain himself from crying, but he could not. He cried for the past twenty years of his life. They were long years which he crossed with difficulty and struggled to reach the beginning of a comfortable path for himself and his family, but his wife was the first destroyer, disappointment, and a professional of misfortune.

He asked himself, "Was my poverty back then what allowed her family to commit such foolishness?"

Or was there a conspiracy that was agreed upon, and Jawad was chosen as a victim who could be easily fooled? Everything could be forgiven for Jawad except for the stab from a family he had always been loyal to. He would wait and be patient, as time would either take revenge for him or put him in a place where he would be able to take revenge for himself.

Jawad recovered from his shock.

Did fate make him aware of this truth at this time as a good sign, or an evil one?

Why did Jawad feel sad for a confession he was waiting for and was almost certain of?

Why was he sad? Was it because his past years were mostly filled with sadness and oppression? He should focus on the priorities of his life from this moment on; much of his life had been lost already.

He would not let the shock scatter him away.

Destiny weaves a tale of British wool.

He told Yona of what had happened.

She listened to him, but did not ask about the details. Instead, she said, "I want to confess something to you, too."

He said, "No, don't say it."

Yona laughed and said, "Forgive me, because I thought that you were making up stories about your instability in your home to justify our relationship. You did not inform me of one real serious behaviour that justified this during our conversations. All your stories were speculative and did not include facts, but now I realise that you were suffering and hiding inside you a huge amount of doubt that was apparently true. I want you to never be sad. God wanted that, and you are a believer. Consider what happened war damage. There is no family left in Syria that has not been harmed; thank God that you discovered this here and you did not discover it in Syria. Let fate produce for you another film for a new life in this country that has opportunities which will make you forget the dark days that you have been through."

Yona left Coventry for Glasgow, Scotland, to start a new journey in terms of the geography of the new city and the feelings that had become completely confused. But a simple smile of joy began to appear on her lips as she obtained her temporary residence as a refugee in Britain, and Jawad became aware of an issue that had always been a nuisance for him, but he did not yet decide on what to do; all possibilities were available.

Jawad, in turn, returned to Manchester after informing Yona that he had changed his mind concerning settling in southern Britain and that he would move to Edinburgh, which was just about an hour away from the city where Yona would settle if Jawad obtained the residence permit that was delayed because of Jawad's answer to the investigator's question whether he was with or against the ruling regime in Syria, and he said he was with it.

The investigator was surprised. "Are you with the regime?"

Jawad answered, "Yes."

She asked, "Why are you here then, and why are you with him even though he is killing his people?"

He replied, "First of all, the regime did not kill its own people. Rather, it kills those who disturb the State's system. I think this is the right of any regime in any country. You are currently working in the police force; if any citizen or group of citizens kills you because you work for this institution, will the government or regime be silent about it? Of course not. All security departments will mobilise to arrest the perpetrator, even if battles erupt between the State and criminals, and many civilians are killed. I want to ask you something else: does the State's insistence on arresting criminals and saboteurs mean that it is anti-democratic?

"Did the regime, as you say in Syria, kill its sons before the chaos, destruction and crime committed under the name of a revolution?

"Secondly, if you think that overthrowing the regime is the solution to have democracy, then I tell you that the Islamic organisations recruited from abroad, and that have been blacklisted by you and by all countries, will not bring any kind of democracy to Syria. As for the chaos that will afflict the country in case the regime is overruled in Syria, you have realistic evidence, such as Iraq and Libya, which have not stabilised so far despite changing the regime.

"Allow me to ask another question. Is the one seeking asylum refused because he is with the regime and accepted if he is with extremist Islamic organisations?

"Let me tell you, if this is the case, this means that any country that accepts such a thing will one day suffer from its decision and regret it. The issue is not who is with the regime and who is against it, the issue for many people who have applied for asylum is the price. Do not be surprised; yes, the price of death has become very cheap in our country. Fleeing from the chaos that was created with agendas for multiple interests is the reason. It is true that the regime usurped power, but the real democracy that brings a new ruler is not yet available in the Arab countries, so Syria is no different from Iraq, Libya or any other country. There is a domination of power in all those countries, and I think that the change will not be in this way, and the experience in Libya is a living example.

"Then the answer to your question is yes, I am with it, if its alternative is sabotage, the rule of terrorist groups, loss and chaos. But if the alternative is democracy, the rule of law, the absence of authoritarianism and the application of the constitution in the republican system in its entirety, then of course I am against it, but this is a kind of fantasy that you will not find in Syria or in all the Arab countries and dictatorships."

Whoever sees rape every time he looks in his mirror is the ruler who has usurped power.

This answer delayed Jawad's temporary residency because his file had to be checked more than necessary. They knew who he was.

Syrians seeking asylum in European countries are often not within the circle of conflict. They are searching for a homeland, for a spot on this planet where they could sleep without fear of a war that lasted for a long time, more than they imagined, which had turned into an image of a bleak future. Everyone was eating away at everyone because the war had made people lose values and morals.

There is no one in the Syrian war who fights ideologically or out of love for the party he belongs to.

Those calling for freedom do not know anything about it. They have taken it as a symbol of oppression and exploitation of people, and they even killed the innocent. For them, freedom was to seize power and exercise supremacy over the rest of the people as the system is now.

Those who call for patriotism do not know that the homeland is not a stone or a tree, but a human being. This being inside this geographical spot, who has lost respect and many rights due to the arbitrariness of many officials using the authority desired by many to achieve social ostentation and quick financial revenue. Positions in Syria are sold, and many officials were appointed to positions they paid for.

Therefore, before the war broke out, the fleeing Syrians lost the basic humanitarian needs: housing, food, electricity, heating. They lost being treated as human beings because of a government employee who understood that his mere work in the government entitled him to practice impoliteness and thus they were the ones also responsible for it and thus Syria lost its identity as a homeland. They searched for a homeland that would secure the elements of patriotism for them. Nothing in Syria was fine.

All sectors are backward and those in charge of them are, too. The government did not notice that the loss of the citizen's confidence in his country is a catastrophe. The greatest disaster was that they did not realise that a country without a citizen was a deaf stone that would not benefit them even if they stole it.

The general condition of the lives of the rulers of the Arabs is surprising. Their countries are wealthy, yet their people live in a constant state of losing their basic needs to live. Corruption lives with them as a friend and crushes and flogs the capabilities of their peoples. Regimes that only care about accumulating money and exercising the instinct of supremacy. The homeland belongs to them with all that is in it. Their behaviour deprives them of the pleasure of making others happy, and turns them into outcasts among the immortals, living under the illusion of greatness, unaware of the assassination bullet.

Yona called Jawad. They did not meet for two months. She told him that the next day she would go to the council to get a house or be placed in a camp with those who do not have a home. She added that she was afraid of this, because she had spent two months with a family of their acquaintance, and she was starting to feel like an unwanted guest because her stay had gone on for two months. She had been waiting to receive a house of her own during this period, but nothing happened. Jawad wished her success and told her that he would not see her until the approval of his residence, or the refusal was issued.

Jawad had dark circles under his eyes. He did not see sleep well after the shock he received from his wife. He had been trying hard all this time to overcome this ordeal. He hoped to meet the Syrian young man who smoked hashish to take one wrap that might help him sleep, which had left the port of his eyes like a ship lost in a stormy sea. But the young man obtained the residence permit and left for London.

Never give up on anyone who you may need, even if he is an unclean fraud.

On the morning of the second day, Yona called Jawad, crying heartily. Jawad tried to stop her, but she was saying that they had decided to put her in a hostel, and she was very afraid and did not want to go because she did not like the one she was in before. It had been full of people of different nationalities and the bathrooms were dirty and used by everyone. Jawad tried to stop Yona, but she kept talking. "I might stay there for months, because it is difficult to give me a home. There are families who have priority."

Jawad interrupted her, saying, "Please, just listen to me. I want to tell you something important. My residence was approved today and I was trying to contact you to tell you this."

Yona was silent and lost between tears and joy. She laughed and cried with happiness. Jawad only heard two words: "For real?" Then she said, "Tell me that you are not lying to calm me down, please."

"It came, I swear to God. It did."

Finally, news that made Yona's heart happy. Now Jawad had turned into a reality, not an illusion. She tried to escape from him when she decided to leave Damascus, but before she left, she said to him, "Please follow me. Life may be happy in Europe, but I will not see anything beautiful without you. Please try to go, even if to another country, and even if you are only a friend."

Today, Jawad was legally here. Near her and with her, even if their relationship was not clear yet. In the past days, Yona used to blame herself for asking Jawad to follow her, but she now sensed that the Lord spoke to her with her sincere and loving heart to save Jawad from waging into a losing revenge.

She said to him, "Go now and I will call you back later. Now I am going to get my room. I hope it will be better than what I expected."

The end of August in 2015. Any changes in Jawad's life had always taken place in August by chance, and a new stage in his life had begun now.

Jawad called his Damascene friend Yaman, who came with him from Belgium to Britain in a truck, and who obtained residency two months earlier and was now trying to settle in Edinburgh.

Yaman was little in everything, except when it came to his ambitions. He was cunning enough to get what he wanted, and often pretended to be stupid because he knew that most people enjoyed giving lectures and feeling superior to others. He would feign surprise whenever someone gave him information, even if he knew it ten years ago. 'No' was not in Yaman's dictionary, and neither was 'I know'. However, he abundantly used the word 'Me'alem' — the word for master or teacher in Arabic. He was a djinn who would simplify everything for you to get what he wanted from you. Jawad met that kind of people during his long years of work in Damascus, and he knew people always said that this kind of person was clever because it never mattered the means through which you got what you wanted, as long as you got it.

The two agreed that Jawad would come to Edinburgh in the evening to go together to the hostel in which Yaman lived alone in a private room, and on the second day he would take him to the council of Edinburgh to apply for accommodation, as was the custom.

Yona called shortly after, laughing after she sent several pictures of her room in the hostel to Jawad. It was a better room than Britain's four-star hotels, but she said that visitors were not allowed to enter. Jawad stopped at this word and told her, "But Yaman will host me at the hostel tomorrow evening in Edinburgh!"

Yona replied, "The laws for men may be different."

Jawad added, "Most likely. Yaman would have asked about this, as he is one of the most careful people I have ever met."

Jawad thanked the Lord for this day, which brought news that made Yona happy. He said to her, "Thank God, it seems that things are starting to improve, and tomorrow I will arrive in Scotland, and if things settle down and I find lodgings, I will visit you on the second day and we will spend the day together; then I'll return to Edinburgh."

Jawad arrived in Edinburgh. It was a bit rainy and cold. No summer comes to Scotland.

The city was bustling with people, even though the time was ten at night, and this was surprising in Britain; people usually returned to their homes before six in the evening and slept before ten, except rarely.

Edinburgh, the beautiful ancient city, resembled Damascus, with a small hill in the middle of the city, as if it was the small Qasioun Mountain in Syria, and instead of the radio building over the top of Mount Qasioun, there was a large castle in Edinburgh.

The streets of Edinburgh are old, as are the alleys of Bab Sharqi and Bab Touma in Damascus.

Jawad asked Yaman, "Why is the city bustling with people?"

Yaman said, "Every year, throughout August, there is a festival and celebration in the city called The Fringe. It brings thousands of tourists." Jawad felt that his decision to choose this city, which he first heard about from the movie *Braveheart*, was a right one. This was what Jawad loved: heritage and a lively and bustling city.

The two arrived at the hostel at eleven o'clock at night, but the official did not allow Jawad to enter!

Yaman asked why, and the answer was that visits were only allowed from ten in the morning until five in the evening, and he was not allowed after that. Yaman did not know that and did not inquire about the matter. Jawad had nowhere to sleep. He immediately called Yona to book a hotel room for him in Edinburgh, and Yona hurried to book one for him, because he was very tired from his trip. But it was all in vain, since all hotels were fully booked for the festival. She found a room for him in a hotel at the cost of two hundred and twenty pounds. Jawad told her that he would spend his night at the station. "Buy me a bus ticket to go back to Glasgow tomorrow morning." Jawad spent his whole night walking the streets of Edinburgh, which he began to hate before he even loved. Yaman left him to return to his room, because he was not allowed in after twelve. The city was cold and the night was long, and the station was closed until half past five in the morning.

Jawad returned to Glasgow, where Yona was.

Was his return a new sign of a decision not yet taken?

Jawad arrived exhausted and went to a mall to rest and eat something.

Yona asked him, "What are your plans now?"

"I don't know," he said, "but I could rethink everything and plan again so that I wouldn't go back to Edinburgh."

Yona was surprised because he was the one who insisted that Edinburgh be his city.

She asked, "Why?"

He said, "I trusted my little friend, but he preferred to sleep warmly and was afraid of being punished if he slept outside his hostel. Such a friend cannot be relied upon. I know that I am a little selfish, but in the matter of friends there are not many options. I trust one type of friendship; a friend is the one who wishes for you more than he does for himself and sacrifices everything for you; you are number one for him. Therefore, Yaman cannot be relied upon to follow a long journey, as he needs a crutch, and he is one of the people who only wants to take and not give back. I want to stay in Glasgow with you."

Yona's eyes flashed, and she said, "You want me to be your crutch and I want you to be my cover."

Jawad laughed, saying, "You and I don't know that we are two. Let's look for a place for me this night. I may need two or three days."

Jawad spent his first night in the Glasgow mosque and the servant of the mosque served him breakfast in the morning and told him, "We do not accept anyone to sleep here, but if you need another night, you can come back." Jawad thanked him.

The Jordanian-Palestinian interpreter of Yona's lawyer was able to secure him a temporary room rented by a young man. After two nights, Jawad found a hostel to sleep in.

During these days, Yona began to prepare the necessary papers for the unification procedures for Jawad's children, who were happy for their father to obtain the residency. In a few months they would see him and would live in Britain as semi-citizens. They would finally escape from the war that had been going on for a long time. There was nothing left for them in Syria to depend on; even the people, especially their relatives, began to take advantage of them. The holidays passed without an aunt or uncle knowing that there were three children without a father who might need something.

Also, Yona needed to bring her mother from Damascus.

Yona's burdens were endless, since she was the one who knew English very well. As for Jawad, he was unable to talk, although his persuasive abilities and word manipulation were among his most important artistic talents; but now he was mute in all the meanings of this word, and deaf, too. He only heard voices, but without distinguishing what was said. Sometimes, he could understand something from the features of the speaker. Despite that, the Scottish people were co-operative and friendly and helped anyone, regardless of their colour or race. They were people who respected animals more than the Arab peoples respected each other.

Jawad worked on the necessary procedures needed for his children, then all that was left to do was to wait. As for Yona, she was informed by her lawyer that the request to bring her mother was rejected.

She came to meet Jawad in his private room in the hostel in the morning. She was planning to bring her mother by smuggling her to Britain, but her mother absolutely refused to cross the sea in a small boat between Turkey and Greece. She discussed this issue with Jawad and they both agreed to bring her to Turkey, and there she would meet an acquaintance of her family in Istanbul, who would help her cross safely to Greece by land.

Yona's married sister, residing in Damascus, obtained approval from her husband for family unification and began preparing to travel. Yona's mother, a lonely woman who was over fifty-five years old, was preparing to set out on a journey of unknown fate. That was very difficult, because this road was fraught with many difficulties, but there was no other way for her but to take it. She had no other choice, and she must cross this road to reach her two daughters and live with them.

Yona's mother was suspicious of Yona's relationship with Jawad before Yona left, but she rested from this obsession after Yona travelled. However, she did not know now that Jawad was planning with Yona to bring her to Britain, which confused Yona, because Jawad wanted to send one of his relatives to take care of her mother after her arrival in Istanbul. Yona refused that at first, but then she relented after everyone abandoned her mother, even the family friend in Istanbul, who said that he had left the city.

Yona's mother arrived in Istanbul and was received by a friend of Jawad who booked her a hotel room and brought her some necessities. In less than twenty-four hours, she would take a trip in the trunk of a tourist car across the Turkish-Greek land border. It was not an easy journey at all for her as she was arrested and returned to Istanbul exhausted. She tried again after several days. In her second attempt, she was also arrested, and despair began to take over Yona and her mother, whose decision to return to Damascus became the best solution after a week of torment on her own.

But how would she live alone without her children?

Yona persuaded her mother to be a little patient because her return meant that Yona would return, too, because she did not want her mother to remain alone in Damascus, especially since Yona had used all the family savings to reach Britain.

Jawad called Yona's mother for the first time after he agreed with Yona that he would try to convince her to cross the sea.

To break the astonished silence which struck Yona's mother when he called her, Jawad said, "I don't have much time. I want to tell you something brief. You will cross the sea in a big boat with a man who will accompany you. He is absolutely better than me and will protect you until you reach Greece, and then he will continue his way to Sweden after he is assured that you have left for Britain. You have no other choice. Trust me and I hope that you will not try to do that on your own, because people have become greedy and you are now alone and it is easy to be robbed by bad guys on the road. I want you to only follow the man's instructions and to trust him as if he was Yona."

She asked him, "Are you in Britain?"

"Yes."

"Are you sure I will cross the sea?"

"If there was an iota of danger to you, I would not accept that you do that. The man will reach you in less than an hour. His name is Bassem. Together, you will go to someone who will call you to pay the security deposit. His name is Abu Nasser. When the meeting takes place, call me and let me talk to him; then the departure time and place will be agreed upon, and, God willing, in less than twenty-four hours you will be in Greece."

Indeed, after making all the arrangements, both Bassem and Yona's mother arrived at the starting place and boarded the ship. During the cruise, Jawad called his friend to reassure Yona, who was worried, that all was good and that things were going according to plan. Jawad asked Bassem, "How is Yona's mother?"

Bassem replied, "She became the doctor aboard, distributing lemon and salt to the passengers because they were vomiting from seasickness. I think that her state of mind is better than mine. Don't worry. God willing, we will arrive safely."

Yona did not fall asleep that night until she was assured of her mother's arrival to safety. She hugged Jawad and said, "Thank you. You saved us all. Without my mother, I would have gone back to Syria, and my sister's life would have been troubled if she stayed in Britain. She would be worried about us in Syria and the raging war there. Today, you gave me what I wanted. Although my mother may be worried now because she knows you are in Britain, it does not matter. What is important is that she crossed the sea."

Jawad asked her, "Will you marry me?"

Yona was shocked by Jawad's suggestion, and her tired eyes from the lack of sleep were suddenly fully open, staring at him. She did not utter a word.

Jawad said, "A few days ago I learned the truth about my wife. It did not occur to me that her whole family were perfect actors and professionals in the art of role-playing. An entire family whom I dearly loved more than my own and to whom I gave everything. But my knowledge of this only came to me after I left Syria. As if God did not want me to be involved in a crime, so he kept me away, and the timing coincided with the beginning of preparing a plan to end our relationship!

"And now your mother knows that I am here, but she is occupied with so many things, so she was not able to think about it much because she is psychologically stressed and needs a straw to survive. God facilitates everything and at the right time. They are signs that lead us to the truth, but we do not know, as Paulo Coelho said in his book, *The Alchemist,* that signs will take a person to his destiny. Therefore, I do not want your answer now, but I wanted to tell you that God does not only take us to what we want, but to more than we do."

Yona said, "I don't need time to answer. Yes, I agree. This is a dream. A dream of owning the moon, a dream of irrationality. How can I not agree, when I was playing with the word 'marry' in my fantasies and it fled from me and disappeared like swarms of small fish in the heart of the ocean. I was looking for it in the words of astrologers and the daily horoscopes on the Damascus radio in the morning. What you asked me has no two answers and no choices. We have a great and intimate love story that went through all the challenges of life, but I did not imagine that a day would come, and you would ask me to agree to marry you. I saw separation and pain as the end of a story that was long and has grown more than we were able to take care of it and end it peacefully.

"Don't wait for anything. I am yours as soon as my mother gets here."

Jawad said, "Consider her arrival my dowry for you."

They hugged and fell asleep, each embracing the other.

From the small island of Kalmenos in Greece, after eating a meal of fish, Yona's mother and Bassem moved to a huge boat, where they were transferred to Athens, to begin their attempt to leave by air to Britain.

Jawad asked Bassem to come to Britain as well, as he needed him as a friend he trusted. Bassem was the younger brother of Jawad's friend, who had died early. He was an example of a pure human being: honest, truthful, and loyal. A calm man.

Jawad needed someone to lean on. He was also alone in a strange country where he did not know anything, with no friend, no brother, not even a relative. Bassem agreed to secure Yona's mother first, and he would leave after being assured she had arrived safely.

In the first attempt, Yona's mother was unable to leave. As for the second attempt, it was a kind of wonder that had not happened before with any fugitive. Yona's mother had lost her boarding permit, and the staff began to help her search for it at the airport, including security! In the end, a new board pass was issued for her, so she crossed the most difficult crossing gates from Europe to Britain, which was highly monitored. Yona's mother miraculously boarded the plane.

Another strange coincidence was that she and her eldest daughter arrived in London a few hours apart without any prior planning for that. Yona's mother was very happy but worried, because she did not know how to tell her daughter who met her hours later at the airport that Jawad was with Yona! This news needed strength of heart, and her mother did not want to disturb the joy of their arrival.

Yona and Jawad went out to eat lunch, which cost them fifteen pounds. It is true that Jawad had some money, but it was still in Damascus. Yona saved everything she got to buy whatever her mother needed when she came, because she would definitely need a lot of things.

Yona's mother stayed with her eldest daughter in London and left in the morning to arrive in Glasgow in the afternoon. She was also greeted by Jawad, who was puzzled by her reaction when she saw him, but she did not express anything except that she thanked him very much for what he had done. Jawad took them to the temporary house which Yona had received, and he returned to his house, which he had also received, and they agreed to meet for lunch on the second day.

Yona was finally with her mother.

As for Jawad, he spent his night alone. It seemed that he was facing another battle, despite Yona's consent to marry him, but the struggle to obtain the consent of her mother and older sister was not an easy thing. Yona would not be able to overcome all these barriers, as she was a small pony unable to determine the height of her mother's eyes and the brutality of her sister, who Jawad always described as extremist. It was impossible to accept the idea of marriage.

Yona's sister did not look like Yona in anything. She was free from all restrictions, wearing the shortest shorts and posting her pictures on social media. She did not accept new ideas or discuss them. She had a self-confidence equivalent to the hatred of everyone who had suffered a catastrophe in this world as a result of convincing an extremist that by his suicide act he will swim with the mermaids in the sky. She was the one who suffered from the brutal crime of an Islamist who detonated his car bomb to go to heaven, and the price was the blood and death of her family members just because they were passing through that area. Muslims were a point at which she would stop. She lived in a state of false psychological stability. The monster of that day never disappeared from her imagination. He etched hatred in her memory similar to the inscriptions of the writings of the pharaohs: immortal, removing all the joy of the past and killing everything beautiful in her life. She believed in fate, but could not accept the idea of losing a father, a brother, and a family like the rest of the people, because an idiot wanted to go to heaven. Her life was an illusion where she did not see people and they in turn did not see her. She would tell her only child the story of the greatness of her grief and consider him her world. She never discussed, but rather imposed her opinions and data.

After she learned from her mother that Jawad was behind her arrival and that he was in Britain, she called Yona to ask her about that. Yona said that Jawad was also the one who guided her husband to reach Britain after he was stuck in Europe. Her sister asked her, "Does this mean that you were seeing each other during this whole period and you did not cut off your relationship with him in Damascus?"

Yona replied, "Yes, we did not break off the relationship, not even for a single day. Even when you were spying on our conversations through your work in the telecommunications company. It only cost Jawad fifty Syrian pounds for a new SIM card in the name of his driver for my cell phone to get rid of your prying ears. I want you to know one more thing: Jawad and I are getting married!"

She hung up. Her sister called their mother, who was devastated at the news and quarrelled with Yona, then called Jawad and asked him to meet outside the house the next day. Jawad agreed. He already knew the reason from Yona, who had called him and informed him of what had happened.

There, on a bridge over the river, thoughts were racing in Jawad's head before Yona's mother came. Many choices were passing through his mind.

Should he be quiet or be loud as usual?

Would he allow himself to quarrel with a woman who has been afflicted by fate and great calamities that shook all her being, or should he give in to her requests, no matter what, and forgive the fate which had put him in a place where he was powerless?

He wanted to defend his love as a knight who wanted his love to win during the coming days. He loved Yona's mother, who was unusually generous and tactful, but she loved herself, too.

She appeared from afar, walking towards him with trembling steps. He welcomed her. She did not answer his welcome. He asked her to sit on a chair across from the river.

He said to her, "Go ahead, I see that you are not well."

She cried and begged him to leave Yona alone. "You promised me in Damascus that she would have a brother and that your relationship would not continue. You are a married man, and you have children and are about her father's age. I think this is enough. You have to stop this farce, so please leave her alone. Yona is a reckless girl who never knows what she's doing."

Jawad interrupted her and said, "Are these just the reasons, or is the main reason that I am a Muslim and this is reason enough for you to be ashamed?"

"Yes," Yona's mother answered. "Yes, it is a great shame and disgrace that I cannot imagine. Have mercy on us and leave us alone. The whole world has religious considerations, and you also have foundations in your Islamic religion that you cannot cross. Rules govern all your daily actions and you do not cross them. Why do you want me to go beyond that?

"Yes, this causes us a big problem in front of the society in which we live. How do I face my family and her father's family? What do I tell people: my daughter married a Muslim who is twenty years older than her? That he is married or divorced and has three children! Which of these misfortunes do I begin with when anyone asks me about Yona when I get back?"

Jawad said, "Answer them that she married the one she loves, without going into details. Haven't you ever loved? Doesn't the word love mean anything to you?"

"What do you want it to mean, Mr Jawad?" Yona's mother replied. "Do you want her to erase a shame that people will talk about for a lifetime? What nonsense and what love are you talking about? Love lives in a right place, not in a dungeon. This story must end and stop in any way and at any cost. If I had to, I would kill my daughter and myself and I would not agree to this matter."

Jawad said, "It seems that you came to live in Britain, but you still carry your blind fanaticism. I think that if a man came forward with the same specifications as me, but was a Christian, you would accept him. The issue is only this bigotry that was planted in your minds and confirmed by what happened with you on that black day. You are right, I will not be able to get rid of my religion nor exonerate myself. But fate may want to prove to you later that Islam has two sides. In any case, I do not want to philosophise matters before their time, and I will clearly summarise what I have for you. I will not leave Yona except in two cases: if I die, or if she wanted me to.

"Try to accept the idea, and I beg you to discuss it with your eldest daughter, who spoke with Yona yesterday and wished me death. Tell her that death is something from God, but the blackness of hearts is something we make ourselves. That her lightning sword does not grow beautiful flowers, but fills the lands with black dirt. Tell her that her son will have a Muslim cousin, and I think that her son will not care about his cousin's religion because he will grow up in a civilised environment that is not governed by religion. Tell her to try to show herself as the light of the sun who shines with tolerance, warmth and understanding to greet the roses of the fields. She is the light which appears for a moment after lightning, a moment of pride and arrogance, and that she only produces buried fruits that do not differ from the mud of the earth, except for their price.

"In this country, gays marry, and black and white people as well. Here, the creature is respected for his actions and not for his religion. Please, do not consider what I will say as a threat, but consider it a challenge. Yona, for me, is something too big for anyone to take, even if this someone is her mother or her religion. We will continue our path and you will have a chance that may be a year to accept the idea or discuss it, but after that I will not take your opinions into consideration, and I will marry Yona even if you still refuse. I am sorry that you did not get what you wanted from the meeting, and I hope to see you soon and to find that you have understood the meaning of the love which unites me and your daughter. It is true that this love is reckless and does not recognise customs and traditions, not even within the boundaries of logic, but it is strong so that it can live among everyone who wants to prey on it. It can wrestle anything. It is the only dragon surviving, because it has not been defeated."

Yona's mother left for her house, where Yona was waiting.

She told her when she entered the house that Jawad told her that the decision was in her hands, so if she left him, he would move away from her. Yona did not say any word to her mother, but she allowed her thoughts to swim towards the crazy Jawad who threw his fishing nets in Yona's water full of love's fish. He would surely catch the food of his soul as long as Yona was alive and would not give up on him.

She remembered that Jawad once told her, "When love enters your heart, do not close the doors and windows for fear it may escape from you or that someone will see you, because when love enters you, it occupies you and controls the place. It occupies and usurps your entity without leaving. In you is a light that transcends all barriers and turns you upside down.

Makes you a naughty child who loves everything. You will even get injured, no matter how old and conscious you are.

"Love makes you a saint after you were a disbeliever. You know the meaning of life, you will be saved for it, and you will abandon any corruption within you. Love will make you a righteous contemplator, and then you will understand that any love is the lesson of creativity in life. Love is the only one who shows you the purity of the soul. Love is the word of God, which he throws on his servant when He loves him, making him enjoy life and become satisfied with everything in it. Love is the key to thanking God for everything. Love is to be convinced that madness is a healthy state."

Love is the only currency that cannot be counterfeited.

Yona did not answer her mother because she was satisfied with what she achieved and understood that fate and days would throw up bright stars that light up the celebration of their love. It was enough for her that her mother and sister knew about them and they no longer hid anything, and that a fierce fighter can triumph with the huge sword of love which he carries.

Rama, Yona's friend, called Yona and consulted her that she and her brother-in-law, the engineer, were thinking of leaving Damascus for Germany. She had found a person in Damascus who wanted four thousand euros for each person to take them to Germany. Life in Damascus had become unbearable, not only for security reasons, but for economical ones as well, even though she worked, but her monthly salary was no longer enough for her to live on for only one week. Yona told her to call Jawad and that he would help her more because he had friends who went to Germany.

She called Jawad, whose answer was, "If you intend to, do not hesitate. The road may be a bit arduous, but most of the time it does not last more than a month and you get to your destination. No one left and did not arrive, except for those who died at sea, and this is a fate that no one knows. Death is in Damascus and its farms produce more crops than any other region in the world."

Rama left Damascus and arrived in Germany within a week, and she was elated with this achievement, as she crossed from Greece on foot to

Germany, which is not an easy thing for a girl of her age. The risks were much more than in the airport.

Jawad's children left Beirut airport after their mother took them to the airport, because it was not possible to take off from Damascus International Airport. The security situation had become very complicated in Syria, and the State was now unable to control the burning places because they extended over entire Syrian areas and were close to the capital.

Syria was astonishing in the war it waged. The army was fighting on a thousand fronts. The conflict was between European and Arab countries and America combined, with the Syrian regime, Iran and Russia on the other side. No one knew why these countries were looking for democracy and freedom for the Syrian people.

Each of these countries, whether they were with or against the regime, had a goal hidden under great slogans such as freedom, democracy, non-US expansion, and support for weak nations. The biggest calamity was that all those in Syria and even the world knew that they only cared for their interests. What most provoked the intellectuals in Syria was what was happening in the corridors of the Security Council and the United Nations. A farce that was followed by another farce. Any intellectuals knew that those countries were gangs that did not care for any kind of humanity.

The Syrian people, with the exception of the intellectuals, practice sarcasm in all situations, even the most chilling, and believe in themselves in a strange way. They did not understand the issue of having any stranger interfere in the affairs of their country. No one can forgive this act, and that receiving money from abroad is treason, and summoning foreign armies is a betrayal that the people did not understand. The Syrian people did not understand that all those parties were fighting on their lands.

What is worse than that is that each of them believes that killing the other is a victory. The ugliest form of war is that the regime defends one thing with all its tools, which is to stay on the ruling chair. The protesters are all concerned with uprooting the regime to practice the same thing the regime was doing. Within this bloody scene, the most heinous human massacres were done. There was a third party, who was not concerned with who sat on the chair; it only cared for living in peace. This group, which was the majority, suffered all kinds of oppression, such as captivity and looting.

Jawad went to the airport to meet his children. A year had passed without seeing them. He longed for them, but he was also very afraid of this unknown world in which they would begin their new lives.

A new country and a new language. He wanted them to excel, like all parents wished, but the situation was difficult.

He had previously drawn a plan for their school life in Syria and was able to provide them with the foundations of stability, but the circumstances were changing. He did not know much about this country and did not even master its language. He remembered the stories of his ancestors when they were forced to migrate from the country — the Caucasus — to Turkey and then to Syria, to settle in the border city of Quneitra with Palestine. They established their villages, but sooner than later Israel occupied the Golan, so they migrated to Damascus to rebuild their lives. And now he is migrating to Britain, as many Syrians have been distributed in all of Europe. To be born at the age of forty years is impossible, but it is a title for any person who emigrated. The Circassians are four generations that did not rest of displacement yet.

Jawad sat in the waiting area at the airport. There was less than half an hour left for the plane to arrive. He browsed the news on his mobile phone, and watched a news broadcast by an international news agency about a crime committed against the Syrian people, as the news claimed. Jawad knew the truth of what happened, as he was a resident of this area before he escaped to Britain, and he was fully aware of the reality of what had happened. A militant armed Islamist group tried to enter Damascus from the east, but the government forces were able to stop them, as they learned of the attack through their intelligence, and they suffered losses. It was a massacre committed by the regime against civilians, as some shells fell on nearby buildings while fighting. The shells were from the attacking side. This is how the news was transmitted, and the viewer was the poor man from the area of the event.

Any news has two sides, so do not believe any news.

The plane arrived. Jawad's eyes were watching on the arrival door until his children came out, accompanied by an officer from the airport security.

Jawad hugged his three children at once and everyone cried. The female officer also cried over a scene she was not used to seeing and was sorry because she had some answers she needed to ask Jawad about.

The first question was, "Are you okay? Do you need any help?"

Everyone who works in the field of security in Europe is qualified to be a saint. They take pride in your humanity with their kindness. As for the security in the Arab countries, it is the one who provokes all human brutality. They have the ability, in their filthy ways, to turn the saintly citizen into a savage criminal who rouses the beast from within; even if he was dead, they had supernatural abilities.

His children were very happy, but sadness flashed in their eyes. They had left their mother in circumstances they did not understand exactly. There were many troubles that were going on in the family. Some aunts spoke in a bad way about their father, and another aunt said to them, "She is your mother, no matter what she has done, and you have to respect her."

They had asked, "What did she do?" No one answered them.

They came without the joy of arriving or leaving the battlefield unharmed. They came with the bodies of children lost in the chaos of neglect.

But Jawad insisted that they be successful in their lives and complete their higher studies, even if this was almost impossible. He wanted his eldest son to pass high school and enter university, but the two girls had no fear; they were superior in everything, and their success might be easier than his son, who had only one year to apply for high school exams.

Days passed.

Jawad and Yona began studying the language in a private university at the expense of the State. Jawad's children entered school and every day they faced more difficulties than the day before. It was difficult to rebuild yourself to adapt to a completely new world.

Jawad's friend who accompanied Yona's mother also arrived and became a resident with Jawad until he got his own house. God sent him as a companion for Jawad.

They were cold days with their weather and news. There were many disputes between Yona and Jawad. A struggle to make the decision that suited her best; either to stay with Jawad or leave him and end the relationship. But the days passed quickly, despite all of these problems.

Yona was floundering in making a decisive decision that was more difficult than the issue of life and death. Should she leave her absolutely opposing mother and sister, who knew nothing in the world but herself and did not try to argue with Yona or even discuss something she wanted? She did not stand by her younger sister, as she would put the family in a disaster. Yona also did not stop thinking about her big family, her uncles, the people of her village, the name of her late father. How could she get out of her skin completely and go to Jawad, who was like a dream to her? It was the love that answered her needs as a female. He was the one who wrote to her every moment and described her in terms far from the imagination. He was the one who mixed the ugliest words to extract a love poem from them. Jawad who painted Yona's face in a thousand ways. He was the one who mixed the colours of Carmen's painting with his blood and drew a painting that had nothing which followed the standards of art. But he knew that Yona would understand that painting. It was Jawad who tried to do everything to make Yona happy when it was impossible for him.

She told him one day at the beginning of their relationship, "I don't care that you are married, that you are older than me, or that you are a Muslim. All I care about is that you stay close to me, for without you death is better. I am with you. You came back to life as a fox. You were able to be in everything in my life. I see you in everything in my house, in my necklace which was a gift from you, my pyjamas, my wall painting, all were from you. I don't know what to wear before I ask myself whether you will like it or not. The smell of your perfume nests inside me. I look around me all the time, expecting to see you, because you used to surprise me in places I did not expect."

These were the words that brought tears to Jawad's eyes. With them, Yona strengthened the commitment of love in her heart.

For a whole year, Yona kept trying to convince her mother, but to no avail.

In a few months, she decided to marry Jawad by the beginning of next winter. Jawad agreed, and they decided to travel during this period together with Jawad's children to Spain and France. Rama, who was in Germany, would meet them in Germany. It was a dream trip that the two of them dreamed of despite everything. However, there were lumps in Yona's heart, who lied to her mother and told her that she was going to visit her friend in

Germany, and so she left. Jawad was also floundering between pleasing Yona and his children on a journey that the two sides looked on with caution. They did not like Yona's presence, and were trying to find anyone to blame for their family's problem and for losing their mother. Yona wanted to approach them cautiously, but avoid any clash with them, because this would be reflected on everyone with pessimism.

Jawad was in the midst of all these bubbles that might explode at any moment. He was trying to find himself and get back on his feet again. Before they travelled, he was sent by the employment office to a factory of chicken meals. He went to the factory at two o'clock in the afternoon and returned to his house at eleven o'clock at night. This factory, which was somewhat similar, according to Jawad, reminded him of Guantanamo, because of the procedures they had to go through to enter it. They had to work inside at a temperature of one below zero and with materials that were separated and shocked. Jawad's fingers almost fell off when they froze more than once. He spent all the time standing, and no one had the right to blink or talk to anyone, and even if you took a break for a quarter of an hour during the eight hours, it was not paid. The British did not pay an hour's wages for those who drink tea and talk during work.

As for Yona, she worked for a shop in the main bus station in Glasgow. The owner of the shop was a Pakistani who immigrated to Britain fifty years ago. He learned how to practice his sadism on his workers, as he took revenge for his hours of work with the ruthless British.

In this atmosphere, Jawad was planning a small project that he could work with, not to earn profits, but only to work under his own management and cover his monthly expenses, but how? Yona was his guide. She was the one who started the search journey. Finding a shop for rent in Britain was not an easy thing. In particular, you had to get used to the coldness of their procedures. They did not rush into anything. Yona was a mass of energy that continued and corresponded tirelessly for months to get a licence to open a shop from the council of Glasgow.

Jawad, Yona and Jawad's friend joined together to open this shop, and within two months they were able to open the doors of the shop and named it Beit Zaman, after the name of the cafe that brought them together in Damascus; but only a few people entered it and pessimism was a main feature on everyone's face. But soon fate helped them and signs started to indicate that the store was going in a good direction.

Yona informed her mother that she would work with Jawad. This proposition was like a volcano that erupted with lava on Yona, after which she decided to marry Jawad, carried her belongings, and came to Jawad's house, fleeing from her mother's reprimand.

She said to Jawad, "I am tired and I want to marry you. Choose a time to go to the council." They decided that their marriage would be on 6th June 2019. Jawad's friend and his wife witnessed the procedures in Glasgow council.

After that, they spent a night in a hotel overlooking Loch Lomond. The hotel where Michael Jackson and Churchill stayed to relax and breathe the purest air on earth. As for the natural views that surrounded them, they made one fall asleep with their magic. When they arrived at the hotel, the receptionist, who was looking at Yona's pants with admiration, greeted them. The day before, Jawad had placed sparkling plastic stones on Yona's jeans, not for anything, but for a sense of celebration and that it was a special day. The wedding ceremonies and arrangements began and ended!

And it goes on.

A love story that began inside the walls of the old city of Damascus with a moment of madness within the rubble of a thousand impossible ways, which walked the path of death, war, alienation, and heaps of thorns of rebellious lovers. It removed all that was said about obstacles, customs and traditions. Fate obeyed its path and made things easy for it to move towards its goal. All the raging black waves were left behind, miraculously saving the two lovers and giving them peace in a distant port. God willed to reward their patience and faith in Him and granted them what they wanted.

Yona is now living with Jawad in one house for the first time, with the knowledge of her mother, who stopped talking to Yona.

Yona lives an unstable life, torn between pleasing Jawad as a husband, and his children, who do not talk to her because they consider her to have stolen their father from their mother. But it is the mentality of teenage children who only know what they want to know and there is no power in the world to convince them that Yona was not a party in the issue that concerns their mother's divorce. The children agreed not to talk to their father, not to talk to Yona, and to avoid her and consider her non-existent, believing that they were putting pressure on her to leave the house or leave their father.

They do not know the size of the love story that unites Yona and Jawad. They do not know that Jawad only sees their behaviour as that of teenagers, and that he is able to endure it for years without being affected by it. He was once responsible for approximately seven hundred employees and was able to absorb this huge number of contradictory personalities. How can he not comprehend his own children, no matter how fortified their castles of arrogance are? He will be a knight who will storm their fortresses and surround them with a brave love to make them understand that they will not get anything from the world except what the world wants to give them.

In an atmosphere that bears all the illogical behaviours, Jawad and Yona now live, but fate has given them this job to work from morning until late at night. They return to the tense house, wanting nothing but sleep. There are no holidays in the shops in Britain as in other European countries, and this helps them not to think about the calamities surrounding them, and the work's fatigue and problems remove the special tensions and turn them into something secondary to their insistence on the success of their small project.

Yona's mother asked her to come to her to solve a problem related to the house. Yona was afraid of any reaction. She met her for the first time a month after she left the house.

"Did you two marry?"

Yona replied, "Yes, I married him."

"Leave the house then and consider yourself motherless."

Yona went home faster than was expected. She cried all night.

Yona had been living a messed-up life for seven years, but that month was the toughest one. She used to think about how to choose one of the two paths, and today, after choosing love, she only thinks about how things are going with her family and how she can win Jawad's children, and also how to be a wife to Jawad like other wives.

Yona did not think of a wedding, a ring, a white dress, and music to dance to. She did not think of a honeymoon, not like other girls. Yona, who fought everything for love, was now standing at the beginning of her true story. Would she be a successful wife? Or would the experience of living with Jawad during the coming months be proof that she chose the wrong path and that she should go back to where she came from?

Jawad, after he ridiculed his children's behaviour and left the matter of the success of his work in the hands of God, also began to look at Yona without offering any sympathy. He wanted her to know everything, or perhaps the worst of things, so that her next days would be less tense. He did not offer any suggestions, and he even just stood next to her as if she did not make the decision.

He was now in the position of a spectator, as if the whole story was a movie presented in front of him. He wanted to put everything in its rightful place. Since he started fighting life, he did not know lies and did not like to pretend to be something he was not. He wanted everyone around him to know what they should do without him. He asked them, because dictating orders would cause revolution anywhere, so he followed the policy of silence with everyone.

Everyone now considers him an enemy, but Jawad has an experience with life, and he is now at the top of his happiness. He loves them all, including Yona's mother, who hates him. She is right in that, as she has lived all her life among the Christian minorities in Syria who devotedly cultivate in the minds of their daughters that marrying a Muslim is the biggest shame on one hand. On the other hand, Jawad has a quiver full of obstacles, and any one of them is undoubtedly a disaster. Yona's mother, who is close to reaching the age of sixty, cannot bear Yona and Jawad's recklessness and disregard for all customs and traditions and jumping above what is logical. She is right and Jawad realises that, but he only wants to please her for Yona's sake, which is what Jawad cannot do, even if he wants to. The decision is not in his hands alone. Maybe he wants a new family. He lost his small family, even his big family and his brothers. He lost his friends, his homeland, and all his property. That is why, today, he wants a new family in this lonely alienation. He wants a pure and white family in which neither side can hide anything from the other. He wants loved ones, not shapes and numbers. He wants an integrated family that is at the same time different in thought, belief, and upbringing, and this seems almost impossible. But he insists on it. He wants to reunite Yona with her mother, sister, children, and his only friend in one family. He wants to break the laws of life and break religious fanaticism and boredom.

But can he, or does the story of intolerance continue because we believe in the ideas of those who preceded us? Is it really logic, or is it the ego that controls the mentality of everyone who says it is logic? But Yona has now jumped with one foot towards non-sectarianism and defied everything because her only motive was love.

Yona and Jawad sat in one of the cafes overlooking the river on their day off. Jawad looked at Yona, who surprised him with a question, "Are you happy now?"

"Yes, I am happy with the way our love overcame this hardship, and you must know that when I look at you without speaking, it means that my words are unable to describe the state of love that rages inside me, and this, in the world of love, is an indication that love has matured."

Yona answered him, "But I fear tomorrow. We have crossed the red lines and burned logic."

Jawad stopped her and said, "You are right, everything should go according to logic; but **when love interferes, we can practice some anomalies.**

"There is no problem in the world that cannot be solved by talking to a loyal friend. How would it be if he was a lover?"

He always wondered!

Yona got married without a wedding, without a white dress, without a ring, and without any kind of celebration, and without anything that a girl dreams of on her wedding day, even a song. Yona married, yes, but does this lover deserve to sacrifice her dream day for him?

Does this beloved who carries all the obstacles of the world deserve to risk her life for him?

Was Yona too young at the age of thirty to understand what she was doing?

No, she knows very well what she is doing. She is not like her sister, who only cares about appearances and what people might say. She is not like her sister, who remained silent and stopped talking to Yona and considered this her punishment. She was supposed to reach a solution at any cost. This solution must be not to stay away from her only little sister in this life. She preferred to withdraw and be content with her husband and child, and her famous phrase that she says to the mother became, "Don't tell me anything about Yona; do whatever you want with her."

The sister lives in London, five hours by express train from the city of Glasgow, where her mother lives. As well as Yona and Jawad. She no longer visits her mother, arguing that she does not want to see anyone who knows about her sister's marriage because this will be a great embarrassment for her.

Yona is not like her mother; even the short years of her life taught her many things after the death of her father and brother. She learned that life is just a story. You write it, not who surrounds you. She does not care about the words of people, relatives, or anything. She writes her story with the ink of love. With the love she lost after losing her father and learned afterwards how to extract it from an irrational relationship, yes, but she gives ink that she wants to write with. She wants to live where she rests, not where customs, traditions and people's words rest. She knows exactly where she wants to go with her.

You are not always supposed to know where you are going, because your heart is the one that leads you sometimes and the heart does not know the logic.

Her mother said one day that she would kill herself if Yona married Jawad because she could not bear this shame, and Yona considered this shame to be her beautiful cover, which perhaps, after thinking for a whole year, she concluded was better than staying within the circle of the illusion of traditions and religions.

When Jawad, Yona and her friend Rama stood under the Eiffel Tower during a visit to France, Rama said, "I remember once when we were sitting in the cafe in Damascus and you told us that one day you would take us to the Eiffel Tower. Back then I thought that you were just saying things, because none of us were planning to travel; but now, we stand as you promised us and I do believe that a dream you uttered came true. How do you predict the future?"

Jawad answered her, "I am not a djinn, nor a witch. I do not know for sure the unseen, and I did not plan for all this, but fate seems to have made me say that and led us to be here."

Yona said, laughing, "Do you remember, Mr Jawad, that you told me that you would take me to Italy, because I told you that it was the only country I wish to visit?"

Jawad answered her, "By God's willing, I will in the summer of next year."

On the day of the beginning of their eighth year of their love story, they arrived at Rome airport, then Florence and Pisa, and finally they were embracing in a gondola from the city of Venice, floating above the water of love.

Jawad said, "I kept my promise, and I want to tell you another prophecy."

Yona asked, "What do you want to say?"

He said, "There will be no sadness in your heart. Whatever troubles you, the curtain will soon be closed, and relations with your mother and sister will gradually return."

Yona said, "That's what I wish. I miss them and I know I'm out of balance with you because of this dilemma."

After their return from Italy, events really accelerated, and Yona's relationship with her mother began to gradually return to its tracks, and she visited her sister in London on her son's birthday at an invitation from her. Yona was surprised and almost flew from joy; a year had passed and she had not seen her.

And with the beginning of the year 2020, which began as a hopeful year, but then took an unexpected turn with the beginning of the Corona pandemic and the spread of panic and death. The world has proven that science is weaker than what they thought. Is Corona a weapon or a bat? A question raised.

This horror that the world has experienced as a result of the Corona pandemic is the same horror that the Syrians have lived through for ten years. Death that surrounded them from every side. Lack of materials. Fear of shells that only God knows who sends them. This fear and horror made the Syrians ride the sea of death and seek refuge in other countries. Not a single Syrian wants to leave Syria at all. Whoever left it was like someone who was oppressed because he was a prisoner in his home, afraid of Corona.

Whoever left it was like one who was afraid of mixing with people because of the fatality of Corona.

Whoever left it was like any one of you, wishing to stay alive.

Corona is a small global example of what the Syrians are suffering from.

Corona did not end and the quarantine imposed on people did not end, but an event shook America and led them to march in millions opposing racial discrimination after a white policeman killed a black man. The marches turned into a state of violence. In other countries, chaos began, too. Syria's economy collapsed and also America and other countries swayed. Trump and Assad, their days are numbered, and a Russian dragon and bear are watching the scene.

Do the problems stop or go on?

Will the war stop or go on?

Does life stop or go on?

Does the bad go on? It will go on.

The world flounders. It may change, but if the world loses love and affection, it will turn into a savage one.

The story of Yona and Jawad did not stop.

It is still going because she defied everything. Each of them believed in love and injected it with courage. Whenever life weakened them with its trivial issues, they took their antidote and injected themselves. The years that their love crossed were not normal. This love was their patron and their peace in a new world.

They believed in love, and they reached more than they wished for.

Life has many stations from which we can learn a lot. We can do a lot of planning and a large amount of learning, but all of that is nothing but filling in the voids of fate.

Destiny leads us to where we are with the handling of a divine secret. We continue to think that we are making ourselves.

Yona and Jawad sent a copy of this book to Samar and Soliman before it was published.

Both read it within twenty-four hours.

Samar said, "I loved it, and I hope that you will allow me to keep the electronic copy that you sent me because my name in it has not changed, but I wonder why you and your wife changed your names."

Soliman said, "I hope that everyone's names will be changed in the story because I do not want my name to be mentioned."

Yona got pregnant and they both agreed to name their baby JAN, as its meaning in Hebrew is 'God is generous', as God has been generous with them in everything.

Accordingly, everything written above is true, except for the names.